D1391878

MORNINGSTAR

MORNINGSTAR

or

The Vampires of Summer

Peter Atkins

HarperCollins*Publishers*

HarperCollins*Publishers*
77–85 Fulham Palace Road,
Hammersmith, London W6 8JB

Published by HarperCollins*Publishers* 1992
9 8 7 6 5 4 3 2 1

A catalogue record for this book is
available from the British Library

ISBN 0 00 223908 6

Set in Linotron Sabon by
Rowland Phototypesetting Ltd
Bury St Edmunds, Suffolk

Printed in Great Britain by
HarperCollinsManufacturing Glasgow

Dedicated to the memory of
Barbara Taylor Owen

Imagine . . . that I could hold in my hand, as a
book, the heart that has ceased to throb. Should I
not read there something which the world had
never read, during all the long years it dwelt in it?

– The Forsaken of God, William Mudford

Ils reviendront ces dieux que tu pleures toujours!
Le temps va ramener l'ordre des anciens jours;
La terre a tressailli d'un souffle prophétique . . .

Those gods you mourn forever will return!
And time restore the way of ancient days;
The earth has trembled with prophetic breath . . .

– Delfica from *Les Chimères*, Gérard de Nerval

CONTENTS

Prologue	Corrida	11
Part 1	The Morningstar Murders	15
Part 2	Frost's Secret Ministry	71
Interlude 1	The Sleep of Reason	123
Interlude 2	Of the Vampire and Its Glamour	137
Part 3	The Twilight Dance	143
Epilogue	Ephemera	233

CORRIDA

The one that was bleeding was bigger and stronger, but he was a stranger in this place and the red light confused him and the yards of polythene caused his feet to betray him.

Of the many cuts his body boasted, the one above his left eye, though small, was very productive and his wiping hands could not keep pace with the blinding flow of his blood. His left arm, in any case, dangled uselessly beside him; split deep as it was from shoulder to elbow, its only functions now were to send rhythmic telegrams of agony to an already panicking brain and to piss distressingly large amounts of bright red blood onto the polythene sheets on which he tried to run.

The other cuts were insignificant. Though two or three, in fact, were quite vicious enough to scar him for life, they were not disabling, and that was the only criterion here – here in this circle of red light and torment where life meant running and slipping and being or not being cut. Any thought or memory of a life prior to this, a life of house payments, of arguments and reconciliations, of painful loss and healing love, had been put to flight by the same charge of adrenalin that had removed the concept of futurity from his mind.

Twice rage had gotten the better of fear and twice he had charged, bellowing, at the graceful, slick bastard who was doing this to him. And twice he had received the serious cut – the tactically blinding one to the forehead, the cruelly crippling one to the arm. The other cuts arrived as almost playful punishments for when he was clumsy enough or frightened enough to fall over. He was often clumsy. He was very frightened. He was going to die and he knew it.

The Matador was different. The Matador moved with sure

steps and little sweat and his knife danced as gracefully as he. He felt no pity for the lumbering animal trying hopelessly to avoid him or foolishly to attack. He felt only contempt for its easily summoned sweat, blood, and breathlessness. There was little sport here. This one had no idea. There. It was down again. Sent tumbling by its own blood, slick on the polythene. Knife arcing elegantly beside him, he flew at it, marked his passing with a thin, red signature on its cheek, and stepped back.

The figure on the floor felt his cheek stroked and waited for the cold, sharp stinging that always followed. It wasn't long coming. He put his good hand up to his face and touched the wound. The tip of his middle finger disappeared inside his face as his cheek opened moistly for him like an eager lover. He screamed. And for the third time the scream was born of fury not of terror. Blind to danger, blind to pain, blind at last even to the possibility of failure, he scrambled to his feet and ran roaring at his tormentor.

The distance between them was too short and the demands of his rage too great to allow for confusion to take a proper hold of his mind, but he did have time enough to register a brief, animal surprise at the response of the Matador to his charge. Throwing aside the knife, which skidded away across the blood-slicked polythene sheeting, the Matador stood perfectly still and awaited his attack with lowered arms.

He didn't need the invitation that this gesture implied; his momentum and his hatred threw him forward anyway. He smashed into the Matador and, the blood having filled his eyes again, groped blindly for something breakable to seize. Then he felt it.

Not a knife, but equally sharp. Not steel, but equally insistent. He felt the piercing, the puncturing, the rupturing. He felt the blood well to the wound as if eager to leave his tortured body. He felt the Matador hug him tight as if the making of death, like the making of love, was a mutual endeavour. Strangely though, at the last, he felt no pain. It was as if his mind, knowing it could no longer act on his body's signals of suffering, was leaving the phone off the hook, having already gotten the message. He decided to scream anyway – almost as a point of principle – but he found his mouth was full of blood, and by the time he'd spat, swallowed, or choked it away, a scream seemed for some reason to be not worth the effort. A little like breathing. Or thinking. Or being.

A short time later, at one end of the room, a set of double doors opened. Another man entered the room, a tall man, a stone-faced man, a man whose build was a little too stocky to suit entirely the costume in which he was dressed – which was a chauffeur's uniform of soft black leather.

He glanced quickly around the room to be certain all had gone as expected. It had; his employer was seated, the other was dead.

The chauffeur moved forward. In his right hand he held a large black plastic waste bag into which, with a minimum of ceremony but a fair amount of effort, he placed his employer's bloody handiwork piece by piece.

Folding over the top of the bag, he then dragged it along the floor, the polythene aiding the smoothness of its journey, and out into the corridor beyond the doors.

Leaving the bag behind, he re-entered the room and began to fold the polythene sheeting in upon itself, a trick he performed swiftly and with the efficiency of familiarity; despite it not yet having attained a state of stickiness, none of the blood escaped onto the highly polished wooden floor that was revealed as his work progressed.

When this second bloody bundle had joined the first in the corridor, the chauffeur, playing with a couple of light switches by the doorway, exchanged the red light for white and looked carefully around the room to ensure that his confidence had not outstripped his cleanliness. But he had been diligent; the room was spotless.

The Matador was still sitting calmly at the far end of the room. He remained silent as the chauffeur saw to the bringing in and the laying out of replacement polythene. Once this was done, the chauffeur, back in the open doorway, took hold of the two bundles of trash and, for the first time, looked directly into the eyes of his employer.

'You know where to take it?' the latter asked.

The chauffeur nodded.

The Matador made a small gesture of dismissal and watched as the chauffeur closed the doors behind him. He stood up and walked across his room to the double doors. Reversing his employee's action with the light switches, he once again flooded the room with redness and then placed his mouth close to a small intercom that was adjacent to the switches.

'Next,' he said.

PART ONE

THE MORNINGSTAR MURDERS

September 21

It was after the event.

Summer was disappearing in a slow decay of brown desiccation. San Francisco had seen its first fogs and was resigned to more. Along Liberty Street a slight breeze blew, mild in itself but full of the promise of the cold to come. Carried on the breeze was a single passenger – a discarded leaflet from the Castro Theatre advertising a series of films by Jean Cocteau.

From his fourth-floor window, Donovan Moon watched the flier's progress. Watching it was his latest excuse. Stuffing receipts into an envelope for his accountant had been the afternoon's best – it had taken at least an hour. Tidying his pencils wasn't so good. There are only so many variations on making three look neat. But this was promising; every so often the leaflet would ground itself or wrap itself around the base of a lamppost, and Donovan, in spirit, would be right there with it – urging it to resistance, encouraging its self-assertion. Each time, though, the wind would find a corner that wasn't battened down sufficiently and off it would go again.

Donovan, if asked, would reply quite confidently that he was not wasting time. He would explain quite patiently that it was all part of the process. He would insist quite indignantly that he was waiting for an important thing to happen, and then he would admit quite reluctantly that what he was waiting for was the moment when the self-loathing generated by prevarication finally outweighed the fear that kept him from his desk.

The leaflet was now well advanced along the street. Despite Donovan being pressed firmly against the glass of his window, despite his face being distorted into flatness, despite his eyes aching with the strain of being forced so far to the right, the leaflet was undeniably at the edge of his field of vision. And then it was gone. It had failed him. Let him down badly.

'Bastard thing,' he said. 'Bastard fucking thing.'

He turned away from the window, picturing revenge scenarios: a stray mongrel pissing all over it; stray stilettos catching and tearing; suffocating and geographically unlikely snow trapping it in place and slowly – very slowly – reducing it to pulp and dirty water. They helped. A little. But his feet were still moving, his legs were still carrying him, and here he was – back behind the desk instead of between it and the window. And there was the chair. And there was the tape recorder.

Moon lowered himself into the chair, pushed it back slightly, and raised his legs to rest his feet on the surface of the desk. His manner was easy and confident. Hell, he'd even light a cigarette before he . . . no. He caught himself. Matt, his lover, perched on the sofa across the room, face buried in a magazine, had been tactfully silent through the whole of the afternoon's performance, but Donovan knew the rhythms of his patience intimately. One more unnecessary task, one more act of avoidance, one more cigarette, and . . . what would it be? The quiet cough? The theatrical sigh? Or even – God forbid – the low-pitched but admonitory use of his name? Fuck it. He snatched at the tape recorder. He turned it on, cleared his throat, and began to speak.

'To begin, a declaration: She was no child of the night. No daughter of darkness, she came to him with spring. In the streets, skin braved exposure and stores closed in sunlight. In homes, windows declared a truce and allowed what was left of the wind into what they'd spent a winter protecting. In classrooms, children began to feel that there might soon be a day on which they might begin to feel that the last day of school could hide from their impatient search no longer, that soon the doors of summer would be opened. In people's faces, colour crept back and in people's conversations, subtexts of delight, in a thousand different voices, said "Summer's coming."

'And in the fields the wasps were waking.

'It was early in –'

'Donovan.'

18

'It was early in –'

'Donovan!'

Moon switched off the tape recorder but kept his feet on the desk. Looking across the room at Matt and scowling slightly, he asked, 'What?'

Matt smiled, said nothing.

'What?' Donovan repeated, his voice a careful mix of inquiry and annoyance.

Matt raised an eyebrow.

'Fuck you *and* your eyebrow,' Moon barked. 'Put up or shut up. What's the problem?'

'Well . . .' Matt said slowly and carefully.

Moon raised a warning hand. 'But tread softly,' he said, 'for you tread on my art.'

Matt seized the opportunity that Donovan's joke offered and rushed ahead, a conciliatory tone wrestling with a sarcastic one as words tumbled from him. 'But that's it, Donovan. That's exactly it. It shouldn't be. Shouldn't be art. I mean far be it from me, mere broker of insurance that I am, to advise famed journalist D. Moon, winner of – how many Pulitzers is it, now?'

'None. Fuck off. Go on.'

'– as to the correct approach to his latest project . . .'

'But . . .'

'*But* . . . do you really think Commissioner Schulman is going to care for your purple prose? He's –'

'Matt, please! I bleed easy.'

'Yeah, yeah. But Schulman, Don, Christ! Those elegant silver hairs hide a hard head. You know that. He's a street cop who made good, not some college boy.'

Donovan waited a beat or two. He stared at Matt across the uncomfortable silence, his face the perfect blank that he always employed to mask perfect and unwelcome understanding. He was going to play this one to the limit. 'So?' he said.

'*So* . . . I just think it would help if you'd bear in mind that you've been asked to write a confidential report for a police commissioner rather than to provide a sample of overblown style for some creative-writing class. Just the facts, ma'am, just the –'

'So now you're a literary critic. Jesus! If I'd wanted the ghost of Edmund Wilson, I'd have asked for it.'

Matt hid a smile. He knew Moon's techniques very well, and recognizing the surrender that sarcasm attempted to disguise, he consciously softened the mood. He let the smile out gently and, in a much quieter voice, said, 'I'm glad you didn't.'

There was a moment's silence and then Moon slowly returned Matt's smile. 'Yeah, so am I,' he said. He paused, sighed, continued: 'And I know damn well you're right. I think it's what we in the psychiatric trade call overcompensation. I resent the fact that it's my accidental role as a witness that made Schulman ask for this rather than my talent – or lack of it – as a journalist.'

'I don't think it's that at all,' said Matt, still speaking gently and carefully.

'No?'

'No. I think it's what we in the psychiatric trade call repression. You're avoiding the facts because the facts still frighten you.'

Moon let that one hang in the air a few moments. Then he sighed, took his feet off the desk, stood up, and crossing the large main room of the apartment, sank heavily into the leather armchair directly opposite the long sofa on which Matt reclined. 'The facts still frighten me . . . yes,' he said. 'Yes. That's absolutely true. The facts still frighten me.'

June 12

Fact: When Stephen Lumby was being slaughtered, he lost as much sweat, induced by mortal terror, as he would have lost, given his mild obesity and his general aversion to exercise, on a two-mile run. This is approximately equal, in terms of expended energy, to the calorific cost of a relatively leisurely bout of sex. None of the investigative team assumed for a moment that the particular passion Lumby had undergone would have manifested itself in ejaculation, but this in any case would have been impossible to check, because by the time the corpse was discovered, the genitalia were missing. So were the eyes.

Fact: Although the majority of Katharine Elizabeth Ferritti was found in one piece in the litter-covered doorway of a deserted hardware store near Turk Street, smaller pieces of her were still being discovered by sewer workers and street cleaners up to two months after her killing. At a rough guess, the portions of decaying matter that had once added up to a thirty-one-year-old computer programmer covered an area of fifty square miles. Three teeth and a nipple had been mailed to a national newspaper.

Fact: Edward Higgins was three days short of his ninth birthday when, in neatly severed sections, he was placed through the bars of the lions' cage in the city zoo. He had been named after Eddie Cochran and his father called him Summertime.

Fact: Lumby, Ferritti, Higgins, and nine other people were all murdered during the first eleven days of June. Saturday the seventh had been the busiest; within its twenty-four-hour duration, four people had died in four separate attacks. None of the twelve victims was related to, or acquainted with, any of the others. Apart from two men who worked different shifts in the same canning plant – a plant that employed over five thousand people – no occupations or professions were found to be common. The ages of the dead ranged from Higgins at eight years old to Carol-Anne Peters at sixty-one. Mutilation was common to all the cases, but the nature of the mutilation was not only various in its perversity but wilfully perverse in its variety.

Apart from the instinctive assumption that twelve unrelated and astonishingly violent murders in eleven days would be stretching anybody's coincidence theory a little too far, there was, according to the media, only one thing that let the police know they had one lunatic, rather than a dozen, to deal with.

Fact: In all twelve cases, on the available surface nearest to the body or the major part of it, scrawled in the victim's blood or, where possible, in a disgusting mixture of the victim's blood and excrement, was a single word.

Morningstar.

Morningstar: From alley walls, store windows, and bedroom furniture, via two-point Roman type, colour photographs, and TV screens, the word made its way to its natural home – the cage labelled 'Terror' in the human heart. Once there, it fought for space with its fellow triggers of anxiety, overpowering those – like Manson, Gein, or DeSalvo – whose real power was already history, wrestling with those – like cancer, terrorist, or fallout – whose tenure was long-term but whose threat was not always immediate – until finally, because of its freshness, because of its mystery, it became, for these people, in this city, at this time, the fear that rattled the bars of its cage the loudest.

Morningstar: Like a hit record's melody or a new slang expression, people were surprised to hear it spring to their lips before any conscious decision to utter it had been made. Once spoken, however, once spat out into the safety of conversation, its power seemed to lessen and people grew eager to speak it.

22

But the relief of the uttered fear is the transient relief of the freshly squeezed boil; beneath the suddenly smooth skin, pus already regathers.

Morningstar: The newest name for the death that walks, that shops and smiles and calls you neighbour.

It was fucking unbelievable.

Un-fucking-believable. Pete Munro had a head full of incredible news – news about the maniac who was making this whole city sweat, news that he was selflessly to give to his friend Donovan Moon (if he could just *find* him), news that had the potential both to revive Moon's comatose career and to shock even further the shocked citizens of this town – and was he somewhere having his back slapped, his hand pumped, his glass refilled? No. He was standing here on an unshaded street corner at twenty after four on a hot June afternoon having to listen to this dipshit cop – at *least* five years younger than he was for Christ's sake – give him grief about jaywalking. Jaywalking! Where'd the fuck he think they were, Los Angeles? *Nobody* in San Francisco waited for the little green man if the roads were clear.

'*Nobody* in San Francisco waits –' Hold it. Not a good tactic. The narrowing of the cop's eyes told him that. Don't lecture anybody in a uniform unless you've got one with more stripes. Don't lecture. Don't condescend. All Pete wanted was to get away as soon as possible, find Donovan, and dump his amazing discovery on him. Humility, that was it. Humility and lies. Pete started again.

'Officer, you're right. I'm sorry. I just wasn't thinking. As you probably saw, the road was very clear and . . . See, my brother – he's in the service – he just got into town. Haven't seen him for nearly a year. I was hurrying. I was wrong. I apologize.' Pete looked at the cop with what he hoped was the right mix of respect and solid citizenness.

The cop took it for about three seconds and then shifted his own gaze to the road junction. 'People think it's a joke,' he said, the weary wisdom of the urban warrior in every syllable, 'but it's not just *your* life. You hurry across here . . . to see your brother . . . car comes down Twenty-third, makes a left a little faster than he should . . . maybe his mother's just back from basic training in Berlin . . . swerves to avoid you, doesn't see the other car that's −'

Oh, for fuck's sake. Pete tuned out. He weighed the situation. What would it cost? Twenty, maybe thirty dollars? The hell with it. It was worth every penny to get this bore out of his face. 'Why'n't you give me a ticket?' he said, cutting across the multiple-death scenario the cop was still busily constructing.

'What?' the cop said, more surprised than annoyed.

'A ticket. Write me a ticket. Come on. I was wrong. I did it. I want to pay. I want a ticket.'

Thing is, it was true. He managed not to laugh, but the situation was suddenly both amusing and exhilarating. He *did* want a ticket. He wanted to frame it and laugh with his friends. He wanted to be able to refer to his criminal past. He wanted to be able to claim he broke the law to jump-start his friend's floundering career. Shit, yes; the story burning in his brain was hot as hell − he could probably stiff Donovan for the fucking ticket, anyway.

The cop − thank God − was wasting no more time in word-play. The pad and pen were already in his hands. But he didn't seem very happy. Presumably half the pleasure of writing the things was the accompaniment of whining remorse he could normally expect to hear. This one couldn't be much fun. Pete, on the other hand, was having a great time. Donovan, he knew, would appreciate this, too, once he managed to *find* him. The cop asked him his name and he gave it cheerfully, helping him out with the spelling, his mind already recrossing the road, backtracking around the neighbourhood, busily wondering where Moon was.

Moon was in one of his favourite positions. In fact, discounting those that relied on more than his own body being involved, it was probably number one: buttocks on padded leather, feet on shining steel, knees against varnished mahogany, elbows resting on more of the same, frosted glass cool between his palms, amber liquid warm in his throat. Moon was sitting at a bar.

It was 4:25 in the afternoon. Donovan was musing on this very fact. An odd sort of time. Too late to do anything constructive, too early to go home. An odd time for people. And therefore, he declaimed internally, proud of the deduction, a time for odd people. He wasn't sure if he could make that one hold up in logic class, but, hell, it worked for him. A time for odd people. A time for an odd drink. Or two. He liked logic. It was irresistible, and used wisely, it never left your glass empty.

'Hey, Sam!' he called, his voice a little louder than necessary – apart from himself and the bartender he was paging, there were two men in the bar, the jukebox wasn't on, and the TV was muted.

Sam, in front of that muted TV, turned from the rerun of 'My Favourite Martian' and made his way up the length of the bar. 'Hey, Don!' he replied, and stood awaiting instruction, short, round, balding, the same hopeful look he had directed at his clientele for twenty-five years on his face. 'Astonish me,' it said. 'Ask me for Kierkegaard's line on ethical subjectivity. Ask me for three eggplants and a tomato. Ask me for anything but a Jack Daniel's.'

'Gimme a Jack Daniel's,' said Donovan Moon.

A little more of the light went out of Sam's life. 'Anything in it?' he asked hopefully.

'Yeah.'

'Yeah?'

'Yeah.'

'What?'

'Another Jack Daniel's.'

Sam took a tall glass, filled it with bourbon and ice, and handed it over the bar with all the stoic patience with which his seventy-six-year-old mother awaited the coming of the Messiah.

Donovan took the drink and sipped, giving Sam his straight face for as long as he could manage. 'Was there anything else?' he said eventually.

Sam pursed his lips slowly and shook his head. He had half turned away when he remembered and spun back round,

26

suddenly eager again. 'Hell, yes there was. Pete Munro was in here looking for you.'

Donovan's nod was qualified by a quizzical twist of the eyebrows. 'Did he say why?' he asked.

'Said he had something for you. Excited. Didn't say what it was, though. Didn't tell me. Why tell a lousy barkeep anything?'

'Yeah, right,' said Moon, ten years' experience having taught him that brusqueness was the best way to deal with Sam's self-pity. 'Is he coming back?'

Sam shrugged, a theatrical gesture expansive enough to suggest a whole world of possibilities. 'Who knows?' he said. 'I told him you'd probably be in later. So he says maybe he'll be in later, too. Maybe he will. Maybe he won't. Who knows?'

'Who indeed knows?' said Donovan, voice rising to a mock gravity to match the seriousness with which Sam regarded the issue.

Sam nodded wisely and wandered back up the bar to wonder what Ray Walston was up to these days, leaving Moon to return his attention to the contents of his glass and to begin a serious attempt to get on the outside of it.

It wasn't that he doubted Sam's word. It wasn't that he doubted the usefulness of anything Pete might have for him – Munro had put several things his way in the past that had led to short-term solvency. It was just that it had been a lousy few weeks and Donovan always found that it was never wise to anticipate a change in fortune until the cheque had cleared the bank.

It was another half hour – and another long drink for Donovan – before Munro returned. Pete, now the proud possessor of his jaywalking ticket and a small sense of moral victory over the forces of authority, had tried another couple of bars and a phone-booth call to Donovan's machine before coming back.

Opening the door – a foot still on the sidewalk, a hand still on the door frame – he cast a glance around the room. A married man, Pete had reached – almost unconsciously – that stage that some married men arrive at where a reason other than alcohol is necessary to get them into a bar without some small nag of neurotic discomfort. Moon was Pete's excuse tonight, and the light that came on behind his eyes when he recognized his friend's back was not powered exclusively by the story he had to tell him. He let the door swing firmly shut behind him and strode to the bar, hoisting himself onto an adjoining stool.

Donovan's eyes left the display of bottles behind the bar to look over his left shoulder at Munro. They saw the usual great cheekbones, the usual ill-conceived moustache, and a characteristic if infrequent look of eager delight on the face. Despite an attempted casualness, this eagerness spilled into his voice as Pete spoke.

'Hi,' he said. 'Sam tell you I was looking for you?'

'Eventually,' Moon replied, face twisting into a benign grimace of the well-you-know-Sam variety. 'So . . . what's happening?'

'Donovan, you will not *believe* what I've found out —'

'Marie's pregnant again, but this time she swears it's yours?'

'No, she swears it's *yours* — and that *would* be funny, right?'

They smiled, Donovan signalled the bartender for a drink for Pete, and the rituals of insult and affection over, Munro's revelation began.

'Okay. So you know about the Morningstar murders, right? Jesus, what a stupid question. You and everyone else in the state. Yeah. But what you *don't* know —'

Pete broke off to stare pointedly. Sam, having served the drink, stood, eyes focused somewhere in middle distance, the picture of a man with no possible interest in somebody else's conversation.

'Hey, Sam, you wanna watch TV or what?' Munro said, and waited to see Sam take a pace or two back down the bar before turning back to Moon's amused glance. He continued. 'Right. Now, wait, let me start . . . yeah. You know Marie's sister is screwing a guy in the records office of the police department?'

'It doesn't distract the rest of the staff?'

'Huh? Oh. Okay, a guy *from* the records office — but, hey, I'm glad you're paying attention. Anyway, this guy — Walt, I think — told Laura —'

'In strictest confidence.'

'Yeah. In strictest confidence. Just like Laura told Marie in strictest confidence and Marie told me in strictest confidence and I'm trying to tell you . . . Now – you wanna know or you wanna crack wise all night?'

Moon swapped his grin for a suitably chastened expression.

'Okay. So the story, going by the papers and TV, is the only link the cops got for the killings is this Morningstar thing, right?'

'Right.'

'Wrong. They got more. A lot more. But they ain't saying. And some of the top media guys? They got it, too, but they're co-operating. An ace to let the cops spot any copycat work, see?'

'Yeah, yeah.' Donovan sneered. 'I know the syndrome; a corpse is discovered, complete with graffiti, but the police know it wasn't really Morningstar that did it because the left foot's third toenail wasn't painted blue. Fantastic. Victim's still dead as shit but San Fran's finest have the satisfaction of knowing it was a different crazy made him that way. Great.'

'So you're a philosopher. I'm impressed. But do you know what the blue toenail in *this* case is?'

Donovan sighed his heavy sigh, the sigh he kept in reserve for moments like this, moments that required him to refer to the tenuous grip he had on what was a pretty low rung of his professional ladder. 'Pete, I'm a free-lance. I generate my own work and place it – if I'm lucky. I'm not privy to editorial secrets at the best of times, and frankly, for me these are *not* the best of times.'

'Hey, I don't know that? That's why I'm here. The guy's caught, the facts break. The facts sell one day's papers, the feature articles sell the next's. Am I right – that's how it works?'

''S how it works.' Reluctant to believe anything good was coming his way until it'd actually paid for next month's groceries, Moon was still hooked. Pete's excitement was obvious and contagious. His own cool was melting faster than the ice in his bourbon.

'So if you get the facts now,' Pete said, 'you can steal a jump. Start work tomorrow. Or tonight. Contact editors. Book space.

Do whatever you do. I don't know. Recall the great wackos of former times. Explore the psychology of this one. 'Cause I tell you, Don, this guy is a classic.'

Moon smiled wryly. 'I think we already know that, Pete,' he said.

'Yeah?' said Munro. 'You don't know the half of it.'

Donovan allowed his eyebrows to speak for him.

'I'm just going to say one word to you,' Munro said, and then he paused, enjoying his silence and filling it with a sip of his drink. He stared into his friend's face. 'Vampirism,' he said.

For one glorious second he thought he'd impressed Moon into a stunned silence, but then the silence and Moon's stone face broke together into derisive laughter.

'Vampirism,' Donovan said, after his laughter had passed and he had sucked the few drops of spilled whiskey from his shirt cuff. 'Oh, come on. What? Bite marks on the necks? Big deal. He's not the first, you know. Lots of lunatics choose that one. Lots of 'em drink the blood, too. He do that? And what's with the daylight attacks? Hasn't he read the books? Hasn't he seen the films? Hasn't anyone told the poor bastard all little vampires should be tucked up nice, safe, and sated in their bijou coffinettes during the day?'

Munro refused to be provoked. He stared at his friend for a beat or two after the outburst, and as Moon sipped his drink, amused eyes glittering at Pete over his glass, his voice was calm and quiet and slow. He was playing this very well. 'No, Don. You've got it quite wrong,' he said. 'That's not what I meant at all. It *is* a common wound that links the victims, but it's not neck bites. No. In each case the initial cause of death was a massive rupture of the heart – caused by the violent insertion of a large sharpened, wooden stake.'

Now he had the reaction he wanted. Now Moon was silent. Now Moon was stunned.

'Followed by decapitation.' Munro rewarded himself with a long swallow. 'Oh. And he stuffs their dead mouths with garlic.'

4

The lighting rig swooped, stabbing beams of mood-controlling colour across the dance floor. The music pounded, multiple speakers pulsing visibly as the powerful sounds pushed the woofers to the limit of their response. People swayed, dipped, strutted, and preened, lifted beyond themselves by rhythm and light. There were several good dancers out there, but Chris Tempest's eyes remained fixed on the guy in black leather as he smoothed his way between them all, coming back to the table from speaking to whoever it was to whom he'd had to speak.

It was the shape and the clothes that had caught her attention, of course, but it was the hooded eyes and the conversation that had held her. She really hadn't intended to desert the girls – they'd made a deal about that before hitting the club – but sometimes stuff just happens. And he'd happened. She'd go over later, make nice, make jokes, make it all right again. At the moment she just wanted to make sure he was safely back at the table before she hit the rest room. There was lots to do yet – like confirming his name and giving her number – and she didn't want to lose him to the randomness of nightclub mingling before these things had happened.

He paused at the foot of the steps that led from the floor to the raised seating area and turned his head back to survey the crowd through which he'd just walked. It was strange, Chris thought, the way he looked at them: face impassive, head panning smoothly on his shoulders like some flesh-and-blood video camera, taking them all in. He didn't dwell on the women (yeah, okay, she was checking that), in fact he didn't dwell on anybody; just registered them in passing as if he was looking for somebody or something that he'd recognize when he saw it. He was an artist, he'd told her that, so it must be part of his gig to study people, but it bothered her. Hey, I'm here, she wanted to shout, you already saw it, tonight it's me. Whatever the hell it is. But she didn't need to, because now he was coming up the steps and smiling at her as he lowered himself back into the seat.

Good. And now it was her turn to play the wanderer. She smiled apologetically as she got to her feet, gestured at the rest room, and mouthed 'Two minutes' over the roar of the music. He nodded and she started to walk, glancing over at the girls' table. Heather, Jane, and Anne didn't notice her, and Shelley wasn't there. She checked the dance floor. No. Good. Two birds with one stone. She'd smooth it over with Shelley, whom she was closest to anyway, in the judicial chamber of the ladies' room.

Shelley Masterton knew a secret.

She knew one of the great hidden truths of the world: Women's rest rooms are always nicer than men's.

The reason this truth is generally unknown is natural enough: Men, for the most part, have experience only of their own rest rooms and women only of theirs. The reason Shelley, despite being neither a designer of public conveniences nor a cross dresser, was in possession of this truth was also natural enough: Her next-to-last boyfriend had loved to talk.

More specifically, Adam loved to talk about women's hidden lives. He wanted to know how they spoke about men when men weren't around. He wanted to know if they swapped notes on lovers' capabilities and peccadilloes. He wanted to know if menstruation was as terrifyingly weird as he thought it was. He wanted to know what their bathrooms looked like. From the age of seventeen he'd always requested of his dates, on their first return from a nose powdering, a description of the rest room. It hadn't taken many such inquiries before he'd realized the sexist conspiracy that condemned men to stained porcelain and filth while providing for women little palaces of relaxation. And through the succeeding years and the succeeding partners, he had never tired of telling them how lucky they were, of alerting them to this secret.

So Shelley knew. And in the ladies' room of the Mask of

32

Venus, desperate to pee, she was summoning up this knowledge as a source of comfort. The men's room must be worse, she was repeating to herself, the men's room must be worse. Not that she was capable of imagining how it *could* be. This place was astonishingly disgusting.

The toilets in two of the cubicles had cracked or overflowed, and so the cheap linoleum floor of the public area was covered in a thin film of water – at least she *hoped* it was water – and thanks to the numerous shoes that had padded through it in the course of the evening, in places this watery substance had coagulated into little black puddles. The paintwork seemed almost contemptuous in its slapdashness and the wallpaper had either been there for thirty years or somebody's sense of humour was out of sync with her own.

Shelley tried to make allowances. It was two in the morning and the club was busy as hell. She was sober as a Methodist sermon – maybe *all* clubs got this bad this late, and drunkenness normally hid the fact. And the Mask of Venus had only been hip for just over two weeks. Prior to that, it had been home to some serious late-night activity by the S&M crowd and – what did *she* know? – maybe clean toilets just weren't an issue with them. Maybe the management hadn't yet had time or money to cater to the new clientele, the young and monied who'd followed their braver number into this edgy part of town to experience the frisson of recently departed sleaze.

But allowances or not, this bathroom was the pits. And the club itself wasn't so great. She wasn't having the best time of her life. She was sober because the thought of an early-hours cab search in the environs of Turk and Polk streets had been enough to make her volunteer to be designated driver, but the problem with *that* was the amazing discovery of just how stupid, banal, and wholly pathetic friends could be when they were drunk and you weren't one of their bright, startling, and wholly admirable number.

The tampon machine, which sported almost as many rust spots as did the mirror over the wash-basins, had two handwritten notices pinned to it – one, presumably official, read OUT OF ORDER and the other, presumably not, read BREAD ROLLS

AVAILABLE UPSTAIRS IN CASE OF EMERGENCY. Shelley thanked Christ that the girls' night out that had brought her here hadn't taken place last week as originally planned. She was wondering just how pressing, after all, were the arguments of her bladder when she heard the main door to the bathroom open behind her.

'*Dream Angel*,' Bobby Corvino and the Fiasco Brothers' first hit from many years ago and now back in the clubs and on the charts thanks to a scratch remix, swelled momentarily in volume until the door swinging shut muffled it again. Shelley turned, eager to share her disgust in the hope of dissipating it, and found herself looking at the smiling face of Chris Tempest.

'Hey, Shelley!' said Chris. 'You guys having a good time?'

Shelley should have been annoyed. Chris had been one of the main instigators of the night and it'd been planned in strict accordance with the philosophical principles of Cyndi Lauper – the Girls Were Gonna Have Fun. No men. Just drink, dance, and conversation. So when Chris had vanished within half an hour of their arrival with nothing but a purred 'Well, will you just look at him?' Shelley and her other three female colleagues from the video distribution company had been more than a little pissed off.

But Shelley liked Chris. It was difficult not to. Chris lived her life almost completely to the pulse of the pleasure principle, and though this entailed fecklessness and unreliability, it also meant that she met the world with an affectionate optimism that was both contagious and charming. And what the hell, Chris was a friendly face in a palace of slime and potential disease, so Shelley bit back recrimination and smiled. She also spread her arms to draw attention to their surroundings and widened her eyes.

'Good time?' she replied. 'Sure. I love being reminded that taking a piss is so shameful an act that it requires appropriately degrading decor.'

'It *is* pretty scuzzy,' Chris acknowledged with a laugh as, unlike the frozen-with-disgust Shelley, she walked through the slimy film on the floor to stand in front of the mirror.

Shelley watched her watch her reflection tug and smooth at its clothes and felt the usual pang of envy at the apparent ease

34

with which Chris could look great. She was dressed, as always, completely in black. The Lycra vest, sleeveless and scoop-necked, sold her slim figure convincingly, while the knee-length pleated skirt, flared and lace-covered, tempered the sales pitch of her appearance from a shout to a flouncy seductive whisper.

Chris patted at her Louise Brooks haircut and ran a quick moistening tongue over her full and startlingly red lips, which were one of the two flashes of colour in a consciously pale face, the other being her large grey-blue eyes.

Shelley flicked her own eyes – green and quite beautiful – across to her own reflection. She was slim and firm-bodied, her hair was an appealing blonde mass that framed her face to perfection, and her outfit – a sheer silk blouse and a tight and sexy short skirt – while not as . . . decisive . . . as Chris's, was both flattering and attractive. She looked good, she knew. But she also knew the time and effort she put into it. It wasn't only the long-term things like the cripplingly expensive health club she belonged to or the rigorous approach to eating, but the fact that she took an hour to get her hair right, that she took twenty minutes to make wardrobe decisions, and that once dressed, she'd practise in front of her mirror to establish just how freely she could move without running the risk of striking unflattering poses.

And that kind of thing showed. It wasn't obvious. Nothing at which a finger could point. Nevertheless her . . . deliber-ateness . . . was somehow apparent when contrasted with Chris, and that made her envious. Envious of Chris's approach to life. Chris improvises, she realized, the rest of us rehearse. And this sudden awareness of something she'd always under-stood instinctively led her safely back from envy to affection. As Chris turned back, the gestural grooming having taken all of three seconds, Shelley smiled.

'You look great,' she said.

'Thanks,' said Chris. 'So do you.' She tipped her head slightly in mock coquettishness. 'Wanna fuck?'

Shelley laughed. She wanted to come back with a witty answer, but Chris saved her by continuing to speak as she headed for one of the cubicles.

'Hey! Just kidding. Besides, I know they tell you a full bladder is good for your orgasm but – personally speaking – I've always found it a *hell* of a distraction.' She closed the cubicle door behind her. It sprang back about half an inch from the frame.

Shelley stared at its cheap marble-effect veneer in shock. 'Jesus!' she called out. 'You're not going to *go*, are you?'

The door was pushed against the frame again from the inside. 'Shit. No lock. What a dump,' Chris muttered, then, louder: 'Of *course* I'm going to go. You can only cross your legs so long. And I ain't pissing in the parking lot. Not in *this* neighbourhood.'

'But, Chris . . .' Shelley faltered. What the hell was there to say that only complete sensory deprivation would keep someone from knowing anyway?

'What?' said Chris. 'Disease? Jesus, I don't sit *down*. Whaddaya think? I'm *crazy*? There's always a coupla inches between me and the seat in places like this. Kind of a conceptual condom for moments of nonsimultaneous intimacy, know what I mean? Anyway, it's real good for the thigh muscles. Should try it sometime.'

Shelley thought about it. What the fuck. She let herself in the adjacent cubicle. Hey, whaddaya know, she was lucky. She had a lock. She clicked it into place, hiked up her skirt, rolled her pants down as far as her knees (any further and she might as well have pissed in them herself), and crouched in position.

Chris's voice came over the connecting wall. 'You can brace your arms on the walls if your legs object too much.'

'Right,' said Shelley, and giggled. She felt absurdly liberated, like smoking your first joint or giving your first French kiss.

'And whatever you do, *don't laugh*,' Chris shouted, tone serious as a driving instructor. 'You'll never get the aim right!'

The giggle broke into helpless laughter. And Shelley didn't get the aim right. And it really didn't matter. Chris banged on the wall.

'What's so funny?' she asked.

'Well . . .' Shelley began, fighting her hysteria. 'It's just . . . just that . . . oh God, I'm sorry . . . it's . . .' Finally she blurted it out: *'This is the most fun I've had all night!'*

Chris got it then. Laughing as much at her friend's laughter as at the incongruity of what had inspired it, she was reduced to a giggling fit of her own. The mutual laughter made adjusting clothes and opening doors more difficult than normal, but eventually they stood facing each other outside the cubicles.

'"Most fun I've had all night"?' said Chris. 'Jesus, Shell. Has it been that bad?'

Shelley smiled, shook her head. 'It's been fine,' she said. 'I'm just too sober.'

Chris nodded. 'Always an error. And what? The intoxication of midair pissing has come to save you?'

'I guess.'

'Glad to have helped. I owed you one for dumping you all. What can I tell you? It's that old devil called love again. Or at least his first cousin – you know, the illegitimate one?'

'Uh-huh,' Shelley said. 'So what's the current incarnation like? He *looks* good.'

Chris nodded enthusiastically. 'He looks *great*. Killer eyes. He's a painter. He –'

'Yeah. Right.'

'No. I really think he is. We went into the other room for some food and talked and, you know, he really seemed to know stuff. I mean, my bullshit meter didn't even flash *once*, you know?'

Shelley smiled for her friend. 'Is he nice?'

This time the nod was slow, with a wry smile and a note of nervous guardedness in the voice.

'Oh yeah. Yeah. He's nice. Real nice. Maybe too nice, you know? I mean, you know what I mean – if he's that nice, how come he's here on his own? Why isn't he taken? And the answer is – he probably is. I mean, you musta been there, Shell. You know the type of guy I mean. They come on all single at you, but by the third or fourth date there's always that phone call they just *gotta* make. Business, you understand. Quiet, whispered voice. And you just *know* there's a confused woman at the other end.'

Chris stared at her friend hopefully, waiting to be contradicted.

Shelley smiled sympathetically. 'Well, sure. I mean, that *hap-pens*. But not always. Maybe he just split up. Maybe you got lucky. I mean, go for it, Chris. At least until you *know*.'

Chris smiled, patted Shelley's cheek gently. 'Hey, kid,' she said, 'you sound like me.'

Shelley shook her head. 'No,' she said. 'No, I really don't. I just don't have that Debra Winger throatiness. God knows I've tried – cigarettes, whisky, the works – it just won't happen.'

Chris laughed. 'C'mon, let's go. I don't trust Anne. If she sees I've left him alone, she'll be over there telling him I go down on the entire male staff every lunchtime.'

'Don't worry.' Shelley followed Chris to the door. 'The truth can't hurt you.'

They were laughing again as they went back into the club.

*   *   *

Shelley sat next to Jane. Her good humour restored by her encounter with Chris, she kept a carefully non-judgmental smile on her face as she glanced at the completely unconscious Heather, sprawled back in her seat with her mouth unattractively half-open. She also did her best not to look disapprovingly at Anne, engaged in a long distance tongue-gyration contest with a bearded blond of large build and Valium eyes who was leaning on the bar sucking in his stomach and assuming his luck had changed.

'I saw Chris,' Shelley said to Jane, not because it was important but because it took her attention away from Anne and Heather and their practical demonstrations of the virtues of abstinence.

'Bitch,' said Jane, managing the difficult trick of slurring a word that had no sibilants.

'No,' Shelley replied, shaking her head and smiling. 'She's okay.'

'She ran off! No guys, we said. Girls' night out.'

'Well, yeah. But, hey, at least hers is a painter not a basket case.' Shelley gestured with her head to the tongue comedian at the bar.

Jane gave a slow laugh, her eyes moving from the guy to

Anne and then back to Shelley. She nodded. 'I guess,' she said, then banged the table for emphasis. 'Hell, yes. If you're going to dump on your friends, do it with style, right?'

'Right!' Shelley agreed, and then, making another gesture with her head, directed Jane's attention across the room. 'And look, at least she's letting him check us out.'

Jane swivelled in her seat to look across the dance floor to where, at a table on a raised area, Chris was standing. She was behind the chair that held her conquest, crouching down slightly, one arm across his back and on his shoulder and the other pointing across the room at Shelley's table.

The guy raised his hand slowly and then sliced the air in a crisp gesture of salute, his face creasing into a smile. Shelley and Jane returned the wave.

'What do you think?' Shelley asked, through her long-distance smile.

'I think I woulda dumped on us, too,' said Jane, and then, one hand to her mouth, called across to Chris. 'Way to go, Chris! Give him one for me!' She broke into drunken laughter despite Shelley's slapping arm and mock-outraged cry of 'Jane! For fuck's sake!'

'Well, exactly,' Jane said, turning back to face Shelley. 'I mean – don't you think?'

Shelley threw another glance at the table where Chris and the guy had returned their attention to each other and smiled slyly. He *was* really good-looking. Slim but broad-shouldered, the face skeletally drawn against all-but-perfect cheekbones, long-legged, and packaged in tight black leather, he really did invite the kind of blatant sexual response Jane had given. Facially, he laid claim to a territory somewhere between the asexual perfection of the young Alain Delon and the sensual let's-do-it-right-here-and-let's-do-it-right-now look of Ray Liotta in *Something Wild*. A mop of hair so black it could come only from a bottle or from Oriental ancestry sat atop the head, framing it in nonchalant perfection.

His chair was pushed back at a perpendicular angle to the table and he was spread over it in wide-legged ease and confidence, one arm leaning across the back of it, the other resting

39

on the table, where his fingers beat out a casual rhythm on the side of his glass. His head leaned in towards Chris, who was leaning forward over her half of the table, her arms crossed beneath her. Their eyes were locked on each other's as they engaged in a conversation of smiles and promises. Something about his eyes . . . Shelley tried to remember something Chris had said about his eyes. Yes. Killer eyes. Something so fleeting as not even to be called a thought flashed through Shelley's mind and she was suddenly aware of an unfocused anxiety.

She was about to try to recapture whatever had prompted this when Jane's voice, raised in incredulous complaint, pulled her back.

'What? Again?' Jane said. She was referring to the Bobby Corvino record, now receiving what seemed like its twentieth play that evening.

Shelley smiled. 'It's the deejay. He looks old enough to be Bobby's brother.'

'He looks old enough to be Bobby's *father*,' snarled Jane. 'Fuck, he looks old enough to be Casey *Kasem*'s father!'

'Well, count your blessings, kid,' said Shelley. 'At least he hasn't borrowed his son's sweaters.'

Jane laughed and, as Bobby and the Fiasco Brothers moved into their close-harmony middle eight, began to sing along in a loud and parodic imitation of their doo-wop loops and swirls.

'*I dreamed I saw her in an e-le-heh-heh-vay-ator.*

I looked around; she was gone . . .'

'"Gone. Gone! GONE! Oooooh!"' sang Shelley, effortlessly ascending the scale with the backing vocals. The girls locked hands across the table and swayed in time to the record.

'"But she must pick somebody sooner or la-heh-heh-ter, so why . . ."'

'"I . . . I . . . I!"'

'"Cannot I . . ."'

'"I . . . I . . . I!"'

'"Be the wuh-huh-hunn!"'

They laughed, let go of each other's hand, and grabbed at drinks as Bobby and the boys flowed into the crooning refrain of 'Dream Angel' without them.

Shelley stole a cigarette from the pack belonging to Anne, who had moved over to the bar to join her blond friend. She took a deep drag and asked if Jane felt like dancing.

'Sure,' Jane said, pushing her chair back.

They danced. Whatever Shelley had been trying to remember had gone from her mind and she didn't think about Chris again until she heard the morning news.

It was 3:20 in the morning and the streets were neither well lit nor welcoming, but Dino had called this area home for eighteen months now and he was in any case drunk enough to be past nervousness.

He was also, though only five-seven, in every other sense a big man – broad shoulders, barrel chest, and upper arms nearly as thick as a slim girl's waist. But he didn't look for trouble; nor, on those occasions when it looked for him, did he particularly enjoy its company. Consequently, when he first heard the rhythmic clicking coming down the cross street towards the corner he himself was approaching, a small needle of anxiety managed to pierce both his drunkenness and the self-confidence his size lent him. Somebody was wearing cleats on their boots, he thought, and walking like they owned the street.

He remembered what Steve had told him – and Steve was from New York and his uncle was connected – about how violence doesn't advertise, about how if somebody showed you their weapon, it was a sure-as-shit sign they weren't going to use it. So somebody who walked to the accompaniment of metal clicking on concrete was probably a somebody who wasn't a professional. So that was good. But that didn't allow for the lunatic, of course. That didn't allow for the crazy whose hunger was not for drugs or food but for human pain itself. That was the kind of maniac who *would* advertise, who would walk down streets in the small hours beneath erratic lighting, making just as much fucking noise as he fucking wanted because he really didn't give a shit, he'd kill anything that was stupid enough to walk his way. And Dino watched TV. Dino read the papers. He knew San Francisco had its very own psycho at the moment. For one horrible frozen second, Dino knew he was in the proximity of Morningstar and the sensible nervousness he had been feeling gave way to a stab of genuine scrotum-shrinking terror, a mortal fear such as he hadn't felt since junior high and the Donnelly brothers.

Then – before his fear had even had time to break his stride, let alone send him speedily back in the direction from which he had come – he heard the other footfalls. The quieter, softer footfalls that marched in time with the confident clicks. And all his fear disappeared.

Jesus, Dino breathed to himself, it's a girl. It's a guy with his girl. What an asshole.

He was happy to insult himself. He was happy to have been stupid. He turned the corner. And there they were, still a few yards from him, a guy and his girl. Arms linked, they walked towards him, interested only in themselves.

God, Dino thought without malice, it wasn't even as if the guy on his own coulda given him any trouble. Okay, he had a few inches on him – the guy was about six foot – but a single punch from Dino would have had him eating hospital food for at least a week.

They were both dressed in black. The girl was gorgeous. Dino smiled at them as they passed. The guy nodded guardedly and the girl mouthed a silent hi wrapped in a heartbreaker of a smile. Dino kept moving as the sound of the cleats turned the corner behind him and began to diminish into the night.

He'd walked maybe another block when the big car crested the hill a block or so in front of him.

It swelled into view over the artificial horizon of the steep street, silhouetted against the night sky, its headlights dimmed. It moved slowly, the sound of its engine a low, purring whisper that seemed pregnant with a potential roar.

Dino paused in his walk as the car coasted past him and followed it with his eyes and a turning head as it moved elegantly and mysteriously down the incline of the streets towards the corner he himself had just turned.

Dino could tell the car was old. He could tell it was fucking expensive. But it was neither of those things that registered most with him. What held him rooted to the spot was the unusualness of its being here at all. There was something almost

43

spooky about its slow, implacable progress through these deserted streets at this quiet and lonely hour, something that suggested purpose, something that recalled in an oblique fashion the deceptively leisurely tread of the confident predator.

Was it trailing the couple he'd – Dino stopped himself as he came to a sudden understanding. A slow smile of contempt crossed his face. He almost wished he *had* decked the guy. Of course; the car was *his*. He was probably some actor or a rock star. Some fuckin' rock star in homeboy drag walking the bitch home because it was the homeboy thing to do while the expensive limo tailed them in case things got a little *too* homeboy for the phony's comfort. Jesus! Punk chic and cleats and a forty-thousand-dollar set of wheels. What an asshole.

Dino stood there a moment or two longer as the car turned the corner and disappeared from his view. Then, shaking his head in the kind of disparagement that only envy can produce, he turned on his sneakered heels and headed home.

'Well, the cabs aren't exactly lining up for our custom, are they?'

Chris's voice broke the unstrained silence they'd lapsed into since passing the heavyset guy on the previous street. There was no annoyance in her tone, just an amused statement of fact. Karel – for that was his name and she'd already checked the spelling and she'd already made all the jokes – grinned embarrassedly.

'Er . . . no. No, they're really not,' he admitted.

'But – now, correct me if I'm wrong – wasn't it you who said you knew the best way to walk to find one?'

'Yep. That was me.' Still smiling, Karel nodded his head in a cross between vigorous agreement and shamefaced admission.

Chris didn't reply, except to echo his smile and to press her arm a little tighter against his. Karel spoke again.

'Fact is, I'm really in no hurry to put you in a cab.'

Chris turned her face towards him. He was looking at her in a sidelong glance and there was a question in his eyes. Chris suddenly stopped walking, pulling him to a stop with her. He

44

angled his body towards her and looked down at her upturned face.

'Fact is,' she said, 'I'm really in no hurry to be put in one.'

She raised one hand to his cheek and stroked at it delicately and slowly. Their eyes locked. Karel leaned his head forward as Chris's rose to meet it. Eyes still open, they brushed their lips together. It was a fleeting and dry contact and they broke it off temporarily, moving a few centimetres apart to refocus on each other's eyes. Then, arms winding languorously about each other, they pulled themselves to each other, body pressed against body, as their mouths, now wet and open, renewed their acquaintance.

Chris could feel the hard wiriness of his body pressing insistently against her as his hands on her back pulled her to him. She felt his erection bloom as the kiss continued. She loved that. She couldn't help it, she always had. To feel that palpable evidence of desire, to have it confirm whatever promises flirtation may have made, was always a sweetly exciting moment for her. She brought her tongue into play, licking delicately at the inside of his mouth, as a discreet but eloquent acknowledgment of what was happening.

She felt his chest swell as he drew in breath through his nose and pressed his own tongue forward to meet hers. The pressure of his hands grew stronger, the urgency of his desire more apparent.

They held the kiss for twenty seconds. Chris felt her heart beat excitedly, felt the rush of her blood, felt her nipples tingle and tighten, felt herself growing moist. She wanted to go home with him. She wanted to feel him lose himself inside her. She wanted to lose herself in him. She wanted them to dissolve into each other, to disappear together, to coalesce and emerge re-formed and complete.

She broke off from the kiss and leaned back in his arms, looking at him, her eyes proclaiming all these unspoken wishes.

Karel was hyperventilating, his breath expelling itself fast and frantic through his flaring nostrils. There was a new fire in his eyes, a fire of furious lust and an excitement beyond containment. 'Why wait?' he said. 'You wanna wait? I don't wanna wait.' His voice was low and intense, a husky and desperate edge to it. The words seemed almost unimportant, merely sonic indicators of the language his body and blood were speaking.

He hadn't let go of Chris when she leaned back from the kiss, and now he lifted her from the sidewalk, thrusting her to him as he suddenly moved forward in a half run, propelling her with him before she had a chance to speak.

Chris, semibreathless from the force of his action, which had smashed her into his body without warning, found herself looking over his shoulder at the retreating ground behind his heels as he carried her on. Her head was a wash of racing and confused emotions – disappointment, anger, surprise, and outrage – but gaining on them all, rapidly taking lead of the field, was a debilitating panic that sealed her mouth and kept her body frozen through those vital seconds during which a cry or a struggle may have alerted interest even in this deserted stretch of town.

By the time she had recovered even a modicum of composure, Karel had carried her thirty or forty yards into a dark and narrow alley that separated two factory buildings on the same block. Suddenly their flight stopped; he put her back on the ground and, placing a hand firmly on her chest, pushed her back against the dirty red-brick side wall of one of the buildings.

'Karel, no! What the fuck are –' was all Chris managed to get out before he raised the hand that had pushed her and, seizing the top of her vest, ripped it open. Her breasts came into view and her cry gave way to a gasping sob as he stood back briefly to look at her.

'Beautiful. Your breasts. Beautiful,' he murmured in the same breathy growl he had last spoken in. He moved back towards her.

'Fuck off!' Chris screamed, anger finally displacing paralysing fear and lending her strength. Forming her right hand into a fist, she swung her arm viciously through the small space that separated them. It was aimed for the side of his head and it was a good swing. Had it connected, it would certainly have gained her enough time at least to start to run. But it didn't connect. Without moving his eyes from the panic-fuelled rise and fall of her breasts, Karel raised his left arm and seized her wrist. He pressed himself to her, sandwiching her between himself and the bricks. His other hand squeezed its way between their bodies and tugged at the front of her skirt as he buried his face in her neck and began kissing it feverishly.

Her voice muffled by his shoulder, Chris tried to call out her outrage and distress as she felt his hand ripping, ferreting, finding, and pawing at her. Reality concentrated itself into this tiny tableau of aggression and selfish demand. Her eyes were focused on the impassive and disinterested bricks opposite her face and she almost found space to be startled by the clarity with which they burned into her consciousness. She could see every tiny detail of their texture, every crack and every line. The world was somehow simultaneously shrunken and enlarged for her as her senses pulled everything into a tight close-up. She could smell his excitement. She could taste her fear. She could hear the rushing of her blood and the thrusting rhythm of his excited breath. Then she heard something else. Something on the fringes of her consciousness. A slamming, metallic sound. A car door closing. A car door closing somewhere back in the real world, where life had detail and multiplicity and wasn't a small primal tableau of taker and weeper, of demand and helplessness.

Chris, frozen and numbed by the assault itself, suddenly began to sob, and the cause of her tears was this sense of involuntary removal from the wider world, this hideous reminder of how reality could be shattered, how the self could be dragged down protesting to dance its ritual prehuman steps in an atavistic ballet of user and used.

Karel's breathing slowed. The hard assertive pressure of his body against hers lessened and he moved back slightly. 'Chris? What's wrong?' his voice said, and it *was* his voice, not the low animal growl she had last heard from him.

Chris blinked away some distorting tears and his face came into focus, a face at once confused and concerned. 'What?' she managed to get out between her gasps as her breathing slowed. Relief waited in the wings while incomprehension did its number first, but Chris could sense its presence and was

47

gratefully patient. Karel spoke, his voice as confused as hers.

'Didn't you . . . ? I mean . . . I thought . . . ?'

His eyes, which seconds before had been burning black jewels of madness and passion, were nervous pools of apology. Chris couldn't believe it. She couldn't fucking believe it! Relief came and went quickly, to be replaced by blazing rage. She could hardly spit the words out through her clenched teeth she was so fucking angry.

'What the fuck do you . . . ? I . . . You thought . . . ? You bastard! You bastard! Are you *completely fucking crazy?*'

'No,' said a voice marginally warmer than an Alaskan midnight. 'He's something worse.'

Chris gasped in shock. Karel's head swung around. Then everything happened very quickly.

Chris had half a second to take in the large shadowed car parked at the end of the alley and the tall man standing between them and it, and then the static moment exploded into action.

The newcomer, from a terrifyingly calm standing start, suddenly leaped forward, his body leaning back gracefully as his right leg shot out with heart-stopping speed and awesome power to slam into Karel's chest. Karel, breath blasting out of him, flew backward, lifted clean off his feet, to smash against the wall opposite Chris.

Even as Karel landed, and before he could fall to the floor as he surely would have done, his attacker had recovered his footing and was moving forward purposefully but calmly, his left hand drawing something from inside his jacket and pressing it to Karel's shocked and fearful face. The man stood well back from Karel, his arm at full stretch and pressing hard, keeping Karel semi-upright by its tension.

Chris could smell the ether from her position several feet away. She saw Karel's eyes roll up into their sockets and close. Before she could even think about responding, the man's right arm pointed at her and his head turned to her.

'Stay,' he said. He took his hand and the chloroform-soaked cloth away from Karel's face. A single word, slurred and terrified, slipped from Karel's mouth before he, completely unconscious, followed its example and slipped to the ground.

'*Matador*,' he said.

The man stepped back and turned to look more fully at Chris. He was in his mid-to-late forties, well built, besuited, and had eyes a king cobra would envy in their fixed implacable coldness. Chris didn't like to look at him and she didn't like him looking at her. She pulled the torn vest together over her chest and kept her arms wrapped around herself, partly to hold the vest in place and partly because her own arms were the only source of comfort she could find in the situation. She didn't even know what the situation was. Had this guy *saved* her? Or what?

'Did you . . . did you save me?' she asked, her tone as flat as his eyes, her inquiry a genuine request for elucidation.

'Yes,' he said, 'I saved you.'

'But . . . I don't know . . .' Chris said carefully. 'He . . . he'd *stopped*. It was —'

The man cut her off. 'I saved you,' he repeated. He looked beyond her, farther down the alley towards the parked car. There was an almost imperceptible gesture of his head, a tiny flicker of expression on that stone face. Chris began to turn her head slowly in the direction of his glance in order to see to whom or to what he was signalling, but realized he was moving towards her. She snapped her head back to find his eyes again.

His expression hadn't changed. His right hand was reaching into his jacket. He was very close to her. 'Unfortunately,' he said, 'you've seen me.'

Then he slit her throat.

The knife had appeared, his arm had flown, and her throat had opened in one smooth sequence that rehearsal couldn't have bettered. Chris certainly had no time for specific fear of the knife. She didn't even see it. Or hardly, she realized with surprise, feel it. Her neck felt very cold immediately afterward, but by then she was busy watching the man Karel had called Matador turn away from her and bend over the unconscious body of the painter.

She realized she was sliding down the wall as feeling began to disappear from her body. She realized that the hammering in her head that was both deafeningly loud and inconceivably distant was as unreal to the world and as real to her as the sound of the sea when shells are held to the ear. She found she could call that sound, too, and the hammering gave way to a deep timeless roar. *Listen, Chris*, her mother was saying, *listen. Take it home and keep the sea with you always.* Her eyes failed. Everything was black. She realized she was dying. But she held on to her previous thought. She dwelt on the sea as a sweet metaphor for whatever unknown tides were pulling at her now. She would let them carry her, held by their swell, until they took her to whatever shore they would. She hoped there would be music. She hoped she wasn't bleeding too much. She heard footsteps coming up the alley, but she didn't see the chauffeur. She was riding the waves. She was gone.

June 13

*B*rrrrring

'Yes?'

'You said to call. Is it . . . ?'

'Convenient? Yes. Speak.'

'The woman's brother-in-law was observed in a bar late yesterday afternoon. He spent more than an hour with the subject.'

'So I may assume the information has been passed on.'

'Well, I can't guarantee that. This method is –'

'That wasn't a question. It's been passed on. The dissemination of information is an engineering problem, no more no less. People are like ball bearings. Grease the path and they go where you intend. The money's already in your account.'

'Then I guess that's everything. Just keep my mouth shut, huh?'

'That is entirely your decision.'

'It's professional ethics. I –'

'I have no interest in pursuing this conversation. I don't buy silence. I pay for assistance. Silence I guarantee by other means. Do I make myself clear?'

'Perfectly. But you misunderstood. I wasn't –'

'Good-bye.'

Click.

It was early evening. Matt was doing drinks with a client over in Sausalito, and so Donovan was alone in their apartment with a dinner-cooked-from-frozen, a large black coffee, and a racing mind as he switched on the TV to catch the six o'clock news.

The lunchtime news had had nothing for him. Nobody had

been butchered for nearly fifty hours, and so Morningstar had been relegated to third, behind more bombs in Paris and a record divorce settlement. There had been nothing new in the report anyway, just a voice-over listing the same grim statistics while beneath it the same footage of a harried Commissioner Schulman – fighting his way down the same City Hall steps to a waiting car, still silently mouthing the same 'No further comment. No further comment' to the silently pressing crowd of microphones, cables, and cameras – replayed itself.

Moon had spent the morning in the morgues of various newspapers reading all the reports on the killings. All afternoon he'd given some serious phone time to contacts and acquaintances in the media and law enforcement. Zilch. Nothing. *Nada.* So here he was back with the TV, getting his facts like any other sap. On screen, the picture cut to a location report.

'Oh fuck,' said Moon.

This was new. It was familiar, but it was new. The ambulance lights, the yellow police-department plastic bands sealing an area off, the mass of people, some busy, some curious, the zipped body bags – all the regular set-dressings, props, and extras were there. But the location was new – the base of a statue in a city park. The leading player was, as ever, absent, but his latest costar played the usual still, silent, and severed role.

The voice of Waverley Garrick, the station's top news anchorwoman, emerged over the location noises, and after her first few words, her professionally concerned face replaced the documentary footage. Waverley – Donovan knew for a fact she'd been christened Jean – was as glamorous and beautiful as any prime-time soap star and was just as routinely dismissed as an airhead by many among the public, but Donovan rather admired her ever since he'd seen her slice up a particularly slippery senator over a pollution cover-up. And he liked green eyes.

'In a bizarre twist to the series of brutal slayings which have become known as the Morningstar murders and have terrorized San Francisco for the last eleven days, police have this afternoon admitted that they don't know whether the unknown killer's tally is now thirteen or fourteen after two bodies were discovered during the course of the day. Here's Martin with the details.'

Moon stopped eating and sat a little further forward in his chair. Two bodies. Was one of them the first of the copycat killings Munro had implied the police had expected? Or was it some other problem? Here was Martin with the details.

Martin Freeling was a bluff broad-shouldered redhead who had started off as a sports reporter and had somehow graduated to hard news. The station's PR called him the Face America Trusts. Donovan had once had drinks with him and had quietly decided he wouldn't trust the man to unzip his own fly without a studio manager talking him through it on a headset, but, hey, what did he know? One of Freeling's monthly paychecks could probably buy Moon's whole neighbourhood, raze it, develop it, and still let him eat sushi all month. Tell us about it, Martin.

'Thank you, Waverley,' Freeling said, flashing her a smile that was curt enough not to seem inappropriate, given the topic, but confident enough to validate America's trust. His face became set and troubled as he continued. 'Police chiefs today admitted to puzzlement after two killings in the San Francisco area last night.'

On the inset screen behind his head appeared a black-and-white photograph of a smiling young woman. Pretty. Stylish. Bobbed black hair. Donovan felt a wave of pity wash over him.

'The first victim was a young woman. The body of Chris Tempest was discovered early this morning. Her throat had been cut and she'd been left to die in an alleyway.'

Freeling paused for a second to shake his head slightly in disgusted disbelief. The picture of Chris was replaced by a colour shot of a skeletal-faced young man in a black T-shirt. 'From the testimony of Ms Tempest's friends, who'd been with her last evening, suspicion for this slaying centred initially on this man. Karel Voedicher, a young avant-garde painter with a growing reputation in the art world, had left a nightclub with Chris Tempest in the early hours of the morning.

'Police had already initiated a search for Voedicher when, in a bizarre turn of events, his mutilated and dismembered body was discovered shortly after midday several miles from where Tempest had been found. He was confirmed later to have been a victim of the lunatic killer Morningstar. A much-loved piece of public art located near his body had been defaced with the maniac's signature.'

The TV image cut to a two-shot of Garrick and Freeling as Waverley interjected, 'But that's not all, Martin, is it?'

'No, it's not, Waverley. What may have been a simple but horrible coincidence of one killer being killed by another now seems less likely; autopsy findings have revealed that not only did the victims die within an hour of each other but that the knife which ended Chris Tempest's life was also one of the weapons used on Karel Voedicher. It seems probable, the police are now saying, that Tempest, too, though not mutilated in the same trademark way, was a victim of Morningstar.'

Waverley's perfect face creased into an expression of bemused horror that Donovan granted the benefit of not looking rehearsed. 'It's awful,' she said. 'Something has to be done.'

Freeling nodded, his face grim. He turned towards the camera directly as the studio cut back to his head-shot. 'That's right. If you're watching, Commissioner Schulman, it's not just the city, it's not just the state. America Wants Action. Find this man.'

Waverley replaced Freeling on screen. 'Sentiments I'm sure we all share,' she said, looking earnestly into the camera before casting her eyes down for a beat to allow a change of tone. 'Turning now to the Middle East . . .'

Moon switched off the set via the remote, drank his coffee, smoked two cigarettes, and continued to stare at the darkened screen.

He hadn't mutilated the girl. He had differentiated between her and the boy. Was this the first example of that? Donovan wondered. Or were there a few other unclaimed corpses hanging around the city morgue or already in the ground that had enjoyed the dubious benefit of a Morningstar murder, second class? And what the fuck did it mean, anyway? He just hadn't had the time to go the distance? No, the way this guy had been operating – four kills in one day last weekend was it? – he'd have *made* the time. The decision had to be conscious. The only hypothesis that fit was the crazy one Pete had given in Sam's place. Some required the special treatment, some didn't. Moon let himself run with it.

So Morningstar was some amateur Van Helsing? Some self-appointed pest exterminator leaving roaches, rats, and rabid dogs to the small-timers while he, presumably neither tarnished nor afraid, made his way down the mean streets of Vampire County? Pete was right. As wackos go, this one *went*. This one was a classic.

And what, for fuck's sake, were his criteria, anyway? How'd he spot them? What particular mental fracture could make him perceive an eight-year-old kid as a short-pants Bela Lugosi? And why didn't it worry him that his targets could walk in daylight? God, he was so textbook in his method of dispatching the poor bastards, you'd think that whatever it was that did an impersonation of logic in his fucked-up head would tell him something was wrong when the sun wasn't already doing his slaughtering for him. And why the splatter party afterwards? That wasn't right, was it? He couldn't see Peter Cushing going to town on the vampire's body after he'd finished him off. Or signing his work. None of that went with the dignified anonymity of the literary and cinematic vampire hunter.

But of course Morningstar was a psycho, wasn't he, and anonymity doesn't suit psychos. They might want their family name kept secret so that they could carry on their work without troublesome house calls from concerned policemen or greedy publishers, but they *liked* to smear blood in the world's face, they *liked* to be noticed.

So why bother with the traditional and elaborate ritual first?
Because that was his particular madness.
So why screw it up by smearing the remains all over town?
Because he wants to be noticed.
There are newspapers — the guy can't write? He spells his fucking name out often enough. Why not do the job neatly and let the world know via the mail? Why mess 'em up?
Because he likes to mess people up.
No, he doesn't. He's a vampire hunter. He likes to kill vampires in the time-honoured way. So why mess 'em up?

Because . . . no . . . because he doesn't want people to *know* he's a vampire hunter? Would that make any kind of sense?

Munro had said that all twelve of Morningstar's previous victims were known to have been staked – but no stakes had been found at any of the killing grounds, even though several knives, cleavers, and screwdrivers *had* been found, thrown aside in an apparently careless disregard for any clues they might provide (not to mention the cost of replacement). But *was* it carelessness? Or was it camouflage?

All twelve victims had been beheaded, but three or four heads were still missing. So the force-fed garlic diet could only be assumed to be a constant for the whole dozen. Further; the mouths of those heads that had been found had been beaten to a bloody pulp. In an attempt to hide the contents? Could that really be it? Some crazy attempt to make what the killer regarded as a perfectly proper vampire extermination look like the random work of a maniac? Surely not. That would be . . . clever. Worryingly clever. He'd have to recognize the world's notion of craziness and agree with it to do that, wouldn't he? To throw up a smoke screen of insanity while quietly getting on with his vocation. No. To buy that you'd almost . . . almost . . . have to buy the notion that the first bit – the vampire killing – wasn't crazy, wouldn't you? Wait. Wait. If you try to disguise something by making it look crazy – and you know it *looks* crazy to do so – then you can't *be* crazy, can you? Does the madman try to fool the world by making it think he's mad? The mutilations were undeniable proof of madness. But were they proof of the madness that hides madness – or the madness that hides a terrible sanity?

Donovan breathed out slowly, his eyes blinking at the grey blankness of the TV screen. He really didn't like the way this was going. Didn't like it at all. He put his coffee aside, walked to the five-by-five-foot mirror that sat in silvered splendour above the old-fashioned fireplace, and began talking to himself. A small, silent voice threw in its own reply: 'You want to know what crazy is? Talking to your reflection, that's what fucking crazy is.' But he treated that contempt with the silence it deserved and continued his conversation.

'Look,' he said. 'What do you see?'

'A guy so close to six feet the half inch ain't worth talking about. Good shoulders. Nice haircut. Hell, nice hair – and not receding yet, which is not bad for thirty-six years of shampoo and city life. Strong chin. Shame about the other one. Waist, admittedly non-existent – but what do you expect from a predominantly sedentary profession? And at least the hips aren't actually wider than the chest yet.'

Donovan nodded. His reflection did likewise. It was a fair summary, honest without false modesty, kind without false hope. But he knew that wasn't the point. Speaking slowly, with patient understanding, he coaxed his reluctant self further into its auto-analysis.

'Now look at the eyes,' he suggested.

'Blue,' he replied with *faux naif* evasiveness.

'Look deeper.'

He shuffled his feet and avoided his gaze. But he was insistent.

'Face it, Moon. Those are wise eyes.'

He smiled gratefully. This wasn't so bad.

'Those are the eyes of a man who has seen life. A man who has been touched by it but not mortally wounded. Understanding eyes. Mature. Rational eyes. Rational guy.'

Donovan smirked. Shucks, this was getting embarrassing.

'*So what the fuck are you doing convincing yourself you believe in vampires!*' This last roared, with waving arms and flaring nostrils. '*Idiot!*'

Properly told off, he turned away from the mirror exactly on cue for the ringing telephone, perched on a small table between the long couch and the fireplace. He gave a slight start at its first ring, like an errant pupil suddenly getting an unexpected faceful of platitudes and abuse from a school secretary after the Principal had already done the major humiliation. But he pulled himself together with a quick deep breath and picked up the receiver.

'Donovan Moon,' he told it.

'Good evening, Mr Moon,' it replied. 'This is Jonathan Frost. Tell me, do you believe in vampires?'

7

Two seconds of silence.

'Why . . . this is . . . er . . . this is quite a coincidence, Mr Frost.' He could almost feel the shift in the level of alertness at the other end of the phone line.

'I don't believe in coincidence, Mr Moon. To what were you referring?'

Donovan had, of course, been referring to his meeting with Pete Munro, its consequent considerations, and the absurd synchronicity of Frost's absurd question. Now, however, something intangible yet unpleasant in his caller's tone, something suddenly hard-edged, chased Donovan into a glib lie. Undoubtedly Jonathan Frost was somebody it was unwise to lie to, he reflected instantaneously, but it was too late. 'Oh, it's, just that only ten minutes ago I finished reading the *Examiner*'s piece about you.'

Nearly true, he thought. Nearly true. So near I can believe it.

It was in fact at this hour on the previous day that Moon had gotten about halfway through a five-thousand-word feature article about Jonathan Frost before realizing, as happened often with him, that he had no interest in the piece. An arresting opening phrase, a familiar or respected byline, even a witty caption to an accompanying photograph – something, anything, could regularly persuade him to buy a ticket to someone's train of thought, but it was always the old engine called habit that hauled him helplessly on towards the terminus long after the ride had entered territory that left him cold. It had been like that with the profile of Frost.

Jonathan Frost, it had told him, was a prodigious achiever. Still in his middle forties, he was one of the country's most respected and successful real-estate developers. Neither an architect nor an urban planner by training, he was nevertheless one of the men most sought after when a city wished to remake itself. Described as a 'conceptualist' and a 'motivator' by those who had worked with or employed him, he had risen to a position where he now commanded his own team of specialists and, once given the green light by a city council, could single-handedly oversee every aspect of slum clearance, office-building construction, or environmental cleanup that a city tired of its appearance could wish for.

There had been the obligatory paragraph or two listing the main objections of his detractors – that his austere yet elegant plazas and boulevards, grafted wholesale onto areas that had grown in their own labyrinthine, chaotic style over decades, stripped a neighbourhood of character (a word put heavy-handedly in quotation marks by the writer or his editor). But apart from a surprisingly undetailed summary of his life prior to his first public success – the transformation of a square mile of derelict waterfront property in New Jersey into an upscale mall – the article was a relatively uncomplicated paean to the city's latest, and by implication one of its greatest, residents. Oh, yes, Donovan vaguely remembered – that point in the article having been just about where he'd jumped off the train – Frost had moved his whole team out here and had taken over an entire skyscraper in the financial district, renamed it simply Frost's (nothing as pushy as the Frost Building or Frost Tower) and doubled the price of rentals for floors two to twenty.

'Two pages of flattering nonsense, Mr Moon. I'm surprised you managed to finish it.'

Donovan was pulled back to the present by Frost's voice, its tone less frozen, thawed perhaps by Donovan's lie. 'No, no. Fascinating.' Another lie, but an easy one.

'I'm also surprised you chose to remark on the article rather than on what anyone else might regard as a fairly startling question, if asked seriously – which, I assure you, is the spirit in which I ask it.'

'Oh. Yeah.' Donovan paused, uncomfortable again. 'Vampires, right?'

'Yes. Vampires. Do you? Believe in them?'

Oh, what the fuck. 'Yes.'

'Good.' Frost paused for a second and then continued without further comment on Donovan's admission, as if every day people acknowledged to him their belief in sea serpents, giants, or spring-heeled jacks. 'There's a car waiting downstairs for you, Mr Moon. Perhaps you would do me the service of getting in it.'

'Why?'

'Because I feel you'd be able to do this more comfortably over here at my building.'

'Fine. Do what?'

'Oh, forgive me. Interview me, of course. I'm Morningstar.'

Three flights down to the darkening street – Donovan took the stairs. The apartment he and Matt shared on Liberty Street had originally been the attic of one of the old gingerbread Victorian houses that beautified that area. Despite the house's carefully preserved nineteenth-century style, an elevator had been installed at some time in the 1940s, and Donovan, moving in in the late seventies and instantly acquiring the breath-saving habit of ascending in it, had soon acquired the balancing habit of going down in it, too.

But still he took the stairs as his route to Frost's limousine. He wanted time to calm down. He wanted time to think. But suddenly there was the front door and he had done neither. What he had done, he realized as his hand moved to open the door and deliver him into the night and its stories, was to throw on an attractive but seasonally unsuitable overcoat, long, heavy, and dark brown. He tried to remember what he had on underneath. Couldn't. Oh shit, he thought, and opened the door.

The car was beautiful. He knew that much. He didn't drive cars, knew little about them, and cared less, but every now and then aesthetics conquered apathy and he was forced to admit to the glory of certain models. This was one of those occasions.

The car was long and sleek and its two-tone bodywork of silver grey and midnight blue shone in the twilight. The lights in the rear compartment revealed an interior of red leather and varnished wood. It had running boards. Free-mounted headlights. Moulded tyre compartment in the back. Big. Gleaming. Beautiful.

Moon had no way of knowing that the car was English, a 1934 Bentley. That didn't matter. What was important was that it was a car from Moon's childhood dreams of adventure. The type of car driven by heroes of pulp fiction, whose mythical exploits the pubescent Donovan had assiduously collected in paperback reprints. It was a car to ferry those dark and perfect cavaliers into the twilight testing grounds of rain-soaked neon streets or grim dockside warehouses. It wasn't the model in which Kato drove the Green Hornet, nor that in which the Shadow purged his enemies, but it was something appropriate to them or any other of the Nietzschean Supermen who made the world safe in the 1930s. Spy smashers. Gang busters. Vampire hunters.

Even as Donovan stepped onto the sidewalk and registered these impressions, a rear door was opening for him, though there was no one sitting in the back-seat. At first he thought it was automatic – ('No, you didn't, you thought it was magic,' said the silent voice from his earlier conversation) but then he saw that the chauffeur had leaned back from his front seat and opened the door.

Nodding in what he hoped was a confident and feared was a nervous manner, Donovan approached the car, got in, sat down, and grasping the leather-covered handle, pulled the door shut. 'Hi,' he said to the rearview mirror's reflection of the chauffeur's face.

A slight and impassive nod in return.

'Big old thing, isn't she?'

Nothing.

'Nice, though. Very nice.' You're chattering. Nervous. Shut up.

Nothing.

'Bet she drinks gas like a pervert drinks piss, huh?' Oh Christ.

A raised eyebrow.

'Oh shit. I'm sorry. Let's just drive.'

They just drove.

Night actually fell, Donovan figured, as the Bentley made its first turn, left onto Dolores. The streetlights had long been on, but it was at just about that time that the spaces between them became black, not the deep dark blue that they had been.

Jonathan Frost?

Once they made the right into Market Street, of course, it

was so bright that night attained godhood; you could no longer see it, you just believed it to be there. They had joined one of the major routes through town, and headlights, movie posters, dazzling store windows, and neon bar signs collaborated to create that strange, almost hallucinatory half-world, neither night nor day, that can exist only in big cities and is made stronger in the summer months by the continued presence on the street of shirtsleeves and sweat late into the evening.

Morningstar?

The car skirted a collection of civic buildings, turned left onto Grant Avenue, and cruised north through Chinatown. The Bentley collected more stares now as people on their way to or from restaurants paused to admire or to resent its elegance. Moon, depending upon the nature of the stares, sat smug or uncomfortable in the back.

Vampires?

They cut straight over Columbus, heading for Telegraph Hill, and beyond the Embarcadero, Donovan could see the lights of the cars on the bridge to Oakland forming a glittering and mobile chain over the darkened waters of San Francisco Bay. He glanced behind him, and illuminated on the hill, the stupid phallic nozzle of the Coit Memorial Tower was his last sight before the darkness reinstated itself in the form of the low unlit roof of Frost's underground parking lot. The Bentley smoothed to a stop and its lights went out.

Why me, Lord?

The pitch blackness lasted only a second, of course, before, from a remote in the dash, the chauffeur shed light on the long low cavern into which they had come. This done, he slid smoothly from his seat to the rear doors of the car. He moved quickly. But not quite quickly enough to save Donovan from committing the sin of opening his own door.

'Would you follow me to the elevator, sir?' the chauffeur said, glossing over Donovan's social maladroitness. Without waiting for a reply, he turned on his heels and walked deeper into the parking lot.

Wonder if he's carted dead heads around in that car? thought Donovan as he followed him towards the bank of elevators in the middle of the lot, but as that thought led inevitably to the possibility that he himself might very well recently have been sitting on the same fine red leather on which such pieces of person may have rolled around, he did not pursue it.

Instead he pursued the chauffeur whose pace was as brisk as his outfit was fetishistic. I mean, thought Donovan, *leather*? Does he *know* what signals he's sending out? He wondered further whether the choice of fabric was the man's own or that of his employer, and if it was Frost's, what that said about him. He glanced around as the chauffeur pressed a button to call the elevator. The lot was nothing out of the ordinary, just a big, bland space with walls and support pillars of grey-brown concrete and little in the way of decoration. Apart from the Bentley, very few vehicles were parked there at the moment – one or two sleek and low Japanese machines that were presumably the property of one or two sleek and middling junior executives from any of the businesses that rented from Frost, and a few older American dinosaurs that were presumably the property of janitorial or security staff. A perfectly normal midevening parking lot at the base of a perfectly normal office building that just happened to be owned by a perfectly abnormal serial killer. Hell of a scenario, Moon, Donovan told himself, hell of a scoop. So why would you rather be getting quietly drunk somewhere less interesting? He trotted into the cubicle behind his leather-clad guide.

'Mr Frost is waiting in the penthouse, sir,' the chauffeur explained as the automatic doors sealed them in the small space. Donovan assumed that this was where they were going, though, in fact, the button the man had pressed was unmarked.

The ride was giddyingly fast. They reached the top of a twenty-five-storey building in what Donovan's stomach assured him later, having made its own much slower ascent, must have been less than five seconds.

The doors slid open. Moon's companion stood aside and gestured politely in the direction of the carpeted corridor beyond. 'Through those double doors, sir,' he said to Donovan's back as Moon stepped out onto the plush carpet and glanced quickly around him. The corridor was small and contained nothing other than the double doors the chauffeur had indicated and the elevator itself, the doors of which Donovan now heard close behind him as the chauffeur descended, leaving him alone.

He stared at the dark wooden doors ahead of him, pulled at his sleeves, swallowed, ran a hand through his hair, yearned for a mirror, feared for his sanity, scratched his crotch, breathed deeply, and grasping a brass handle in each sweating palm, pulled at the doors.

Unfortunately they opened inward.

Cursing himself, he pushed. And found himself in a remarkable room.

Remarkable, that is, in its lack of elements to remark upon. It was large, admittedly. It was imposing, certainly. But its size and its ability to daunt the first-time visitor were roughly the norm for the receiving room of any man of power. Donovan felt awkward and embarrassed by the room – the evocation of such feelings being, of course, one of the primary functions of such rooms – but the embarrassment was curiously comforting in its familiarity, the awkwardness almost an old friend.

The room was longer than it was wide. It was very wide. The carpet stopped with the corridor; here a gleaming wooden floor allowed the existence of only two types of walker – those who strode with confidence, enjoying the ringing rhythm that told of their passing, and those who felt like jerks. Donovan, of course, felt like a jerk, but as previously noted, he was, at that particular moment, happy with anything that made him feel at home, no matter how shameful home was.

The first two thirds of the room's length were essentially bare, except that about twelve feet into the room two antique wooden chairs of a plain style faced each other from opposite walls. Between these, as if breaching a psychological electric eye, the visitor had to pass. 'If you really can't make it,' they seemed to say to Donovan, 'you may sit on one of us, singled out for shame like the school dullard.'

After a further fifteen feet of testing ground came the occupied area. The chauffeur had referred to the penthouse and Moon had flashed on an image of himself sinking into a dark leather chesterfield, chomping one of Frost's cigars, and swilling some of his cognac while Frost, tuxedo-clad, told his ghost stories. Penthouse level or not, however, he was clearly in a room in which the dominant aesthetic was 'Office: Spartan.' There was a chair – stranded stylistically somewhere between the Particularly Luxurious Secretarial and the Just-Short-of-Insulting Visitor's – which he assumed was for his use, standing as it did on the same side of the substantial, though non-ornate, wooden desk as he did.

The desk had an inlaid surface of deep green leather and on this surface rested two tumblers. One, the nearer to Donovan, contained what looked suspiciously like a large scotch, the other a colourless liquid that Donovan tried to believe could be vodka or gin or white rum but knew was probably water. The company of teetotallers was depressing at the best of times, but Donovan felt particularly hard-pressed at that moment when, more than anything, he would have liked to have felt he had something, if only a taste for booze, in common with the man behind the desk.

Jonathan Frost was at least as elegant as his Bentley, at least as impressive as his room. By the time Moon reached his table, the executive was on his feet. It seemed to Donovan that the time taken by Frost to stand was equal to that taken by his own nervous crossing of the long room, as if Frost had started to rise as the doors had been fumbled open and, without appearing to exaggerate or deliberately to draw out his rising, had completed his simple movement to coincide perfectly with the cessation of his visitor's tread.

'Mr Moon,' he said, 'please,' and gestured with his right hand in a crisp but expansive manner towards the chair that Donovan had correctly guessed to be temporarily his.

Again, as with the room, it was the almost stereotypical elegance of the man that surprised Moon. There was no denying the aura that Frost exuded – an intoxicating mix of power and refinement – but while it may not have been familiar to Moon the social creature, the journalist in him knew it well. The suit, like the suits of his peers, was neither in nor out of fashion, but the cut was superb, the hand stitching apparent without being

66

obvious, and the cloth itself as unostentatiously rich as a millionaire's daughter.

His other clothes too, elegant in their simplicity, were predictable in their elegance. A pure silk tie of unobtrusive stripe lay comfortably on a plain white shirt of the finest cotton. Donovan couldn't see the shoes, but he knew what they were. The only jewellery Frost wore was a plain gold band on the middle finger of his right hand. The nails of both that and the left hand were trimmed, buffed, and shined just enough to let you know that their owner was no blue-collar labourer. They, like the suit, like the furniture, like the room itself, were . . . Donovan hesitated . . . *appropriate*, no more, no less, to one's received notion of Jonathan Frost and his type. The black hair, too, silvering at the temples, neither brutally short nor romantically long but slicked back into place, was . . . shit, it was just *right*, was all.

Donovan had taken in this impression of his host in less than a second. Frost was still on his feet, his hand still extended towards the chair. His mouth was pulled into a smile of welcome that gathered no support from his eyes, which, while as luminously blue as Paul Newman's, were as flat as if painted in exquisite detail on the surface of his closed lids. Moon didn't like to look at them. He didn't like to think about what secret pleasures might make those pinpoint pupils expand into swollen excitement.

Giving a brief and nervous smile of his own as he moved towards the chair, Donovan looked beyond Frost to the large painting on the wall behind him. While no expert, he was fairly sure that the disturbingly blurred figure he was looking at was the work of Francis Bacon. He almost sneered. Not at the painter, but at the patron. No, he thought. Ten years ago, Frost, you might have convinced me, but now . . . too easy. Even your eccentricity is straight out of some 'What to Own This Year: Pleasures and Possessions for Plutocrats' article.

He was disappointed. He was actually able to be disappointed. He was tempted to open the conversation with a casual 'Frankly, Mr Frost, I expected something a little more off-the-wall from a mass murderer,' but decided against it.

He was confused. He was definitely confused. He was unsure how to relate this . . . ordinariness – elegant and impressive as it was – to a man who had called up a decidedly low-rent journalist out of the blue and, in effect, admitted to fourteen monstrous slayings. Even harder to connect it to a man who was maybe crazy enough to have *done* them. More unlikely still, a man so disconnected that he believed that what he was doing had a kind of moral imperative to it – that he was not a blood-hungry psycho but a fearless vampire hunter. Then there was that other possibility, the one Donovan pretended didn't exist: that Frost *was* a fearless vampire hunter.

He was fascinated. He was, despite nervousness, awe, disappointment, and confusion, fascinated. He was here to listen, here to discover, here to understand. He sat down and, repeating his smile with a little more confidence and raising his generous measure of scotch, decided to start things up. 'Here's to you, Mr Frost,' he said. 'Or can I call you Jack?'

Frost didn't even let a beat pass. He was right back on him. 'It's an old joke, Mr Moon,' he replied. 'Can I call you Shine-on-Harvest?'

Now, *that* was almost unexpected. Donovan smiled more warmly. He had a topper, of course – 'No. You can call me tomorrow' – but the scotch being a fine single malt, the chair being more comfortable than its appearance suggested, the only way out being down twenty-five floors of a darkened and possibly deserted building, and his curiosity being what it was . . . he kept it to himself.

Frost, as if he had followed effortlessly Donovan's temptation to cap his remark and understood perfectly his reasons for resisting it, leaned slightly forward in his chair and, steepling his fingers in front of his chin, spoke again. 'Mr Moon. Any questions you may have on the matters I am about to speak of I will gladly answer. I would ask only that you bear with me a few minutes first while I give you some background on myself and my struggle. May I do so?'

The voice, Donovan admitted to himself, was attractive; consciously low without being ridiculously Roger Moore about it and with a vague mid-Atlantic accent rich in the rhythms of persuasion. He nodded his assent, settled himself more comfortably in his chair, and prepared to listen.

To the left of the Bacon was a large picture window. During the day, it was doubtless possible to look down at the teeming life below, from Telegraph Hill all the way to Fisherman's Wharf, but at that hour and from his seat, all Donovan could see was a framed section of the night sky. A crescent moon was there, and a solitary star. For a brief moment he wondered, poetically and pointlessly, if it was perhaps Venus, the Morning Star, risen early to hear her crazed child tell his tale, and then, shaking his head slightly, he turned his eyes, ears, and full attention back to his host, the killer.

PART TWO

FROST'S
SECRET
MINISTRY

I was born in the heart of chaos (Frost began). No, don't worry, Mr Moon, this is to be neither a metaphysical nor a metaphorical autobiography. I mean that quite literally. From the warm pulses of my mother's womb I was pulled into a world on fire. One second I was listening to her heartbeat, the next to the sound of Hitler's bombs. Ah, yes, I don't think that the researchers the *Examiner* employed managed to find this out – and frankly I would have been surprised if they had – but I'm English. Or I was. I now choose to regard myself as a citizen of the world, but in that blitzkrieg summer of 1940, I was simply one of hundreds of children born to the people of Liverpool, England, despite the strongest efforts of the Luftwaffe.

Liverpool, as you may or may not know, was a major target for the Germans. Two hundred miles from London it may be, but its factories, its docks, were considered important enough by the Reich and its masters for, at one stage, nightly raids. And they were very thorough. Whole streets disappeared. Entire districts woke to devastation. Many people died. Many children's lives were measured in minutes. Seconds. I was lucky.

My mother was already in labour, a midwife already in attendance, when the sirens sang their warning on the evening of my birth. She was at home. Quite common then for deliveries. Obviously moving her was out of the question, and so the midwife, whose devotion to new life must clearly have outweighed her fear for her own, stayed by her bedside.

It was a long labour, I'm told, and by the time I was ready to leap into the world, it was a dangerous one indeed. The raid had begun. Explosions, fire, and screams of pain and despair must have been the counterpoint to my mother's groans and the midwife's encouragement. They must have paused, those two women, even at the height of the one's agony and the

73

other's efforts, paused and found each other's eyes when they heard the whistling sound stop overhead. How strange it must have seemed to them, in that frozen moment of silence and dark expectation, to be so close to life as, suddenly, death came out of the sky. The silence fled, disfigured and torn by a sound as loud as Armageddon and as viciously hungry as the baying of the hounds of hell.

It was a direct hit. But a direct hit on the house next door. The windows of my father's house shattered in sympathy. The midwife released her tension in a long scream. The night turned into a dancing brightness as brick, mortar, and security became flame. And I was born.

The midwife survived. My mother survived. And I, as you see, survived. A happy ending, in fact. But a happy ending a little too close to its alternative for my mother's peace of mind. She wanted to take no second chances. My father was a barrister by profession, but one who had exchanged the bar for the battlefield the day after Hitler had marched into Poland. So he was away from home. I was the firstborn, and no aged relatives lived with us. In short, there was nothing to stop my mother decamping the city as soon as I was old enough to move.

My mother had come from Welsh farming stock before my father had swept her off her feet and into the city and she was still close to a male cousin, Harvey, who ran a small farm in a village in North Wales. When I was barely a month old, it was to that village we travelled.

We stayed there, at the farm, for the rest of the war. The Battle of Britain was in fact won within months of our moving and certainly by 1942 or three we could well have moved back. But my mother was adamant. She regarded my safe delivery and her survival in the middle of that air raid as a special providence and she had no intention of seeming to presume on another by moving back before the war was entirely over. Entirely won, in fact – like most of her generation and class, she apparently was never in any doubt about our eventual victory. I like to feel I take after her in that. And she, as you know, was proved right.

I digress. The first five years of my life, then, despite the initial confused horror – of which, of course, I have no personal memory, anyway – were peaceful and serene. Somewhere beyond my horizons the world was at its own throat but to a babe-in-arms, an infant, a child, the green fields and livestock that filled my vision each day were world enough. Again, I have very little real memory of that time. Isolated pictures. Single afternoons. Smells. Atmospheres, perhaps.

Anyway – the war was over. My father was alive and intact, and by the time I was old enough for school, I was a city child again, back in the house I was born in with reunited parents and, despite the strictures of the postwar period, a far from penurious life-style – my father's chambers having welcomed him back as their only war hero, the other partners being all in their fifties.

But it's Wales I need to tell you about, Mr Moon. It's Wales where the course of my life was to be decided.

Every summer from 1946 to 1952, I returned to my uncle's farm for long holidays. Technically, of course, Harvey was my second cousin, but his treatment of me was entirely avuncular, and as neither of my parents had any brothers or sisters, he became my honorary uncle and his daughter, Laura, my honorary cousin. Harvey's wife had died in childbirth while my mother and I were refugees. My mother remembered her. I don't. Laura was only two years younger than me, so her mother, dead before my consciousness kept score, has no place in my memories.

They were happy summers. Indeed, my recollection of my childhood is based almost entirely on my days there. Strange, isn't it? Ten months of each year were spent in Liverpool, yet if ever I think of where I was, what I was doing, when I was six, eight, ten, it is somewhere green and open. A place of blue skies and peace. Always sunny as well, of course – which is complete nonsense. I don't know if you know Britain, but its weather, particularly in the north, is frankly foul. Yet I have no memory of unpleasant days there. Wind and rain, like city life, have been edited out of my childhood. Perhaps everyone does that? Perhaps that's why, as adults burdened with a present tense perception of reality, we venerate childhood so much.

Why our buried selves grieve for it. In memory's selective scrap-book all childhoods were perfect and every summer golden. 'The happy highways where I went, and cannot come again,' and all that. Do you know Housman? Never mind.

Enough! We have spoken of Arcady – soon we shall speak of the serpent.

From the autumn of 1952 to the spring of 1959, I was away from home at school, and so naturally enough my summers were spent with my parents at home or holidaying with them abroad. I think I spent a couple of weekends with Harvey and Laura every other year or so, but the pattern was broken. In any case, puberty had arrived early on in this period to take me away from my childhood and deposit me in another country. A country whose signs I couldn't read clearly straightaway but one which nevertheless and suddenly felt like home. From the wisdom of thirteen, eleven seems aeons away, its events prehistoric, and its concerns almost shameful.

There were also my new friends, of course. Wensdowne was a good school. Not in the top four or five, you understand, but respected. Particularly fond of it, for some reason, were expatriate parents – people in the armed forces, the diplomatic services, what have you – and so my circle of friends inevitably included boys whose homes were in Africa, the Far East, India. Suddenly the attraction of a family farm decreased dramatically. Six weeks in Wales paled before the prospects of a month in Dar es Salaam or three weeks in Cairo.

It was only in the summer of 1959 that I next spent, or intended to spend, a long time at Harvey's farm. I was looking forward to rediscovering the places, people, and sensations of my childhood, of course, but my place at Cambridge was secure for that autumn, and I confess, part of my reason for choosing to stay with Harvey that summer was simply for the quiet – for the opportunities I would have to make some inroads into the heavy schedule of preparatory reading I had been advised to do. It was law, of course; I was following my father to the bar. As matters turned out, I did little of that reading, nor, indeed, did I take up my place at Caius College that October. But let me not get ahead of my story.

For whatever reasons, then, academic or nostalgic, I arrived at my uncle's farm in mid-July to find Harvey changed little, the farm changed not at all, and Laura transformed beyond recognition. She had a month or so left of her sixteenth year, but she had already outdistanced her childhood. She was a beautiful young woman. Already five feet seven, her girlish fat had disappeared or at least relocated itself to all those places men find most suitable. She had her father's dark eyes and frank stare and a head of black hair, wavy and abundant, apparently a legacy from her mother.

My first sight of her was from behind a mist of steam as Harvey and I entered the farmhouse kitchen, he having taken the car to meet me at the train station in the village. The steam which had obscured her had been generated from the boiling water in the kettle she was emptying into a teapot, and as it dissipated in a second or so and her full beauty emerged, I confess I was stunned. I stammered a greeting and received simply a broad smile in return as she concentrated on her task. I was glad she did. It allowed me the opportunity to look.

She was wearing a woollen sweater that was not, presumably, intended originally to be as tight-fitting as it was – she had simply grown faster than her wardrobe – and a pair of blue jeans, one of the few pairs I had seen at that time. She seemed both ancient and modern, like all beautiful women – younger and fresher than I yet infinitely wiser. Ridiculous, isn't it? She was a busty teenager making a pot of tea, and I stared at her as if I were regarding some mythic creature, beyond time and the world. I didn't want her to speak. I didn't want that time-lessness to focus itself on the mundane concerns of a fifteen-year-old and oblige me to remind myself of the mundane concerns of an eighteen-year-old. I didn't want the spell to be broken. But she did, and I did, and it was.

Conversation, when it came, was as expected. We moved from tea, biscuits, and inquiries about school to the evening meal, the dining room, and a debate on the relative merits of jazz and rock and roll. The latter was strictly to be sneered at as far as I and most of my school friends were concerned – incapable of engaging the intellect along with the emotions, unlike the complexities of a Charlie Parker, for example. It was, frankly, a little working class. Laura, on the other hand, was a devotee and seemed almost ashamed of me for liking a music one could share with one's parents. Harvey said little, as I recall, simply watching, amused, as two children argued aggressively about something as trivial as popular music as if it was of world importance. He was doubtless right, yet I recall nearly every word we spoke. For it was the last conversation I was to have with my cousin. Within three days, Laura was dead.

2

I rose early the morning following my arrival. Early by urban standards, that is; Harvey had already been up three hours when I met him in the kitchen at 7:30. He'd returned for breakfast and I joined him, despite feeling a slight guilt at so doing. He had earned his food, I felt; he'd worked and had a fast to break, while I had merely slept. I said as much, though naturally expressing it as a joke, and he was gracious enough to point out, in an equally jocular fashion, that at least I had risen in time to keep him company – his own daughter was still asleep. Instantly I wondered if she slept naked. Instantly I feared the thought would show on my face. Repressing it as best I could, I asked Harvey if it was unusual for her not to be up at that time, perhaps helping him.

'No,' he said, 'I'm more concerned for her education at the moment. I've got day men, couple of days a week. She doesn't need to help. O-levels next year. Sleep and books till she's passed them.'

I found that touchingly progressive of him and, in an attempt to discover just how far this proto-feminism went, asked if she had any plans for a career. Harvey smiled.

'Well,' he said, 'we're still going through the idealistic stages at the moment. You know: nurse, teacher, overseas relief worker. All that stuff. I don't know. Got a strong interest in architecture. As an observer, of course. An enthusiast. But I wonder ... Not something I intend to mention or push, but ...'

My surprise must have shown on my face, for he laughed a little self-mockingly before continuing. 'Yes. Not, I realize, a field with a great tradition of female achievement. But ... Modern times, Johnny, modern times.'

He put down his teacup in an emphatic manner and drew in

and released a slightly theatrical breath. Discussion of his dreams for his daughter was clearly closed. 'Anyway,' he said, 'what do you think? Long walk? Around the fields with me? Refamiliarize you with your childhood haunts. Get some fresh Welsh air into your sooty Liverpool lungs.'

He stood up, drawing breath hungrily into himself, expanding his chest and flexing his arms in that unselfconscious man-of-the-land way he had. I smiled at him and rose to my feet also. The admiring child in me urged me to imitate the play of his body, but the educated adolescent refused to cooperate. I was happy to walk with him, though. Actually, given a completely free choice, I would perhaps have stayed in the house and spied on Laura getting dressed but I decided against soliciting Harvey's views on this option and, fetching a jacket, followed him out.

It was a glorious Welsh morning, the sun explosively bright but the land still moist with dew and the rural air cool on the skin and almost liquid on the tongue. I felt as though a beneficent and indulgent Creation had distilled my childhood recollections into one perfect representation of nature's beauty. It felt like coming home.

Harvey's land was smaller than I remembered – though I suppose, in fact, the land had remained the same; I had simply grown older and my perception of its limitlessness had changed accordingly. In any case, it still proved quite capable of tiring me by the time we had covered the four main fields and headed back towards the house.

There was a fairly large grassy area immediately behind the house – not quite big enough to be another field – which served as a sort of back garden for the family and visitors, though at the opposite end to the house there also stood on it a very large storage shed. As we came back into the garden Harvey made for this shed, mumbling about something he'd forgotten to pick up. I followed him across the garden and through the big wooden door of the shed.

Harvey, who knew the barn intimately, walked straight towards its far end, but I had to advance a little more slowly, letting my eyes adjust to the sudden dimming of the light. There were windows on both of the barn's longer walls, of course, but there were so many items discarded or kept for occasional use in there that the piles they made had reached and obscured the windows. I stopped halfway into the place, in fact, not knowing if another pile – be it of toys, tools, furniture, or magazines – was waiting to trip me up.

The interior of the barn was, as well as dark, considerably cooler than the open fields, and that, coupled with the inevitably musty smell of such a place, woke an old feeling in me of nervous apprehension. It wasn't only the fear that whatever I might bump into would be malicious rather than merely inconveniently placed, but that buried fear we all have when we walk into a cold dark place with somebody else that suddenly the world will take its mask off and acknowledge finally the hidden drama it has played out with you now that you, as victim, have come to the appointed place. As if Harvey's voice would suddenly echo from somewhere in the darkness, its tone transmuted to a gleeful and hungry insanity, beckoning me forward to dance the final ritual steps of cruelty and sliced flesh.

I could hear Harvey at the far end of the barn rummaging around in one pile or another. I was hoping he would find what he was looking for without calling on me for assistance so that I would be free to walk back into the light without having to confront my fear. Just as his voice called out, 'Ah! There you are!' my eyes caught up with my feet sufficiently to let me see, immediately to my right and at about knee height, a dark, round face grinning horribly at me.

I jumped back in alarm and gasped in fright – fortunately too quietly for Harvey to notice, for, hot on the heels of panic, had come a calming recognition.

'Oh,' I said, 'the Dead Table.'

'Eh?' said Harvey, walking back towards me, swinging in his hand what looked like a replacement blade for some kind of cutting machine. I pointed in explanation at the old table and at the carved vegetable head that sat upon it and had, less than seconds ago, seemed so terrifying to me.

'The Dead Table,' I repeated. 'That's what Laura called it, anyway. When we were little. We came in here once . . . I think

I was about nine and she seven . . . and she pointed to this – which had nothing on it at the time – and announced, "That's our Dead Table," and, once I'd foolishly revealed an interest in what she meant by that, completely refused to elaborate. Now I understand. I mean – judging by that turnip jack-o'-lantern, I assume it's something that you use at Halloween?'

Harvey smiled, nodding. 'That's right. Though it's a mangold actually, city boy. A mangold lantern for a dead soul to rest in.'

'What?' I said, grateful that my eyes had now adjusted completely because his words and the sharp thing he nonchalantly held would probably have driven me screaming from the barn a few moments earlier.

'Old Samhain, Johnny,' he said, losing me completely. 'The meeting time. Old tradition. You light the lanterns. Fill the table with food, place it in the open. Preferably by a gate. The Feast of the Dead. The one night of the year they can come back – renew old acquaintances. The meeting time.'

'Sounds foul,' I said. 'Duck apple and pumpkins are quite enough for me.'

'Yes. Well. Only an old tradition. Must confess I've not as yet met the ghosts of old friends any past October. Just fun, really. Laura always likes it. Anyway, this particular old ghost's house is clearly untenanted.' He hefted the blade he carried into the air and smiled at me before continuing. 'And clearly long overdue for demolition.'

He swung the blade down through the air in a slicing motion into the lantern. I assume his intention was to make a clean and impressive bisection, but he had underestimated the decrepitude of his target. As soon as the blade touched it, the hollow and lightless face collapsed in on itself, crumbling. It was completely rotten.

By the time we went back into the house, Laura was not only up, but out. A note for Harvey, resting against the teapot on the kitchen table, explained that she had gone into the village to the house of a friend, apparently called Sarah, and apologized to both of us for forgetting to mention it the night before. She disarmingly attributed this forgetfulness to her excitement at my arrival, which, though I recognized it as a load of old flannel, nevertheless pleased me no end; I liked the thought of Laura excited. I spent the afternoon in my room, pretending to make a start on my studies.

I heard the telephone ring at about five o'clock that afternoon and was about to go downstairs to answer it – how strange to remember a life without extensions – when the ringing stopped as it was picked up, presumably by Harvey, though I hadn't realized he was back in the house. Faint traces of his voice made their way upstairs to my room, but I could make out no details of the conversation without actually opening my door, which, had he heard it, might have struck Harvey as odd behaviour. I had to wait until six, when, upon my venturing downstairs to find Harvey preparing food in the kitchen, he volunteered information without me having to probe.

'Ah, Johnny,' he said. 'That was Laura on the phone earlier. Afraid you're stuck with just my company for dinner tonight. She was very apologetic. And so she bloody should be. Some kind of misunderstanding, apparently. Sarah's mother. Assumed she was staying to eat, you see. Laura didn't want to offend. Et cetera, et cetera.'

I was just ready to start some serious worrying about whether this Sarah had an attractive brother or not when Harvey's joking promise that he'd give his daughter a good spanking when she did get back set my mind racing in other speculative directions. I quickly initiated inquiries about the food. I'd spent enough time upstairs.

It was nearly eleven when the sounds of a car approaching and stopping, a door opening and slamming, and running footsteps coming closer heralded Laura's entry into the lounge where Harvey and I sat talking. Her cheeks were slightly flushed, her eyes particularly bright. I managed to convince myself that this was due to a glass or two of wine and the night air, though I would have appreciated the chance to confirm this by closer observation. But no. A kiss on the cheek for her father, a kiss on her palm blown in my direction, served both as greetings and as further apologies, it seemed, for her first words were: 'I'm exhausted! I'm going to grab a quick coffee and fling myself into bed.'

And that is precisely what she did. I gathered, from Harvey's amused tolerance, that this sort of behaviour was par for the course as far as Laura was concerned, and it was quite clear that he had no intention of insisting that she come and sit awhile with us or, more specifically, me.

But, though Laura had seen the last of me for that night, I had already decided that I had not seen the last of her.

I waited, eagerness wrestling with caution, until about two o'clock in the morning. All human sounds had ceased. Only the settlings and shiftings of the old and insomniac house kept vigil with me. After getting out of bed, I waited a full three minutes before moving to the door and a further two after opening it before I inched my careful way down the corridor to the place where Laura slept.

I stood outside her door, silent and still, my palm pressed carefully against its old wood. I listened first. Somehow one knows when a house is full of sleep. Snores or other evidence are not necessary. The atmosphere is different from when people are awake. I don't know if boarding-school experience – sleeping in dormitories – heightens that sense, but perhaps it does. Probably it does. Anyway, I *knew* Laura was asleep behind that door, yet still I waited. What if I was wrong? What on earth could I possibly say? 'Oh. Sorry. Wrong room. I intended to sleep with your father'? 'Ah, Laura. There you are. I was wondering if it might be possible to stare at your breasts for four or five hours'? And so I listened first. And after a time, after managing finally to transcend the cacophony of my own breath, the riotous clamour of my own heartbeat, I heard it: the susurrous evidence of breathing. Not a snore, you understand. Nothing like a snore. A baby snore. Embryonic. A snore at the concept level, perhaps. Whatever. She was asleep.

I turned the handle of her door and held it for another heart-beat. There was no disturbance to the pattern of her breath. I opened it into the room. One inch. Two. Six. Twelve. I leaned my body slightly forward to peer around the edge of the door. The door and I were opposite a window – happily uncurtained, open to the moonlight – and between us and it was the stage for the night's performance: a narrow, wooden-frame bed. And on it, lying on her back, face slightly turned towards the window, was the star of the show.

I slid into the room and – my back against the door, both hands behind me around its handle, my eyes never leaving Laura's face, my ears straining still for the slightest alteration in the sound of her breath – leaned the door back into its frame, slowly releasing the latch from the handle, slowly releasing the handle from my hands, slowly resealing us both inside the room. She hadn't moved.

There was a distance of some six feet between the bed and me. I held my breath and covered it in three steps and half a second. Then I stood very still and released the breath slowly and silently, sensing it, *seeing* it settle over her sleeping face. The mouth was slightly open, the rest of the face relaxed, and the luxuriant black hair that framed it tumbled also onto the twin naked shoulders provocatively revealed above the edge of the sheets. My mouth formed the shape of her name. But the silence, like Laura, lay undisturbed.

Slowly my eyes travelled down the length of her sleeping body. On that warm summer night she lay between two or three sheets only, and I revelled in the patterns she impressed upon them. Supine as she was, the swell of her breasts still pressed the cotton upward in a warm and gentle curve, which, once past its peak, fell off more sharply to merge into a flatter area, running undefined above her stomach until her hips, in sudden, urgent mounds, enlivened the cotton topography again. Between the hips came a gentle, symmetrical fall to the smaller, sweeter swelling of her pubic mound, and then the richness of her thighs, legs slightly parted – the distance between them increasing towards her knees, shins, and feet – and luxuriously long.

I held my hand out in front of me and lowered it, slowly, reverently, tremblingly, until it was a foot above her breasts. I could doubtless have gone closer, but from the angle from which I was looking, twelve inches was frighteningly, exhilaratingly close enough. I began to make stroking motions in the air, my hand mapping its way slowly down the area my eyes had recently reconnoitred. My mouth shaped other words now. Promises. Descriptions. I showed her my cock and my lips silently bragged of its power and achievements. I ran my hand back up the air above her body and made alternate cupping and squeezing motions above her breast, staring at her closed eyes and stroking myself all the while.

It was just as I was about to calm myself down, worried that I might be unable to resist lifting the sheets if I carried on much longer, that I became suddenly and overwhelmingly convinced that Laura was awake. Had been awake for some time. I snatched my guilty hand back from the space above her and stopped my self-abuse. I was aghast. I continued to stare, but now horror and shame, not desire, were my motivation.

How I knew, how I could tell that her silent patience was the product of waking rather than sleep, I do not know. She continued to lie still. Her eyes continued to be closed. Her breath continued to be the breath of sleep. But I didn't believe her. The pounding of my heart and the shrinking of my member told me otherwise.

I took one step backward, my eyes still fixing on that languorous deceiver. She moved slightly, as a dreamer would: a small shift of position, a small furrow of undefined expression on the face, a slow shuffling subsiding back into stillness.

I took two steps backward. An imprecise and faint moan came from somewhere deep inside her throat and produced a stronger, though still supposedly unconscious, movement as she rolled gently to her right, facing me.

Three steps backward. She drew one arm up and began to stroke at her neck, her head arching back sensually to offer her naked throat to her caressing hand.

I fumbled for the door handle behind me. Her face rippled into movement again and she began to swallow and gulp, the tip of her teasing tongue probing at the corners of her mouth and sliding across it, tasting her lips. The fingers of her exposed hand began to worry at the sheets.

I turned and fled and was in my own room between my own sheets before she could throw hers dreamily aside, before she could sleepily stretch and flaunt her body, before she could unconsciously run her own hands freely over those areas which mine had hovered above.

I lay awake for an hour and prayed she would have as busy a day today as she had had yesterday.

4

Harvey was gone early again the following morning, doing whatever it is that farmers do in those hours that the rest of the world sleeps through. Anxiety, too, puts us on the early shift and so I awoke. I heard him leave. I lay on the bed. I dressed. I lay back on the bed. I looked at the time. I looked at the ceiling. I looked at the time again. I heard the sounds of Laura rising, Laura bathing, Laura breakfasting, Laura waiting, Laura coming upstairs, Laura's hand on my door, Laura's voice.

'John? Are these the sort of hours they taught you at that school of yours? Do you want a cup of tea? Something to eat?'

I was ready for her. Pitching my voice somewhere between distraction and superciliousness, I replied, 'Mmmm? Oh. Thank you, Laura. I have another chapter or so to read here. I'll be down presently.'

'Can I come in and look at your books?'

I was off that bed, at the door, and opening it before her final syllable. 'Oh. Never mind,' I said. 'I can do that later. Let's go downstairs, shall we? I *am* rather hungry.'

I didn't meet her eyes as I hurried past her onto the stairs, and by the time she caught up with me in the kitchen I had plenty of utensils and ingredients at which to direct my gaze. On the edge of my vision, I saw her lean against the door frame and fold her arms over her chest. I stared intently at the cup I was holding as if it was of urgent importance that I study it for minor cracks.

'So . . . did you sleep well?' she asked me.

I picked up the cup, which fortunately hadn't broken, and gave in. I looked at her childish, ancient face, at her glittering and knowing eyes. She was smiling at me. 'Laura, I . . . I . . .'

'Ah, good. Tea,' said Harvey, closing the back door behind him as he came in. I loved him. Laura rushed across the room, kissed her father on the cheek, and headed out of the door through which he had just come in.

''Bye, Daddy. Got to dash. Johnny'll tell you all about it. 'Bye.'

The door closed. Harvey looked at me. I did an imitation of a goldfish, my mouth opening and closing brainlessly. Harvey spoke first.

'So . . .' he said, in that mock-heavy-handed tone that is the nearest most adults seem to be able to come to a game-playing voice, 'you know something about my daughter I don't, eh?'

Too bloody right I do, I thought as I fumbled my way nervously into the lies that Laura confidently and correctly knew I'd tell for her.

'Er . . . yes. Yes. The – the friend. Yesterday. Um . . . Sarah, is it? Helping each other with homework. Swapping strengths and weaknesses. You know . . .'

Perhaps it was the fact that my confusion had led me into an imitation of Harvey's own minimalist approach to sentence structure that made him accept a story which sounded pretty shaky even to its author. Perhaps he had farmish things on his farmer's mind. Perhaps he didn't care. For whatever reason, his next sentence was not the 'You lying little bastard – you've been sniffing round my daughter's bedroom,' that I expected but instead merely a casual 'Hmm. Girls, eh? What would you do with 'em?' followed by a brisk 'Now. What about that tea?'

At two o'clock that afternoon I was sitting on the crest of a medium-sized hill staring out over the placid blueness of the Irish Sea.

I had left the farm nearly two hours earlier with a packed lunch and a paperback and had struck out, no particular route in mind, on a long walk. I'd walked into and through the village, followed the river through its valley, and taken the cliff walk up onto the hills. My intention, after this break to eat sandwiches and stare at the sea, was to complete the large circle I had begun to describe, following public footpaths over more hills, through more fields, to finally bring myself back to the farm at, I guessed, five or six o'clock.

I've already spoken of the magical time my childhood at Harvey's farm had come to be in my life, of how I never felt more at home than when I was loose amongst that glorious Welsh landscape. Despite that, though, despite the love of openness and greenery engendered in me by my early days there, I was no nature buff. It was the frozen poetic moment that mattered to me – not the cataloguing or the understanding of such scenery but the timeless dreamlike resonance of it. I was no hiker, no bird-watcher or tree enthusiast, and though my representation of myself as all of these things had landed me with an uncomfortably heavy pair of field glasses which Harvey had insisted I borrow, my real motivation in this long walk was, of course, the opportunities it did not present for a confrontation with my cousin.

I looked at the sea. It did not calm me. I looked at the sky. It did not reassure. I felt the warmth of the sun on my naked face. It did not soothe me. I had no idea what to do. I felt completely powerless. Sitting still, letting the weight of my worries settle on me, made it worse. I stood up, sandwiches hardly tasted, and resumed my walk, resumed the drawing of my circle, the physical representation of my emotional avoidance of the problem I had turned the farm into.

I was, I think, already past the halfway point of my walk – and therefore heading towards rather than away from whatever resolution lay waiting at the farm – when a new twist appeared in the knot I already felt to be beyond my unravelling.

A long stretch of the footpath I was using ran alongside a forested area. For nearly all of my round trip prior to this, I had been making my way through open fields or along hilltop paths, but now, on my left-hand side at least, I had tall trees and dense undergrowth for company. It was tempting to walk into the woods, if only for the coolness they promised; the trees, close together, formed leafy canopies, green parasols that ate the light and sheltered any wanderer from the summer heat. Attractive as its green shade was, however, I remained on the main footpath. The subsidiary tracks that ran into the wood all seemed to head deep into its heart, and I was far from confident of my ability to find my way back to my path should the forest wish to take me elsewhere.

I did, however, as I walked beside the cool splendour of the forest, keep glancing within it to see some of its secrets, even if I was not ready to share them. I had seen several squirrels and the afterimage of what may have been a fox before I stumbled upon a secret I had not expected the forest to contain.

I had come to another of those branches of the main footpath. This one shot off from the path I walked on at an abrupt ninety degrees. My eyes could follow it for a hundred yards or so before the density of the woods obscured whatever direction it then took, and at just about that furthest point, I could see a small wooden structure – either a gate or a stile, I was too far away to tell its precise nature or purpose – and standing by it, two human figures. I stopped and looked more closely. Facial features are indistinguishable at that sort of distance – even sexual differentiation is difficult to ascertain – but in 1959, a mane of black hair such as I could see one of the figures sporting could only mean a woman, and as you have guessed, to me it meant a very specific woman. My cousin Laura had also gone walking that day, it seemed.

I repositioned myself behind one of the forest's first trees and carefully reached into the case to remove the field glasses I was now grateful Harvey had insisted I take. I raised them to my eyes. My assumption proved correct. In the white blouse and blue jeans I had seen her in that morning, Laura leaned against the wooden stile – I could see now that its purpose was to ford a tiny stream that ran through the forest at that point. Laura was smiling and talking animatedly, but her hands, usually a vital part of her conversational process, were clasped loosely behind her, between her lower back and the stile. Had she been alone, I could have remained there quite happily waiting for her to do something interesting – scratch herself perhaps, or readjust her clothing, maybe even take off her blouse and wash herself down by the small stream. As it was, however, I was terrified at the possibility that she might do anything like that simply because she was *not* alone. There was a man with her. This, three miles from home and in a somewhat-less-than-densely-populated area, was bad enough, but her companion himself was no figure of reassurance.

He was old. Well, actually, he appeared to be about thirty, but you have to remember I was eighteen at the time and Laura still several weeks away from her sixteenth birthday.

He was tall. In fact, he was probably just six feet in height – in other words I was as tall as him, but my mind, my self-image, had yet to catch up with my biology, and psychologically speaking, grown-ups were all still a foot or so taller than me, whatever physical reality might say to the contrary.

He was disgusting. His skin seemed naturally swarthy and his hair jet black, yet there seemed an ingrained layer of dirt over him that added to the darkness of his appearance.

Like Laura, he was dressed in a white shirt, but with him, the whiteness was something you took on trust – you assumed that given three days of soap and scrubbing, white would be the colour that resulted. Over it, but unbuttoned, was a dark waistcoat that matched the dark trousers, worn into shapelessness, that completed his costume. He hadn't shaved for . . . well, how do you tell? I thought, at the time, it was at least a week, but again there speaks an eighteen-year-old. Two days? Three? He was unshaven. And his hair, nearly curly, was unkempt and not recently cut. He was a gypsy. A vagabond. A tramp. Something.

I was, despite my own unresolved problem with Laura, about to shout out to her when what this . . . creature . . . did next froze my tongue – indeed, my whole body.

He was standing more or less in front of her. Not directly. Not enough to block my view. And, as I watched, he raised his right hand and slowly ran it down her blouse. Not exactly down the front nor exactly down the side. He did it in such a way that his fingers' journey was from armpit to hip, via the rib cage, and that of the heel of his hand was from throat to navel, via the left breast. He didn't dwell on the breast. He kept an even, slow speed all the way down. And when he had reached the end of his exploration, he removed his hand, raised his arm, and did it again. Again slowly. Again evenly. Then once more. Slowly. Evenly. And again. And again.

92

Seven times he touched her like that, and throughout it the rest of their bodies were still. They continued to look at each other's faces and, my God, continued their conversation as if nothing untoward was happening. There was no hugging. There was no kissing. Equally there was no protesting. There was no forcing. It was . . . it was *casual*, I suppose. It was as thoughtless a gesture, both in the giving and the receiving, as when a drunken friend puts his arm around your shoulder, and it ended as arbitrarily as when the drunken friend takes his hand away.

I was paralysed, of course. And paralysed as much by the unprecedented mixture of feelings I was experiencing as by any individual one of them. I was shocked. I was jealous. I was disgusted. I was excited. I felt wronged. I felt guilty. I felt exonerated. I felt condemned.

I was saved from making a decision as to whether I should announce my presence by Laura herself. The interview appeared to be over, the stroking some kind of obscene coda. She was saying something, but I don't lip-read. I could see the smile and the nod, however. I could see the answering smile of her molester. What was being accepted there? What promised?

She moved away from him and began walking up the forest track towards the main footpath where I still watched. One backward glance, a wave of the hand, and then, her face fixed firmly forward, an unreadable expression on it, she headed briskly forward on her way to the footpath, her invisible cousin, and her father's farm.

That night I watched them in the barn. Laura was pretending to be asleep and the tramp was kneeling beside her. He was parting her gown, exposing her breasts, stroking them. I watched, pulse racing, as her somnambulist hand reached up to the opening in his trousers and began to explore.

Suddenly Laura's eyes snapped open, flashing with contempt and cruel amusement as her head swung to find me.

'Oh, how disgusting!' she said. 'Little sneak. Little looker. Little spy. Kill him, Daddy, he's completely rotten.'

I looked up in a panic. I hadn't realized I was on the Dead Table. But it was too late – catching the light and radiating its hunger to punish, Harvey's blade was already swinging downward.

'Tch. Girls, eh? What would you do with 'em?' Harvey's voice asked from somewhere within the piece of rotting vegetation that perched on his shoulders, its cruel triangular eyes and vicious slit of a mouth illuminated from inside by a flickering candle. I gasped in horror as the blade found me. Laura let out a bedlam giggle. Her secret lover hissed. I looked down in time to see my stomach, bisected, collapse into a dry, powdered mess and I began to scream. Which, of course, woke me up.

I was sitting up in bed, sweat already drying on me. The moon was up. The night was still. And the silence of a sleeping house lay all about me. Had I screamed aloud or was the reverberation I could hear audible only to me, an echo from the dream world? The silence insisted on itself and I began to breathe again. My watch on the bedside table told me it was nearly two in the morning and the ache at my groin told me it was time to visit my cousin again.

I drew a robe about myself and left my room for hers in the same careful manner in which I had made the journey on the previous night. Listening at her bedroom door, however, I was unable to detect the reassuring sound of her sleeping breath. What was it? A shallower sleep? Or . . . ?

I pushed the door open, a horrified certainty growing in me. Her room, her bed, was empty.

I walked to the window, which looked out from the back of the house. The bright summer moon illuminated the barn.

Summer it may have been, but the night was cold and the grass felt damp to my naked feet. I walked in darkness and silence, not knowing which I felt the more keenly: outrage, jealousy, arousal, or fear. By the time I reached the barn door, I could already hear the sounds of their movement. Very slowly, very carefully, I took the door inward and slipped into the space that they had claimed. It was darker inside than out just as it was when I'd gone in there with Harvey, but the contrast of the darkness with the moonlight was not as strong as that with the previous day's sunlight and my eyes took little time to adjust.

The two naked people were at the opposite end of the barn to that which held the door and were, in any case, far too busy to take note of my silent intrusion.

A space had been cleared and an old sheet spread on the floor. Laura knelt upon this. Her folded arms, too, met the sheet and her head rested upon them. Her back was dipped and it bulbed upward gracefully to where her hips swayed in splendour above her parted thighs. The animal from the forest was between them, buried deep inside her. He, too, was kneeling but was upright, one filthy palm resting on each of Laura's buttocks as he pushed himself in and pulled himself out of her. They were both making animal noises, breaths like broken sighs jerking out of them in time with his thrusts.

Gradually, the moonlight, sneaking in as I had, showed me more of them. His eyes were for the most part closed, though he would occasionally open them and look downward in order to appreciate fully what he was being allowed to do. Laura, whose face, as I said, was hidden in the folds of her arms, would nevertheless from time to time press her head upward, her

95

throat stretched taut, her mouth opening and closing spasmodically as if she could nearly taste something and wished to be sure of its nature. Her eyes, though, remained closed.

I stood there and saw this and was utterly unable to move – not least because I was seized with such uncontrollable trembling that any movement would run the risk of a noisy exposure of my uninvited presence. I felt hollow and entirely alone. My mouth was dry and my throat hurt. I had to remind myself to breathe and my face felt like I had held it in front of an electric fire for several minutes and had just moved it away: hot, tingling, and tight.

After I had watched them for what seemed like hours and was less than minutes, the creature leaned his upper body forward and lay along Laura's back, his stomach pressed to her, his face, turned aside, nesting between her shoulder blades, and his hands busy somewhere beneath her. Laura lifted her head again in the same stretching, yearning, anticipatory manner I described and seemed to be trying to reach her partner's face with hers. Twist as she might, she couldn't, and I saw her tongue flicking and probing at the corner of her mouth in an equally frustrated attempt to share saliva. He half raised himself again at this point and, taking his cue from her, began to lick at her upper back and neck, occasioning moans of appreciation from her and grunts of response from him. Their increasing excitement drove the male to more frenzied licking and sucking and Laura to more writhing and bouncing, which in turn fired their excitement still more, leading to wilder, even more abandoned movements until, finally, ravenous desire and its determined expression were racing each other frantically towards a climax.

The noises they made were disgusting. They were practically barking now. The male's mouth was growing more bold by the second as teeth demanded a taste of that which tongue had already sampled, and he began to nip at the flesh of her shoulders and back, pinching it between his teeth and shaking his head as a dog will shake a favoured toy or a recent kill.

One of his arms, appearing over Laura's shoulder as he shifted position, reached and rested on the sheet, nestling between her neck and her left shoulder, and she, eager, it

96

appeared, to demonstrate actively her approbation of the new gnawing feature he had introduced into the game, sank her teeth into the muscular meat of his upper arm and worried at it in the appropriate manner. Inspired, the creature chomped down on the soft flesh of her neck, and suddenly, without warning, there was blood. Much blood. Not a trickle, but a wet, rushing flood.

Three screams, strangers to each other and all speaking a different language, shattered what was left of the night's silence. Mine lived the longest, Laura's being drowned in her mouth by her own blood and the male's being smothered by another mouthful of flesh. Mine rang still as the two bodies, locked together, shuddered and heaved in a final, violent harmony and collapsed forward, still entangled, onto the sheet.

As they hit the sheet the unities of their flesh and their movements ended. Laura remained stretched out and still, the only movement on her body being the running of her blood in various directions; down her spine in a narrow red stream, pooling in the hollow of her lower back, disappearing into the crease of her bottom; across her shoulder blade in a wider flood, swelling over the roundness of her shoulder, diverging into three tributaries down her arm; directly from the wound to the sheet, like eager drips from a carelessly turned-off tap. The beast, though, was on his feet again a second after tumbling with her, attempting to locate the source of the third scream. It wasn't difficult. I was still screaming.

The moonlight showed us to each other clearly enough. He saw a frightened boy in a bathrobe. I saw a naked monster disguised as a man. The lower part of its face was completely smeared in blood. But that didn't hide the mouth. It was smiling at me. My cousin lay bloody and unconscious at its feet. I stood before it, horrified and afraid. It was in the company of two damaged children and it was smiling at me. It was very amused. Then it did three things in very quick succession; it ran a tongue over its upper lip and drew some of its victim's blood into its mouth; it grabbed at a pile of clothes to the left of the sheet; it ran straight at me.

I would have screamed, but as I already was, I stopped instead and received his blow in silence. I say blow. I flatter myself. I exaggerate the threat he perceived in me. In fact, he simply knocked me down with the flat of his hand on my chest and was out of the barn before I hit the floor.

I sat up into a world of horror. Somehow, with him gone, the silent, immobile, bloodied voluptuousness that had been my cousin was all the more real, all the more horrifying. She was not moving at all, and the only sound I could hear from her was the rhythmic and liquid noise of blood meeting cotton. I didn't know what to do. Suddenly the door was slammed open again. I froze.

'What the bloody hell's going on? I . . . Oh, my Christ!'

It was a voice I knew. Harvey stood in the doorway, silhouetted before the moonlit sky. Light came from his hand. He was holding a torch and its beam had just found his daughter. My eyes travelled the length of the beam to stare again at Laura. I realized for the first time that her eyes were wide open and were seeing nothing.

'Harvey . . . I . . . There was a man . . . He . . .' In desperation to say it all, I managed not to say anything. I found myself hauled to my feet by the front of my robe, looking up helplessly at the torch raised high in the air and listening to the anguished roar of my uncle, which, though wordless, I knew to be my death sentence. There was no doubt in my mind then, and none now, that Harvey would have beaten me to death there and then had we not both at that very second heard the sound of a motorcycle spluttering into life somewhere near enough to be undeniably on Harvey's land. It was far from the conclusive proof of my innocence I would have wished for, but it was sufficient to stay Harvey's avenging hand at least until the noise had been investigated, and he let go of me at once and ran back through the door, shouting, 'The car! Quickly!'

I followed. A tiny, skulking part of me that in calmer times walked tall and called itself reason whispered at me even then, in that time of mania and passion, that we had chosen vengeance over grief and that some would say we should have stayed with Laura, have covered her wounded nakedness, have carried her back to the family home, have wept for her, but as the Greeks say, revenge is what makes grief bearable, and given Harvey's example, my confused emotions had forsworn their individuality and donned the anonymous, unifying, dangerous cloak called anger. I wanted to see the thing bleed. And I wanted to smile at it as it had smiled at me.

I ran round to the front of the house, moving swiftly, my body no longer responding to the chill, my feet seemingly contemptuous of the damp grass. Harvey already had the engine running and I jumped into the front seat beside him. The car was moving even as I hit the seat, tyres ploughing gravel and grass violently, their urgency a direct translation of Harvey's own. I had to anchor myself to the dashboard as I leaned across to grab at the wildly swinging door and slam it shut.

We had heard the motorbike begin its escape as we ran from the barn to the car, and so Harvey already had a rough idea of the direction our pursuit must take. Straight across two of his fields we went, destroying crops in one and scattering sheep in another, finally smashing our way through a hedgerow and bumping onto the small unlit country road that linked the local farms with what passed for urban life in the area. The village lay to our left, but we turned right to where the road ran directly into the hills. It seemed another life ago that I had come, only fourteen hours previously, to this same point, walked through the village, and eventually circled round through the hills to come back to the farm along the road we were now taking. It was on that walk that I had first seen Laura's violator. Had I said something to her father that evening instead of going to my room to sulk and masturbate, I might have helped prevent the horror and the madness that had come down upon us now.

'Did you see him clearly, boy?' Harvey suddenly snapped, now that he was safely on tarmacked surface and could spare the concentration. For a dreadful second I thought he had read my mind and was referring to my first sight of the creature until I realized he meant had I seen him clearly in the barn.

'I . . . He . . .'

'Come on!' he snarled through clenched teeth. 'We'll never catch the bastard in this thing! We've got to know where he's going. *Did you see him?* Tell me!'

99

I knew he was right. The car was hurtling along, screaming its protest at the unaccustomed speed Harvey was bullying out of it, and had anything been coming in the opposite direction on that narrow country road, we would almost certainly have died, but there was no way we were capable of catching a motorcycle. I did my best, through the inarticulateness induced by distress and rage, to describe the monster: the swarthiness, the hair, the unshavedness, the smile.

'Oh, the bastard! Oh, the filth!' said Harvey. 'I know it. I know it!'

The car didn't slow down, but there was a subtle change in the man who was driving it. It seemed now as if it were no longer a panic fury that kept his foot flat to the floor, but instead a cold and eager anticipation. He no longer worried about whether the meeting would take place, he was simply keen to make it happen at the earliest possible opportunity.

I asked him no questions. In fact, we didn't speak at all, though the remainder of the car journey was nearly half an hour. We didn't want to; had we done so, we knew, there would have been a slight chance that calmness and respect for the law might have found an entrance unguarded by madness and vigilantism, and then where would we have been? Power-less, grieving, lost. Human. No, the night had made monsters of us all, and if it was a madness that sent us screeching down that twisting, unlit highway, then it was a madness most welcome. It was as if, by dipping his mouth into Laura's blood, the monster had somehow *infected* her blood. Her relatives. Us. It was as if, in a way, he had called to us, or to something in us, and now it was answering that call.

6

The car stopped.

We were high in the hills. To our left the ground, heavily grassed, fell steeply down to meet the river. Harvey had pulled the car to a halt at a place where the road met the top of a winding footpath that, eventually and tortuously, reached the valley below. It was not the safest of paths even in daylight, and I was very glad that the moon was so close to fullness and that no clouds obscured it or the stars. Harvey got out of the car without waiting for the engine to die and I followed him.

'Down there, boy,' he said. 'Living like a fucking animal.'

He was pointing down into the valley, but I could see no tent or caravan. Harvey continued, explanation an accidental companion of his need to talk. 'We've all known about him, of course. The Caveman, they call him. Joke.' He turned and looked at me directly. 'Some fucking joke, eh, boy?'

The eye contact was a mistake – that way lay sanity and sadness, those twin cripplers of action – and just as his eyes were beginning to brim he managed to snatch them from the blossoming pain in my own and swung himself round to look at the car. Brusque, businesslike, restored to purpose, he threw open the trunk and bent in towards it.

'Too angry,' he said. 'Should have waited. Got my gun. This'll have to do.'

He had been rummaging around amongst the jump leads and the wire cutters, and as he finished speaking his hands emerged full of what he had been seeking. He turned back to me clutching a heavy-duty spade, a broad blade of sharp-edged but rusty metal mated to a strong and well-worn wooden handle. He held it to him like a piece of the One True Cross, an icon of consolation and a promise of deliverance.

'This'll have to do,' he repeated.

101

I stared, said nothing. We started down the hill.

The cave came into direct view only when we had nearly reached the bottom of the river valley. It was ahead of us, farther along the river's path, and set back on our right, where the hill's descent was steeper and the grass gave way to bare, grey rock.

The night was cool. It was bright and moist, and down in the valley where we were, a wind sang in whispers among the spaces of the rock and the water. We walked alongside the river for fifty yards or so, untouched by the valley's latent poetry, unmoved by the river's liquid dreams, blind to beauty and deaf to its song. Driven only by rage, propelled by a thirst whose only quenching was red and warm and redolent of death, we started up towards the dark face of the hill and the large patch of deeper darkness that was the mouth of the cave. The slope that led us there was covered in small and shifting fragments of stone, and we made our way carefully and as silently as we could, trusting that whatever betraying noise the scree might make would be lost in the rushing of the river, the whistling of the wind.

As we came nearer to the entrance its blackness was broken by flickers of orange light from within. The monster had been returned to its den long enough to revitalize its fire, it seemed. Then came a piece of complete idiocy from me. After leaving the car well back from our goal, after walking without words, after picking our painful way, barefoot, through the sharp and stony path that led here, up piped the smug voice of detached rational inquiry.

'How could he get his motorbike down here? He –'

The rest was cut off by a stinging backhander across my face and Harvey's baleful glare. Instinctively, we both turned our heads to the mouth of the cave and stood very still, waiting to see if my stupidity had alerted the cavity's occupant. But nothing happened. The firelight continued to flicker. The moonlight continued to shine. That was all. After a few more heartbeats, Harvey waved us on. He made one other gesture in answer to my question – pointing up to the top of the hill and the numerous places along it where a cycle could be parked – but what a world of contempt for the collector of the irrelevant detail there was in it. We went on, Harvey holding his spade and me holding my tongue.

The mouth of the cave was vast but misleading. The space it actually led into was more a hollow with pretensions than a cavern. At its entrance the roof was at least twenty feet high, but this sloped sharply downward once we were into the belly of the hill, and where it ended and met the cave's far wall, some eighteen feet or so in, it was barely five feet above the floor. The distance across the space was perhaps fourteen feet, no more.

The fire was set two thirds of the way into the beast's den and was nothing more than five or six heavy branches, deleaved and detwigged, interconnected at their tops like a kind of skeletal and miniature wigwam and set in a tight circle of small stones. Dried grass and smaller sticks had presumably been laid within this structure to start the fire off, but it was now basically the thick, heavy branches themselves that, at their tops, burned in a united and strong flame. The orange glow from this fire illuminated the rest of the cave's contents, but the wind, coming up from the river, threw the flame and its light about so much that shadows shifted crazily across the amber-toned walls of the cave and even the objects themselves seemed to dance. There were bottles, blankets, full and empty tin cans, one or two paperback books, and standing behind the fire and facing us as we crossed into its territory, the beast.

It was dressed now – presumably in the clothes it had snatched up before running past me in the barn – and looked as it had looked when first I saw it in the forest: shapeless black trousers, filthy white shirt, and dark waistcoat. It was also still wearing its smile, or the sneer in smile's clothing it had shown me earlier; amused, contemptuous, and infuriatingly calm. I had fully expected Harvey to rush straight at it and put it down, but its obvious lack of fear, or even surprise, stopped us both where we stood. It spoke.

'Problem, gentlemen?' it said.

I was surprised at the voice. It was one of those voices that, out of some sense of misplaced shame, does its best to hide its education, but educated it certainly was. Murderous vagrant it might be now, but it had probably started life as a son of the gentry. I looked at Harvey. He was staring at the creature, and when he spoke, his voice was as flat and implacable as his expression.

'I'm here to kill you,' he said.

An eyebrow may have twitched a little; otherwise the creature's condescending smirk didn't alter at all. 'Any particular reason?' it asked, as if it accepted perfectly a world in which a reason might not be necessary, but thought it may as well ask.

'Don't play games,' said Harvey. 'We've just followed you across country from my –'

'I only go where I'm invited,' the creature interrupted, the voice still calm, but now with a trace of dismissive contempt that was more enraging than open hostility.

'You killed her, you fucking scum!' Harvey cried, and I could almost feel the tension in his body rise to the point of explosion.

'Don't be stupid.' The creature sneered. 'She always faints when she comes.'

That did it. Harvey screamed in rage and ran at the beast, straight through its fire, scattering the burning pieces of wood, so that they rolled around the floor of the cave like so many discarded medieval torches, one or two going out on contact with the cold stone but the rest still burning and, still swaying to the wind's music, casting wilder shadows than when their flame was one.

The spade raised above his head and held with both hands, Harvey brought it down in a vicious sweep that, had it connected, would have split the creature's head in two, but the thing was fast and stepped to its left, causing the blade to strike only stone. The clanging noise it made was deafening, and the shock it sent up Harvey's arms must have been excruciatingly painful. Nevertheless he reacted swiftly and brought it up in a diagonal stroke that smashed into the creature's hip. Only the upward angle of the blade's attack saved the thing from a crippling, or even killing, blow, but even so we had the satisfaction of hearing for the first time the sweet music of its pain.

104

Harvey straightened himself up and swung the spade behind his right shoulder, ready for the killing stroke when, in one sudden and fluid sequence, the creature crouched, seized a knife from a concealed ankle holster, and sprang at its attacker. Harvey remained stationary with shock and disappointment, spade still poised behind him, as the thin blade found his heart. His killer had the sense to stay close, left arm locked around Harvey's waist, right hand twisting the knife, knowing that even should there be any fight left in his enemy, at such close range a makeshift weapon like the spade would be, at worst, a painful nuisance.

'H-H . . .' was, apart from the blood, all that came out of my dying uncle's mouth.

Was he asking for help? Was it an accidental noise, the dialect of agony? Was it perhaps a race memory of some ancient Celtic courtesy, telling your slayer your true name? I have no idea now and I had no idea then. All I know is that it was that dying stammer that snapped me out of the frozen terror I had stood in since Harvey made his first assault.

I had no weapon. Harvey still held the spade. The creature was armed and clearly competent. Had I wasted time in thought, I would have been lost. Instead I followed Harvey's path straight through the centre of the cave, but where he had simply scattered the burning stakes, I stooped, seized one, and hurled myself at the thing that was still holding my uncle. The force of my run, the charred point that the stake had been burned to, the strength that panic lent me, all these helped, and almost without effort, I slid that flaming stake through the neck of the vile destroyer of my family.

It burst out of the far side of his neck, attended by a fountain of jetting blood, and hideously triumphant, reignited itself on contact with the air. My hands flew from the other end of it accompanied by a gasp that was half disgust and half exultation, and I stepped back to see the creature suffer.

His body shook like a killer in the electric chair, like an epileptic in the grip of his disease, and Harvey, free of his loosened grasp, fell backward. The spade, being freed in its turn, fell to the floor less than a second before him and, stopped by his collapsing body from laying itself flat, embedded itself deep in his dead back.

The creature, meantime, was still standing and still shaking. Its hands were half raised, which, coupled with the open mouth, gave it almost the appearance of a mystic, trembling in the grasp of a vision. Its head, jerking more violently than the body, suddenly caused the still-burning stake to knock against the cave wall the creature was standing by, and the stake was thrust back two inches or so into the wound from which it protruded. Of a sudden and sickeningly, its hair ignited as the flame was pushed into it and caught hold. The vocal cords must have been sheared as the stake made its way through the neck because the creature was making no scream – but I could see the horror and the fear in its dying eyes, and they were good enough. Then the eyes glassed over and I knew it was seeing nothing. I cursed myself for forgetting to smile while it still had sight.

It fell, finally, and the pooling blood from the exit wound extinguished at last both the stake and its burning hair. It continued to twitch, however, and as the killing fury in me abated I was overcome with horror at the scene before me. Two bodies lay on the ground, one skewered both front and back, one impaled through the neck. The latter, though effectively dead, still jerked around like a galvanized frog. There was blood everywhere. It ran from beneath Harvey's back and from the knife wound in his heart. It dribbled, obscenely diluted by saliva, from his slackly open mouth and trickled from his nose. The twitching beast's head lay on a pillow of liquid crimson which was staining the shoulders of his once-white shirt. There was a huge splash of it, which I hadn't noticed before, still dripping down the cave wall in front of which the thing had stood when I slaughtered it.

Making all this worse, however, were the rest of the stakes that had once constituted the creature's fire. Four were still burning and were scattered in different parts of the cave, thus doubling, tripling, quadrupling, the mad shadows of the dead that wind and flame were collaborating in producing. The orange light, the dancing shadows, the tide of blood, the spastic writhing of the speared beast, all these assaulted my senses like a violently efficient drug. I felt at one and the same time exhilaratingly removed from reality and fiercely connected to it.

This epiphany must have lasted all of five seconds before nausea, terror, and the awareness of my freezing, damp, and lacerated feet led me outside to vomit down the slope running from the cave. I puked and heaved long after my stomach was emptied, staring in numb fascination at the watery yellow bile I was producing, and the only thing that stopped me was the sudden realization that it was a stunningly absurd *politeness* that had made me go outside to throw up – as if it was bad form to puke in front of corpses, gouting blood, glassy eyes, and flickering, multiple shadows. I lifted my colour-drained and vomit-flecked face to the magnificent impartiality of the night sky and laughed helplessly for five minutes, the sound of my amused hysteria echoing back and forth across the river valley.

It must have been nearly four in the morning by the time I parked the car back at the farm. I know the sky was perceptibly lightening. In the distance beyond the farmhouse, thin but vigorous filaments of fiery red were already spreading into the star-cloaking blue fringe of a sky that behind me was still black. It promised to be a spectacular sunrise. And it meant nothing to me.

In the passenger seat beside me was the spade – bloodied as promised, albeit with the wrong blood. I had lifted it out of Harvey's poor dead back. It hadn't been the spade I'd wanted, of course. I had foolishly assumed that I was going to bring his body back with me. But Harvey had been a big man. It would have been next to impossible for me to have carried his dead weight across the hill to the car. Reason and resolve weakened by the night's horrors, I had simply left both bodies in the cave and stumbled down to the river and back up the footpath. I wasn't even aware that I still had hold of the spade until I opened the car door. I'd laid it on the passenger seat – for no reason other than needing both hands to drive – and started the car up. It was fortunate for me that it was, despite its curves and bends, a single road that led back to the farm, because in my battered mental state, I would have certainly missed any turns I might have needed to make.

By the time I actually arrived home, though, I must have started to think rationally again, because I deliberately took the spade into the house with me, on the off chance that any casual caller or – and this was already starting to bother me – official inquirer should peer inside the car window. I let myself into the house and made my way upstairs to the bathroom. I had one goal only: to wash my feet clean of my own blood and to wash my hands clean of other people's.

The spade – the blood on it coagulated beyond the point of dripping – came into the bathroom with me and I finally let go of my bloody souvenir when I leaned it against the bathroom wall by the sink. I stripped off my bathrobe and pyjamas and stood naked. I put the plug in the sink and turned both taps on. It was just as I decided that I wouldn't in fact feel clean without a complete immersion and turned my face to the bathtub that I heard the footsteps on the stairs.

I felt colder than I'd felt all night. Frozen. As if my blood had actually ceased moving through me and my lungs and heart had stopped in sympathy. Breathless, stiff, naked, and terrified, I turned completely round to face helplessly the closed bathroom door, beyond which I could hear the slow footsteps approach from the other side of the wall. Then they stopped. And the handle on the door began to turn. I sagged back against the sink, and it was only the shock of the cold marble touching my naked lower back that kept me from fainting as the door swung inward and revealed, framed in the doorway, as naked and as wounded – but empirically less immobile – as when last I had seen her, my dead cousin Laura.

It was terror alone that kept me from screaming as her eyes slowly focused on mine. Her face held all the confusion one would expect from the recently resurrected, along with the shades of other emotions: grief, fear, and, I would like to think, not a little shame. I imagine my own face must have mirrored these quite accurately.

'I . . . I came to wash away the blood,' she said and gestured at her torn neck.

108

In the growing light that the dawn was forcing through the bathroom window, the wound itself seemed less serious than I would have imagined, but the blood had dried on her and her neck was almost entirely covered with the flaky rust it had become, and where five rivulets of it had travelled down her body as she lay in the barn, it looked as though an unnaturally thin, long, brown hand held her right breast in a casual embrace. She looked at me with questioning eyes. I said nothing.

'Johnny . . . what happened?' she asked. Her voice was small and frightened and her question pregnant with foreboding. She took a hesitant step nearer to me. Still I was silent, but I could feel my nostrils flare and the back of my neck prickle. Her face dissolved in a memory of tears. The fingers of my right hand closed quietly and secretly around the long wooden handle of the spade.

'Oh, John . . . hold me, please,' she said, and started forward, her arms reaching out for me.

Her head came off with one sweeping stroke of the spade and flew into the empty bathtub. One jet of blood actually reached the ceiling, but most of it simply showered the body and the floor around it. Very little of it touched me. The body itself did not imitate the dance its lover had performed a little earlier, but simply stood, headless and motionless, for a few seconds before it toppled back and lay almost gracefully on the floor, allowing the still-rushing blood to make for the open door and leave the room as if upset by the scene. I laid the spade aside again and, having removed the head from the tub and placed it and the body by the far wall, began to run my bath.

Frost leaned back in his chair and, as he had done at several points during his long narrative, took a sizeable sip from the glass of ice water on his desk. He looked to his left at the picture window. It was approaching midnight. He had been speaking for almost two hours and was quietly pleased with the thorough attentiveness with which Donovan Moon had greeted his telling. Now he felt he needed a slight stretch of the legs, and so he rose from behind his desk, raised his arms, took a deep and relaxing breath, and walked to his window.

'Laura was lighter than Harvey. I took her to them,' he said, looking out at the night. 'I waited for the return of darkness, of course. But it was all right. I was calm now that I understood what had actually been going on. I burned all three bodies in the monster's cave and then drove through what remained of the night until I crossed into England and, beneath the river via the Mersey Tunnel, finally reached Liverpool.

'I had no intentions of making any good-byes, you understand – it was a matter of expediency. It was simply that at the tail end of the fifties, Liverpool – before the subversion, before the Socialist decade – was still a very busy port. Very busy. And the nearest. Nevertheless, it still took me the best part of a day to find a ship that was leaving immediately and that still had space for general labour. It was easy in those days, you see; work permits, visas, all the paraphernalia, were more or less ignored. If you had a passport and all your limbs, you could effectively set sail on the whim of a captain.

'Michael Gundry was a fifty-year-old seaman with a poet's face leathered by decades of salt and authority. He was tough, cynical, and pragmatic, but hiding inside him there was still the ghost of the sixteen-year-old who'd chosen the sea by romantic imperative rather than pragmatism. He looked at me and thought he saw a similar flame burning in my eyes. He was half-right. The flame was there. What fanned it was beyond his comprehension. But that didn't matter. I'd found my ship. She was called the *Pacific Empress*, and despite her name, it was the Atlantic she was to cross on this voyage; she was bound for New York.'

He turned his face back towards Moon with a quick aside. 'Oh, that wasn't important, by the way. That it was America, I mean. I was glad it was somewhere where they spoke English – or at least a reasonable approximation of it – but as I'm sure you realize, what was actually of paramount importance to me was removing myself from Britain fairly swiftly, and bugger the destination. It might have been days, it might have been weeks, but eventually some form of investigation of Harvey's farm was going to point a finger at me. I played with the idea that three sets of burned bones in a hillside cave might confuse them – might have them believing that the third set were my own – but these pathologists are good, aren't they? No, I had to go. My mission in life had been made clear to me and I could start anywhere. America would do. I jumped ship in New York and began from there.'

From the other side of the desk came the sound of a clearing throat. For the first time since Frost had begun his story, Donovan Moon was preparing to speak.

'Sorry,' he said. 'I seem to have missed something. What is it that you were going to do?'

Moon kept his tone neutral, particularly avoiding irony, and looked at Frost in what he hoped was a convincing imitation of a spirit of clear-eyed and impartial inquiry. He thought he'd blown it when two long seconds passed during which Frost simply stared at him, but then he realized, in time to calm any incipient fear, that Frost's stare was one of incredulity rather than anger.

Frost blinked. Once. Twice. Then he walked back towards the desk and sat down again. Once seated, he waited a further moment before speaking as if to give the journalist time to admit he was joking. 'But surely it's obvious,' he said. 'I was to spend my life finding them and killing them. To stop them doing to other lives what they had done to mine.'

'Who?'

'Good God, man! Vampires, of course! Vampires. Isn't it clear to you that that was what it was all about? Laura was bitten in the neck by some wild thing that lived in a cave and then she rose from the fucking dead! Doesn't that sound familiar to you?'

It did sound familiar, but Frost had asked *two* questions, and regarding the first – wasn't it clear that that was what it was all about? – Donovan was far from agreeing. He had undeniably heard a tale of blood and madness, but – or so it seemed to him – a tale of very *human* blood and madness with little in it to suggest the supernatural. Frost's cousin had recovered from a faint, he would guess, and had woken to a horror more real than the vampire. The fact that that horror was now sitting opposite him and explaining its activities was what stopped Moon from articulating any of this and made him nod his head apologetically instead.

'Of course,' he said. 'I'm sorry. Go on.' Even as he did it he realized that he had played it wrong. Frost might well be insane, but he was far, very far, from being stupid. The cold stare and the ice in the voice confirmed that.

'Don't humour me, Mr Moon,' he said. 'That is not your function.'

Donovan swallowed and nodded. Frost could command fear at a moment's notice. He continued.

'In fact, perhaps I should explain just what your function is – though it would mean getting ahead of my story.

'It's all right,' Donovan said. 'I can wait. Really.'

Frost smiled. 'Very well. Though I'll make it brief. After all, it's nearly midnight and I'm sure you're keen to get back home to your . . . friend.'

The relief Donovan felt at the clear implication that he was to get back home at all allowed him the luxury of also feeling resentful anger at Frost's scarcely concealed contempt for his relationship with Matt. The word *friend* had almost been in quotation marks and the cold blue eyes had been condescendingly amused. Despite the anger, though, he felt that this really

112

wasn't the time, place, or company for a spirited defence of the gay life-style and so remained silent as Frost moved towards his conclusion.

'Upon my arrival in New York, I began to build two careers for myself. One public. One private. But each parallel to the other. To the world at large I became the man who tidied the stages on which they played out their lives. Where there had been squalor and confusion, I put cleanliness and reason. Where there was chaos, I brought order. Where there was darkness, I shed light. I am the man who takes rat warrens and turns them back into cities. What the world doesn't know, however, is that while I am he who demolishes the warren, I am also he who puts down the rat. That has been my secret career, Mr Moon. Exterminator. And I have pursued it as rigorously as that which has brought me fame and fortune.

'Let me tell you about vampires, Moon. They are *everywhere*. I have found them in Paris, in Rome, in London, and New York. I have found them in great cities and I've found them in villages of a few hundred people. In all walks of life I have found them and destroyed them.

'I should, perhaps, disabuse you of any stray notions gathered from popular culture. They are not all from Middle Europe. They are not all aristocrats. And there is nothing civilized about them. Further, you can forget all that nonsense about crosses, garlic, and the rays of the sun. They can walk in daylight, they can hold down jobs, and they do not, unless they choose to, sleep in coffins.

'Cases like my cousin's are extremely rare, but they can happen. I have seen perhaps two or three in my life. I don't pretend to understand that and I don't care; nothing killed by *me* has ever risen again. Scientific analysis can come later. When the world is clean.

'Most people would hold that vampirism is legendary, an invention of folklore if not of literature. Some, more alive to the unsavoury evidence, make claims for a rare disease either of the body or of the mind. But it is not those things. It is neither a myth nor a disease, Mr Moon. It is an ideology. An ideology of indulgence and disorder.

113

'They batten on people. They live only for appetite. They can be young or old, male or female, and of any race you care to name. They are not coerced. It is a choice they make. And they infect by seduction.'

Donovan came back in, clearing his throat again unnecessarily in a nervous response that was the equivalent of the raised hand of a child seeking permission to speak. He wanted to raise one specific issue that Frost seemed to be assiduously avoiding. 'But do they kill?' he asked.

Frost smiled as if indulging a naïve question. 'Sometimes. That's not the point. It is the condition they would lead the world to that is their real threat. Imagine it, Moon, a world of appetite unchecked, of indulgence pursued to its own limit. They are the anarchists of passion. Luxury's terrorists. And their flag is blood and desire.'

Frost stood suddenly and walked again to his window, as if it and his desk were the only places where his secret tongue could be loosened. He kept his back to Donovan and stared straight ahead of him into the darkness beyond his glass. 'For nearly thirty years I've fought them in silence and in secret. *They* know me, of course; they call me the Matador, I understand. But the world has been blissfully ignorant of the blood on my hands. You could search the newspaper files of this and many other countries, and while you may trace, through a number of unsolved killings, the progress of my ministry, you would find nothing to help you make the connections, nothing to let the world know what has really been going on.'

He raised his left hand quickly and imperiously to forestall the question he knew Moon was about to ask. 'So why Morningstar?' he asked rhetorically. 'Why this new and gleefully public persona? Why, after three decades of carefulness, this sudden grandstanding? A fair question. And as the answer to it also involves your role, I'll tell you. In fact, I'll start with you.' He glanced momentarily back at Moon. 'And you can save your sweat; it's nothing sinister. Or dangerous.

'There's fifty thousand dollars deposited in your name, Moon. You'll get the account number and anything else you'll need through the mail tomorrow. It's payment for a job you haven't done yet and it's money you won't touch until you have done it. As long as I'm alive, you won't touch it at all, because I assure you, I will know if you do. It's what would happen were I *not* alive, though, that got you this commission. I needed a journalist poor enough to need that money and with enough integrity not to take it if he felt he hadn't earned it. You made the short list. And when you said you believed in vampires, you passed the audition. Congratulations.

'If I die, Moon, you will tell my story. Documents will be provided. You will serve, in a very much more specific manner, the same function as the Morningstar murders or, rather, the rumours I imagine are already beginning to spread regarding the nature of those murders. The police may try to suppress the relevant details, but the truth will eventually wriggle its way into people's minds via the secret and unsuppressible media – rumour and word of mouth. Everybody will have a cousin who will have a friend who has a sister whose boyfriend works with someone who said . . . You get the picture.

'Your work will confirm and amplify what people have heard whispered. You will help me, posthumously, to inspire by example. If you can reach an audience of thousands, Mr Moon, there will surely be one among them who will choose to take up my work . . .'

Frost paused for a second. His voice had been approaching the territory of the impassioned teacher, if not quite that of the evangelist, and now he pulled back from there, conscious of who he was addressing, and cruised into the state of the cynical pragmatist. 'Oh . . . but don't worry; I'm not seeking propaganda. Should your liberalism, for example, be outraged by my methods, feel free to say so in print; I have no desire to compromise those journalistic ethics I am relying on and I'm not after approbation. Just publicity.

'One practical question probably remains on your mind. Why do this now? In fact why, as a perfectly fit forty-eight-year-old, do it at all? Why not find my own successor and train him in secret to do my secret work? Intimations of mortality? Frankly . . . yes. Exactly that.'

He finally turned to face Moon directly and for the first

time the journalist saw . . . something . . . on his face. Doubt? Confusion? Fear? Something that was a mixture of all three. It lasted barely a second before Frost successfully replaced his mask, but it was there and Moon had the curious sensation of being both frightened and comforted by its presence. Frost continued.

'Something is going to happen, Mr Moon. Something big. And I don't know . . . exactly . . . what it is. But it's why I came to this city.

'It came to me first in the spring. I was still operating out of the east at that time. I began getting . . . signals. In my dreams. Bad dreams, perhaps that's all they were. But I think not. I think they were messages. I –'

'Who from? Who was –' Moon attempted to interrupt but was interrupted himself by the first display of ruffled feathers he had seen from Frost.

'I don't know!' the Matador spat out. 'I'm not a fucking clairvoyant. I'm a soldier.'

Frost paused, got himself back in rein, continued. 'I think they were messages. I think I was being invited. Invited here. Invited to some kind of final confrontation.' His eyes dropped to his desk. He picked up his glass again and took a small sip. When he spoke again, his voice was quieter and lower, as if he were speaking to himself. And Moon knew the question he was asking was one he had been asking himself for weeks.

'What,' Frost whispered, 'what kind of enemy sends messages through *dreams*?'

He had raised his eyes from his desk to look at his guest as he spoke, but Moon knew that the question was rhetorical, that Frost expected no answer. At least no answer from him. He had theories, of course. He was never without theories. Wisely, though, he kept them to himself, holding his tongue while Frost held his.

Frost shifted his eyes away from the journalist to stare down the length of his room, and Moon could almost feel him vanish, as it were, almost feel him retreat within himself to ponder whatever nightmares his dream self inhabited. It was such a profound withdrawal that Moon suspected that were he to be

116

especially quiet, he could stand and leave without Frost even noticing. He wondered how long Frost hit this state. He wondered how long these states lasted. He wondered about the nature of Frost's madness, about the relationship between raging psychosis and silent catatonia. He wondered how long it would take before his irrepressible sense of the absurd forced dangerous laughter from his mouth. Fortunately it was moments only before Frost came back.

The clouds that had covered Frost's eyes as he remembered the dream blew away, and recapturing his usual cold impassivity, he stared at Moon again and spoke with his usual flat confidence. 'But whatever the source,' he said, 'those messages are why I'm here . . . and they're also the other reason for Morningstar's high profile: to let whatever it is know that the message has been received, that the challenge has been accepted.'

Moon could see that of all the secrets Frost had unburdened himself of tonight, this had been the most difficult for him to utter, and perceived that it was its imprecision as much as its alien provenance that caused him this discomfort. The discomfort Moon *himself* was feeling had as its origin the conflict between his journalist's delight at the monster of a story that was exclusively his and his human disgust at the monster that had granted it to him. Half of him was screaming *Scoop!* The other half was simply screaming. Quite apart from this conflict, there was also his quiet conviction that should he attempt to tell the story while Frost was still alive – or even attempt to tell the *police* while Frost was still alive – the Matador would have no hesitation in sending him to join his other victims. Jesus, he wished he was home. It was difficult to formulate a considered response to one of history's great maniacs when the maniac was in the room with him. His disapproval of his scoop's content, his delight at its existence, his determination to tell it, and his dread that he might not survive its telling – all these were genuine responses – but at the moment they were primarily intellectual ones. Emotionally, his response was considerably less complex. He was scared and unhappy. And neither of these conditions was lessened as he watched Frost walk directly past

117

him without another word and head for the double doors through which Donovan had entered earlier.

Frost didn't leave, however. Instead he stopped by the doors and spoke to the wall. Moon saw this over his shoulder. He hoped there was an intercom there. He could see how, away from the room, away from Frost, being told the story by a third party, he might find it hilariously funny to picture the serial killer suddenly breaking off the telling of his insane delusions about vampires in order to have a chat with his wallpaper, but sitting in Frost's chair, he wasn't laughing. As Frost began to walk back towards him he was relieved to see some kind of white object on the wall by the doors that he safely assumed to be an intercom. The relief, though, lasted only as long as it took him to start wondering just what it was that Frost had said and to whom he had said it. The executive's first words were reassuring.

'My chauffeur will be taking you home shortly, Mr Moon.'

But unfortunately, having sat down again, he continued. 'There is, however, one last thing I think you should know – and a practical demonstration seems the best way of convincing you.'

Donovan decided he'd rather Frost had been talking to the wall.

Behind his back, he heard the doors open. He resisted turning around as long as he could, but when he saw Frost nod to whoever had come into the room, he seized the opportunity to make it seem casual and looked over his shoulder. Once again he saw something that managed to be simultaneously laughable and horrid. Frost's chauffeur was laying out long sheets of polythene over the room's wooden floor.

Donovan had a sickeningly precise idea as to the function this plastic sheeting was to serve, but he thought it safest to play ignorant. He faced Frost again, raising an eyebrow.

Frost understood his inquiry and was distressingly helpful in his reply. 'It stops the blood staining my floor. I kill them here, dump them later. It's easier.'

Donovan now felt actually faint. This was too much. He rose clumsily and shakily to his feet. 'Oh no,' he said, both hands emphasizing the denial, 'that's enough. Enough. Believe me, I believe you. But I don't want to see this. I can't see this. I'm going. Now.'

Frost raised his hands in turn, denying the denial. 'Don't misunderstand me, Mr Moon,' he said, his tone as close to soothing as a life devoted to slaughter could allow. 'You are quite free to leave before the termination, but there's something I want you to see first. Something I wish to convince you of. Please sit down.'

His hands' gesture became an invitation, palms dropping toward the vacated seat beside Moon. Donovan grabbed a deep breath and accepted the invitation, sitting himself down and hating himself for doing so, knowing he was only accepting because he was too frightened to force the issue, accepting it as one accepts in dreams – knowing something dreadful is going to happen and, powerless to avert it, playing whatever passive game is necessary in order to defer it as long as possible.

So he didn't turn around as soon as he heard something heavier being brought into the room, but instead kept his eyes on Frost, willing him to talk as long as possible. And he didn't react to the sound of muffled groans behind him, but instead nodded and grimaced and let several other exaggerated expressions crawl across his face, as if he were a ham actor demonstrating 'listening'. And he didn't say anything or even look up when the room became red at the unseen flick of the chauffeur's hand and he heard the doors open and close again as the chauffeur departed. But Frost had little left to say, and when it had been said and Frost had risen to his feet again, Donovan's eyes could find no excuse not to follow him as he walked past the journalist's chair into the centre of his room, transformed by red light and polythene into some kind of ritualistic space.

Sharing that space with him, Donovan finally had to see, was a man about Moon's own age, bound hand and foot, gagged, and unable to rise because of the thoroughness of his binding. There were other things about him, too, of course, things that would normally register, like a receding line of corn-yellow hair, large sea-green eyes, and slightly overripe lips, but in this

119

context Donovan found it difficult to see beyond the prisoner to the man he used to be.

It could have been worse, Moon tried to tell himself, it could have been worse; it could have been a child or an old woman. But it didn't work. A victim is a victim, and pity knows no subdivisions. Frost stood behind the man and, having lifted him into a sitting position, removed the gag from his mouth. The man said nothing. Instead it was Frost who spoke.

'This is Henry Rose, Mr Moon, and he is about to become Morningstar's fifteenth victim.'

Donovan shook his head. It was an all but pointless gesture. He wasn't disagreeing. He had no reason to suppose that the man's name wasn't Henry Rose nor any desire to quibble over the ethics – or the mathematics – of counting Morningstar's two-week total of victims as a separate body count from Frost's three decades' worth. He was shaking his head as a child shakes its head, as a symbol of generalized denial. 'Please,' the gesture said, 'I don't like this.' He was hyperventilating. He didn't like that either. Nor the fact that he knew he'd have to be sick very soon. Worst of all, though, was the crippling shame he felt at the realization that his desire not to *see* this was measurably stronger than his desire for it not to *happen*.

What Frost had said earlier, as Rose had been brought into the room, was this: 'I realize, despite my story, Moon, that you may still be harbouring the suspicion that I am slaughtering ordinary peoplé. Nothing could be further from the truth. But when I tell you crosses and garlic, capes and coffins, have little to do with these creatures, you perhaps ask yourself just how I can recognize them. I appreciate this. And I intend to show you.'

Now, as he stood behind the still-silent Henry Rose, he slapped at the back of his captive's head and said, 'Show him, beast. Show him the mark of your nature.'

Rose spoke. 'Oh, why don't you fuck off?'

Frost grabbed at the back of the man's collar and twisted. 'Show him!' he snarled.

Rose sneered. Though there was the tremor of imminent death in his voice, there was also a tired dismissiveness. 'Just

120

do what you're going to do, you frigging butcher,' he said. 'I'm not playing party games to impress your friends.'

Donovan felt an absurd desire to explain to the man that he was not Frost's friend, that he had no desire to see this proof, that this had nothing to do with him, but even had he seriously intended to shout all this out, he would have had no time.

The knife had appeared as if from nowhere in Frost's right hand, and gripping Rose's hair with his left, he took off the man's upper lip with one slash of the blade.

Rose screamed. Rose bled. Donovan screamed. Donovan vomited. But Donovan *saw*, too. Before the blood descended as a scarlet curtain, obscuring Rose's mouth; before his own protesting stomach hurled its contents to the floor, demanding his complete attention; before Frost slashed at the ropes that held Rose and pushed him away, mutilated but unbound; before all these things, in the frozen second between shock and nausea, Donovan saw.

They weren't new, he could tell at once, for they were as off-white as their blunt and dwarfish companions. One, indeed, looked as if it was in need of serious medical attention – the gum drawing away like that suggested an advanced case of pyorrhoea. They were heavy looking, long, slightly curved, and very sharp. Henry Rose had fangs.

By the time Donovan was able to look again – by the time his stomach had stopped heaving and he was able to take his eyes away from the floor and the steaming evidence of his own disgust – Frost and Rose were circling each other, the one weaving graceful patterns in the air with his knife, the other alternating between growling and hissing out his fury and weeping at the pain of his disfigurement.

Donovan stood up slowly. The vomiting had cleared his head. The overload of horror and confusion had gone. As if purging his stomach had purged him of emotional response, he watched, almost coldly, as they moved around each other. He waited until their circling and weaving brought them close to the edge of the polythene near the desk where he stood, and then he headed straight down the room, running through the pool of red and fatal light, making for the double doors in a crouching dash. He had no fear that either of them would attempt to stop him – they were locked together in their death dance now and were probably not even aware that he was leaving – but he wanted to be out of their insane world as quickly as he could. He no longer felt nauseated. Nor did he feel afraid any more. He simply felt silenced and numb.

The doors weren't locked. The corridor was well lit. The elevator worked perfectly. The parking lot wasn't dark, the car was ready and waiting for him, and the ride home was uneventful. Everything was very normal. He even went to sleep. He hoped he wouldn't dream. Frost dreamed. He wanted nothing in common with him.

THE
SLEEP OF
REASON

There was always the music.

The music would come first – waltz time and lilting. Sweet, distant, and beckoning, the music would sound to his dreaming ears while his sleeping eyes still saw only the void.

Sensation would follow, or emotion; an unfocused nervousness too ethereal to be named as either excitement or anxiety. Then the light show – amorphous areas of colour would explode before his unconscious eyes, the canvas of his eyelids suddenly as big as the world and twice as brightly lit. Invariably, it would begin in crimson. A sudden splash of red that filled his sleeping vision, not growing out of the blackness, not blooming within the void, but replacing it suddenly and completely, so that his body would jolt in physical shock and a rapid heartbeat – his own – begin to accompany the music.

The red would give way, sometimes back to black, sometimes to another colour, but whichever variant of the dream it was, soon the rhythm of the colours would begin and he would be flown – though free of any sense or sight of his body – through a pulsing tour of the spectrum. Always there was the sense of momentum – though no horizons or vanishing points gave any visual reference to this, he felt he was hurtling through endless alien skies, cloudless and immense, sometimes yellow, sometimes red, sometimes green. And the music would grow louder as he sped toward whatever he sped toward.

The anxiety would swell, too, perhaps encouraged by the formerly hidden harmonies that were now apparent in the dream waltz. Dissonant intervals, cracking the music's unity of key at random moments and stabbing into his perceptions with the malice of the undiscovered and the rage of the repressed.

The faster he would go, the more frequently the colours

125

would change and the louder the music would pound – time signature now mutating along with key signature to rob him of all safe reference – until unknown winds were tearing at his incorporeal but responsive face, tearing, whipping, robbing him of breath. He knew, each time he knew, that this would be the last. That this time the dream winds would dismember him, would rip him apart, send him dissolved and desentient into the timeless and unending fury of colour and sound . . .

And each time, at that point, it would stop.

And he'd be standing on the stairs.

And the music now was music again, drifting in from one of the rooms below and nearly drowned in the white noise of conversation and laughter.

The woman standing beside him on the stairs, wineglass in one hand while the other held on to the banister for the support her tipsiness demanded, peered at him strangely through the eyelets of her bird mask. 'Well,' she said, 'don't you agree?'

Frost stared at her, at the long blue silk of the evening dress that clung a little too tightly to her swollen middle-aged body, at the pale arms that had lost their muscle tone somewhere in the last decade, at the beautifully rendered and befeathered raven's head that perched on her shoulders, black and impressive, sharp at the beak.

'Yes,' he guessed. 'Absolutely.'

He was confused. Whose party was this? Why did he have no idea what the bird woman had asked him? He glanced around the mass of people both above and below him on the stairs, at the others gathered in the lobby at the staircase's foot, and at the still more who were moving in and out of the various rooms to which the lobby gave access.

Toad men croaked bawdy stories to wasp girls. Cat women purred in pleasure at the attentions of wolf boys. A cadaverously thin man with the head of a monitor lizard raised peals of knowing laughter from a trio of fish-headed beauties as he demonstrated with drunkenly amused persistence the practicality – and the length – of his reptile tongue. Everywhere, cross-species flirtation was rampant. Laughter and excitement bubbled in the air like the champagne in the glasses, whirled carelessly around by hands too intent on illustrating a point to care about the quality of what they were spilling.

The masks were all uniformly excellent in design and fabrication. There were other costumes, too – the animal motif was followed by only about half of those present – and these, too, were of a high quality despite the relative blandness of their wearers' choices: French maids, cowboys, schoolgirls, and dandies.

The lobby was large, wood-panelled, and hung with paintings. Tuxedoed men with solemn faces moved among the revellers bearing fresh drinks on silver trays. Frost knew he was in an old house, built by old money. But whose house? Whose money?

'Marbled angels in the silence of crystal,' said the woman on the stairs in the kind of offhand tone he'd expect someone to use if they were explaining why a mutual acquaintance was always late for parties. 'Hmm?' she added, as if pressing the point.

Silly old cow, Frost thought, what the fuck is she talking about? But while annoyed derision was one level of his reaction, the woman's words also prompted something else in him – or reawakened something that had been dormant for the few seconds of disorientation during which he'd looked around the party.

A deep – bowel-deep – level of anxiety was suddenly there again in Frost. He was beginning to remember something. Something terrible. He didn't know what it was yet, but he knew he had to get down the stairs. Knew, in fact, that he'd been on his way downstairs when this decaying lunatic had stopped him. He didn't even fake a reply. He simply turned his face away and moved as fast as he could downstairs, squeezing past a group of beast-headed adolescents pressed in a tight semicircle around a Salome clonette coquettishly debating the necessity of her seventh veil.

He had to get away. Had to. Something had happened. Upstairs. They'd find out. And know it was . . . Know it was who? Among this mass of masks, what was his own disguise? As if his waitering skills were so finely honed he could read a guest's unspoken desires, a tray-bearing West Indian stepped out of Frost's path, revealing behind him a large and gilded mirror on the wall at the foot of the stairs.

Frost stopped in his tracks and looked. There was one of those serendipitous lulls in the noises of the party. All the surrounding conversations seemed to come to a natural pause, be it for a renewed breath, a refilled glass, or an exploratory kiss. And so, as Frost stared into the mirror, it was only the strains of the waltz drifting in from one of the rooms beyond – its strict time and haunting melody redolent simultaneously of both order and the beautiful pain of love's transience – that filled the air to accompany his sight of himself.

Of course. He felt better now. He was dressed appropriately. The small black mask, the beret of felt and silk, the reflective dazzle of his suit of lights, and the twin blades by his side all came as a comfort to him. He was the Matador. Just as he should be. The music seemed to caress him, to cover him with a cloak of purpose and dignity. Everything was all right.

Except . . .

What *was* it that was bothering him? He stared more intently at his reflection. There! Something. A clue. Beneath the elegant black curve of his mask, resting on his cheekbone, as neatly placed as if applied by an eccentric beautician was a single tear-shaped drop of bright crimson.

Frost never wept. And if he did, he knew damn well he would not weep tears of blood. So it was from another source . . .

And then it all came back to him. The upstairs room. His host, the Financier, unmasked and alone at a small rolltop desk. The quiet closing of the door as he himself had entered. The knowledge and hate in the Financier's eyes. His own precision as he closed the distance between them. The kill and its accompanying pleasure – the warm, rushing glow as the beast fell beneath his hands. The wiping of the blades.

He was suddenly aware that the conversations had not resumed behind him. He looked deeper into the glass, beyond his reflection. A mass of faces – canine, feline, equine, bovine

– united in the direction of their gaze, stared back at him, the impassivity of their masks failing to disguise the disapproval they all felt for him.

Frost spun round to face them. Not a single one of them moved. Not a single one of them spoke. They all simply directed their attention at the Matador by the mirror. The accusing concentration was doubled in some cases; beneath beadlike beast eyes, human eyes would gaze out from beak, snout, or muzzle. Frost's own gaze danced around the lobby, looking for a single instance of disinterestedness, one impartial partygoer still intent on eating olives or studying flesh. There was no such animal.

Suddenly there was a discreet cough at Frost's shoulder. He glanced sideways. The West Indian waiter was there. He had placed his tray of drinks down on one of the lower stairs and was standing beside Frost, bowing slightly from the waist. From his right hand there dangled a white silk handkerchief, held delicately between thumb and forefinger and proffered as tactfully as had been the cough.

Frost met the waiter's eyes, which were eloquently reassuring. 'If sir will permit . . . ?' they seemed to say, accompanying the request with a twist of diplomatic understanding at this social embarrassment. Frost tilted his head slightly forward, offering the offending cheek. The waiter wiped at his face with a gesture small and subtle, though swift and precise.

The second that the handkerchief left his cheek, offending tear completely removed, the babble of conversation resumed as if it had never ceased. Frost looked up. Nobody was paying any attention to him whatever. He graced his helper with a small smile of gratitude. The waiter leaned forward to whisper in his ear.

'Useless our sparkling horses and Persian women,' he confided, as if offering Frost a tip on etiquette to help avoid such minor gaffes at any future function.

Before Frost could respond in any way, the waiter nodded sagely and withdrew with a slight inclination of his head, pausing only to pick up his tray of drinks before making his dignified way up the stairs.

129

Frost looked around the lobby at the various doors that led off from it. They all appeared to be doors into rooms, not a single one of them resembling a front door at all. In the absence of an immediate exit, Frost headed toward the nearest door, passing unremarked through the crowd that moments before had had all its attention focused on him.

The room he came into was as full of people as the lobby had been and the costumes and masks these people wore as richly detailed as those beyond, but the room was less brightly lit. Outside in the lobby, though Frost had not consciously checked, the light had seemed to be electric and plentiful. Here, the occupants of the room were bathed in the warm oranges and rich shadows that candlelight provides.

Oak-panelled walls were still the most striking aspect of the room and here they led up to and met an arched ceiling high above the revellers' heads. At the far end of the room, set high in one of the walls, was an old-fashioned minstrel's gallery that ran the width of the room. At the moment its three rows of bench seats were empty behind the waist-high barrier of thick wooden columns that had presumably kept any drunken or overenthusiastic musician from toppling down onto his betters in days gone by.

Frost moved into the room, looking around him for another door that looked as if it might lead him outside and away. The only other door he could see, however, was at the far end of the room, below the minstrels' gallery, and promised only another room or, perhaps, a service corridor behind it.

Had the room been less crowded, Frost might have bothered to check the door, but as there had been several other doors off from the lobby, he turned around and headed back the way he had come in.

'Matador!'

The cry was loud and purposeful with a freezing undertone of accusation and it came from somewhere behind him, cutting through the party chatter with the ominous precision of a black fin through water. Frost kept moving toward the door back to the lobby, eyes and ears trying not to register the turning heads and silenced mouths of the other people in the room.

Then, again: 'Matador!'

Still Frost tried to move on, despite the increasing number of stares he encountered as people wondered if he was deaf or simply rude, until some helpful bastard – a fat little falcon-head so stooped by age his beak was at the level of Frost's heart – moved directly in front of him and gestured back along the room. His muffled voice emerged from behind the feathered curve of the falcon's neck, in an understanding tone.

'You're too twar on your bicycle, that's the problem,' he said, and nodded vigorously, the bird head bobbing up and down in unconscious malice as if it would peck through Frost's glittering tunic to the meat and muscle beneath.

Frost turned around slowly. Something strange had happened. The room behind him was empty. Where a moment before the place had been as packed as a shopping mall on Christmas eve, it was now completely deserted. Except, that is, for the person who had called to him.

She was standing in the minstrels' gallery, one leg crossed elegantly in front of the other, leaning forward slightly and putting her weight on her hands, which rested, about twenty inches from each other, on the wooden rail. She was tall, slim, and white-faced except for the slim black mask that matched Frost's own. She was dressed as a harlequin, though, not a matador, in a mask and diamond-patterned motley, and her face, hands, and lower legs were stark white in greasepaint and powder. The motley itself was a loose-fitting one-piece jumpsuit that made little concession to femininity other than in the way it was filled by her body.

She was staring across the empty room at Frost, her expression unreadable to him over the space between them. After a second of silence – the woman neither repeating the cry that had caught his reluctant attention nor elaborating on the denunciation he had inferred from it – Frost glanced back over his shoulder to see if the falcon-crowned midget had any more nonsensical illumination to offer.

That part of the room was empty, too.

And the door to the lobby had been closed.

He turned his attention back to the woman in the gallery.

She hadn't moved, but now, as Frost looked at her again, she straightened up from the wooden rail, stood for a second, her eyes still fixed on him, and then, without a further word or gesture, turned to her side. She walked along the gallery until she reached a small door set in the back wall on the opposite side – and about fifteen feet higher – than the door Frost had already noticed down at his level.

Without any pause for decision, Frost made his way across the deserted room to that lower door and opened it. It led to another lobby and, beyond that, a long corridor. The corridor was out of keeping with the rooms Frost had seen previously, looking more like the bland and plainly decorated walkways one would find in a school, hospital, or other institution. Though his eyes were initially drawn down the corridor and to the deeply shadowed space at its far end, a movement glimpsed at the periphery of his vision caused Frost to turn to his side.

A spiral staircase ran down from the exit of the minstrels' gallery to the floor Frost was on. The brief flash of movement he had seen was the top of the woman's head disappearing down the stairs. Frost crossed to the staircase and looked down.

The section of staircase that bridged the ceiling and the floor of this small lobby was open on all sides and made of wrought iron. As he looked down into its depths, however, Frost saw that the steps became concrete and were lost in the darkness resulting from the tubular stone shaft that surrounded the stairs.

The woman was nowhere in sight. Which was strange because visibility down the shaft was at least twenty yards and Frost had crossed to the stairs almost as soon as her head had dropped below the floor. A voice echoed up from the darkness, sounding very distant.

'Matador,' it called.

The voice was recognizable as that which had cried out across the crowded room, but the tone – perhaps due to the distance and the resonance lent to it by the deep-sounding chamber of the shaft – was different, more an invitation than a challenge, more a beckoning than a demand for confrontation, with the slightest hint of coquettishness. Frost felt at the blades at his side and began to walk down the cold stone steps.

132

Even while there was still light, he advanced cautiously. Though the woman and he were now apparently alone, there was something about her – her confidence, her apparent knowledge of his secret life (the way she had said 'Matador' implied more than a reference to his costume), her disappearance down these steps – that made him wary. As the light dwindled and finally disappeared his carefulness increased. In the first moment of real blackness, he paused on the step he was on and slowly and quietly removed one of the blades, listening keenly all the time. Holding the sharp sword ahead of him, he continued, more slowly than before, step by careful step, ears straining all the time to hear beyond the sound of his own breath and the pulsing of his own heart.

The darkness was so unnaturally total that risking a glance back up over his shoulder, Frost could see no light even from the well-lit lobby above. In a matter of seconds, though, a new source of light appeared. It came from below and was at first simply a reddish tinge to the all-enveloping blackness through which he was descending. It might have been his eyes playing tricks, except that as he moved down stair by stair the amorphous glow became more defined and he saw that he was approaching some kind of cellar space bathed in a dull red light.

Frost could now see the decrepit state of the space through which he was moving. The corners of each stair were packed with filth; decaying matter, balls of dust and cobwebs, mildewed pages from discarded periodicals, were sitting and rotting on each step. Moss, its greenness rendered a deep dark brown by the red light, grew from numerous cracks in the stone walls and in the stairs themselves. The walls were damp, and in several places trickles of water ran down them – sometimes from cracks and fissures, sometimes simply oozing out of the old and porous stone itself.

Frost was reluctant to touch the walls once he had seen their condition, but occasionally, as a foot slipped slightly on the slick and slimy surface of the steps, he would have to steady himself with his free hand against the winding wall. His palm would come away moist and soiled and he would wipe it instantly against the glitter of his costume.

133

All was silence below, except for the occasional liquid noises endemic to damp places – a plop as water fell from roof to floor, a murmuring trickle over stones – and Frost was no longer sure the woman would be waiting below for him.

Finally his feet left the final stair and he walked carefully into the cellar. It was low-roofed and long and the ceiling was of arched stone. Piles of damp debris littered the untreated clay floor, some of them accidental where stone and soil had collapsed, some man-made and forgotten where newspapers, old clothes, and discarded items such as picture frames and rusted tools had been stored.

Darkly shadowed archways in the stone walls led off to other chambers, but of these only one drew Frost's attention. The source of the red light must have been beyond it because the light was strongest there. It pulsed, as if to the rhythm of a heartbeat, against the archway and radiated out into the chamber in which Frost stood. Slowly, his feet catching stickily to the damp and tacky surface of the clay, he made his way to the arch, avoiding the piles of detritus and the small shallow pools of stagnant mildewed water that marked his route.

Carefully, his extended sword preceding him, Frost moved into the chamber. His eyes adjusted to the increased brightness of the light and he stood very still and gasped in disgust. Architecturally, this cellar was the twin of the one he had just left and it matched it, too, in decay. Here, though, was the source of red light and here, too, the apotheosis of the filth that permeated these lower levels.

Against the far wall was a massive and sloping pile of garbage and slime that would not have been out of place in a city dump. Decaying foodstuffs, mud, pulped and rotted paper were packed tightly together in a hill of trash. Frost had an image of being trapped within it – having to claw his way through it, his hands bursting through organic things pregnant with decay and pustulence, his mouth invaded by choking filth – and his throat closed in bilious disgust and he shuddered.

But trash is trash and, in itself, is rarely the source of our horror. What makes us sweat is the notion of the hidden world

134

within it. A dog turd may be revolting, but it is the shit-gorged fly that burrows up from inside it that really turns the trick. A corpse may be both tragic and sobering, but the maggots that hatch and wriggle from the decaying soup of its innards are the triggers of our terror.

And here, too, what froze Frost to the spot was not the pyramid of decay itself but the way it moved. The way its fragile runny surface buckled and rippled in response to buried movements deep inside it. Frost stared more closely at the pile, seeing it for what it was. A major constituent of its mass was chewed, ripped paper, packed together consciously and glued by shit and slime. He was looking at a nest.

And the source of the red light glowed from deep within that nest; from two hollows in the centre, something stared out at him, something invisible save for its glowing red eyes. They shone so dazzlingly that Frost could neither look at them directly nor read anything in them. Nevertheless, their message was clear; Frost felt almost physically assaulted by the pulsing waves of radiated evil and hatred that washed over the chamber and him.

Frost closed his eyes for a second, swallowed, tightened his grip on his sword, and opening his eyes again, began to move forward.

There was a liquid rustling from the nest ahead of him and then the thing inside spoke. 'Matador,' it said, and its voice was the voice of the female harlequin he had followed. Having named him, it let itself dissolve into a low laughter.

Frost took another step forward and then stopped. There was a sudden dampness at the top of his leg. He glanced down and cried out in a mix of fear and revulsion. His crotch was soaked and dripping onto the floor beneath. Though painless and, due to the red light flooding the chamber, indistinguishable in colour, he knew it to be blood. His free hand shook in hesitation. He didn't know whether to cup himself or not.

Suddenly the front of his tight black matador trousers, as if the fibres were rotted by the flow of blood, gave way and a massive spill of blood burst from him onto the clay. He screamed and dropped his sword in shock. He stood watching, the nest and the thing within it forgotten, as the unbelievable continued to happen. The blood, on reaching the ground, ran not into pools but into scarlet sentences, forming into words as if filling pregouged channels in the soft clay. Written in his blood all around him were phrases that hammered into his frightened heart like nails of malevolence. 'The Vampires of Summer,' said one, 'The City of Saint Francis' another, while a third proclaimed 'The Star of the Morning; the Queen of Desire.'

Frost's eyes flew back up, but the nest was no longer there – or if it was, it was lost behind the blinding red glow that was suddenly all he could see. And his body was gone. And the light was all. The light and the movement. And he was flying again, unfleshed, through vast canopies of colour and impossible winds. And everything was confusion and light and a growing nausea. And the colours would give way to a final dazzling whiteness and his hurtling immaterial self would suddenly slam into that whiteness and he would be jolted awake, sitting up in bed, body sweating and head spinning, heart pounding and mind racing.

OF THE
VAMPIRE AND ITS
GLAMOUR

Being a partial transcription of a
hypothetical interview

*C*lick.

Hello. Testing. One, two, three.

Click.

Hello. Testing. One, two, three.

Click.

Click.

Okay. This is Donovan Moon. This is mid-September. And *this* is another in a continuing series of tapes that are trying – mostly in vain – to help me to get my thoughts together. About last summer, I mean. This time . . . well, this time I'm going to conduct an interview. And as Henry Rose was the first vampire I ever met, it's him I'm going to interview. The only immediate problem here is that Henry Rose is dead. Cut to pieces by that well-known expatriate English developer and psychopath, Jonathan Frost. And so, thanks to the miracle of modern imaginative journalism, the part of Henry Rose will be played at this performance by Donovan Moon. The part of Donovan Moon, on the other hand, will be played by me. So, let's go.

DM: Henry. You're dead. So, tell us; what's it like over there?

HR: Well, Don, that's a little difficult for me. You know, we don't have a Freedom of Information Act here, so . . .

DM: Oh, c'mon, Henry. I'm the last living person you saw who didn't try to slice you to ribbons; doesn't that mean anything to you?

HR: Sure it does, Don, sure it does. But . . . you know. I mean, I'm still pretty new here. And revelation is kind of a grey area for us . . .

DM: Hank, I *always* protect my sources.

HR: No. I'm sorry, Donovan, I'm going to have to take a metaphysical Fifth on this.

DM: All right already, we'll change the subject. Let's . . . Hey!

By the way – were you there? That second time I went to Frost's? The last time? Solstice? When it all went to hell? I didn't notice you – but then I *was* pretty freaked out . . .

HR: You think I'd have missed out on that? Hell, no. I was there. Some show, huh?

DM: Ha! Mmmm. Well, that's a viewpoint, I guess . . . Look, Henry, let's not dwell on that, okay? I mean, the reason I'm doing this is to try and find out about *you*. See, I met Frost. Talked to him. Well. Got talked *at*, at least . . . so I figured I should at least hear a view from the other side . . . Hey! 'Other side' – geddit? . . . Nah, scratch that. Cheap joke. What I *mean* is I should at least talk to somebody with an opposing attitude, and as I haven't found any of . . . your type of people . . . in my immediate neighbourhood, I –

HR: Oh, Don, you haven't been looking . . .

DM: Yes. Yes, that's true, Henry. I have *definitely* not been looking. But – for whatever reason – the point is I do not have access to a live vampire and so I'm using you . . . wait a minute. Let's start there. 'Live.' That's true, isn't it? You *are* alive – well, *you're* not, but you know what I mean. You're people, aren't you? Just people. With teeth. Big teeth.

HR: Yeah, right. But even they're voluntary, you know. I happen to like them, not all of us do. They're a bit flash, I guess.

DM: So how did Frost recognize the discreet ones?

HR: Come on, Don. You've read your Lawrence. Murderers, murderees. You did high-school physics. Like and unlike poles. You know. You've been to parties. How does the racist recognize the liberal? How does the pacifist know the warmonger? Extremes know extremes. Maybe we smell each other.

DM: Maybe. Fuck it. Let's get on to the interesting stuff. Tell me about blood.

HR: It's red. It's wet. It's sexy.

DM: Yeah, well . . . is it nutritious?

HR: Christ, I don't know. We don't *live* off it, if that's what you mean. We just like it.

DM: Do you attack people?

140

HR: What do you think?

DM: That's what I'm trying to find out.

HR: Well, like all things, there's probably some truth in those stories. Personally, I prefer a mutually arranged assignation, but there are brutes in every tribe. I don't know. It's not like we're a club or anything. We don't have *rules*.

DM: We don't have rules. That's important, right?

HR:Okay, Don, let's go for it. Forget the blood. Forget the fangs. You don't want to know the how. You want to know the why.

DM: Why?

HR: Because it's the way in which the world makes sense to us. Because living beyond the law is the only life that feels like life. Because propriety rattles and smells of steel. Because all we are is all we have. Because of the glamour of life without denial. Without restraint. Without teachers or fathers.

DM: You were born in a small town.

HR: Yes.

DM: You were schooled to eat shit.

HR: Yes.

DM: But there was somebody . . . different.

HR: Yes.

DM: You'd visit and wonder.

HR: Yes.

DM: And one night. Warm night. Summer night. When nature was singing. They wanted some of your blood. And offered some of theirs.

HR: Yes.

DM: You knew it meant nothing.

HR: Yes.

DM: You knew it meant everything.

HR: Yes.

DM: You said yes.

HR: Yes.

Click.

PART THREE

THE TWILIGHT
DANCE

June 14

Shelley Masterton had been in something like shock for more than twenty-four hours.

Shelley, once she was again capable of lucidity or even coherence, would doubtless have called the numbing grief – a beast of refined cruelty that held her paralysed in its sharp-toothed jaws but refused to bite – by the name shock itself, but what did she know? Shock seemed to be a name reserved for the exclusive use of close relatives of the victim and she had been merely a friend of Chris Tempest. 'Distraught,' the doctor said. 'Very upset,' her mother explained whenever she answered the phone in the room next to the one where her daughter lay.

'Yes. Very upset,' her mother was saying now, followed by a subdued 'thank you' and a quiet and dignified 'good-bye.'

Mrs Katz – she'd remarried when Shelley was fifteen, just eight months after Alvin had run off with the slut from the coffee shop, and often boasted (subtly) to her friends that Shelley had only been without a daddy for less than a year – placed the receiver delicately back in the cradle for the eighth time that day and for the eighth time that day looked around her daughter's living room.

There were books she could have read, magazines she could have looked at, but basically she answered the phone and looked around the room. She wasn't there to relax. She wasn't there to read books. That wasn't why she'd driven in from Redwood City. She was there to handle things for Shelley. To answer the phone. To look around the room.

It was very nice, she told herself again. Very nice, all things considered. Holding *any* two-room apartment in that part of San Francisco – particularly on that pittance her employers gave her – was doing well. But it *was* only two rooms. If Shelley'd stayed in Redwood City . . . well, the Bonner boy – who Mrs Katz knew was still sweet on Shelley and had only married Betty Maugham's more-than-merely-plump Alison on the rebound – had just bought himself a beautiful ranch-style on Sapphire Street and you just couldn't ask for better neighbours than you'd find there; why, Wanda and Mario (three houses up from him) had been among the first to call today and express their concern.

San Francisco. Mrs Katz shook her head. Why her daughter had to bury herself deep in the city that Alvin and she had regarded as something they'd *escaped* from when they'd moved the handful of miles to Redwood in the sixties was something she didn't pretend to understand. But it was something that concerned her. Look what happened! You go out dancing and your friend gets her throat slit! Is that anywhere to live?

Not that Mrs Katz had been particularly fond of Chris on the one occasion they'd met (*She looked like the city*, she'd found herself saying to Etta Bachrach without really knowing what she'd meant, but Etta had said that was a great phrase and Etta spent a lot of time with Mr Carlini who *taught English* at Redwood High), but God knows, she wouldn't wish that kind of hideous end on her worst enemy. Still, though she'd of course agree that people can dress just however they like and other people shouldn't judge them on it, it was . . . interesting . . . that Chris, who dressed the way she did, was the one who had . . . had had it happen to her and not Jane or Heather or, God forbid, her own Shelley.

None of these thoughts, variants on which had occupied her mind for most of that day whenever she wasn't actually on the phone, had she run past Shelley at all. The time wasn't right; she knew that. Shelley needed space and time to recover, and Mrs Katz had no wish to distress her further. Her daughter was distraught. The doctor had said that. She was dazed and confused. She was very upset.

Shelley *was* upset right at that moment, but it was a specific upset; she'd convinced herself for a terrifying second that

146

Ghirardelli Square didn't have escalators and that, therefore, it couldn't be where she was – that her numbed distress at Chris's death had played with her head so much that she'd wandered into a completely different mall. A wave of panic flooded her body and her hands clutched at the moving black handrail to steady herself as she was carried upward.

The people going down on the escalator next to her stared at her as they passed, some of them even turning their heads in order to keep looking as Shelley, face frozen in a terror of dislocation, was conveyed up to the next level.

She looked at them disappearing beneath her, their expressions an assortment of pity, interest, and malicious delight, and hated them for watching, hated them for knowing there was something the matter with her. Then a worse realization hit her. Why was she at Ghirardelli Square anyway?

She had no memory at all of her trip there.

She remembered lying on her bed, deciding it was ridiculous, deciding she had to go out, deciding she had to do something, and then . . . nothing. Nothing until this alarm call-like panic attack that, if nothing else, had at least woken her from whatever trance-like state she'd been in when she'd crossed the city. Jesus Christ, she couldn't even remember if she'd driven or taken the streetcar! Her head spun and she closed her eyes against the chaos, only a nominal and absurd sense of social decorum keeping her from whimpering out her fear.

Her feet hit a sudden obstruction and her eyes flew open just in time to allow her to retain her balance as she reached the top of the escalator and stepped off onto the next level. This act of physical necessity seemed to provide a useful focus and she pulled herself out of the anxiety attack. She stood very still and breathed deeply. It was nothing. It was nonsense. She was here. Therefore she'd gotten here. There were escalators. Therefore there were escalators. She was in control. It was all right.

She moved with the flow of the consumer traffic and found herself at the foot of the next escalator and stepped onto it, ready to be carried to the seventh level.

Were there seven levels in Ghirardelli . . . ? Don't start. *Don't start!*

147

Shelley bit her lip. If the escalator was taking her to level seven, then there were seven levels. The two people who'd stepped onto the escalator ahead of her began adding their own momentum to that of the moving staircase itself and progressed rapidly upward, stepping off the top at a rapid clip and turning left into the shopping areas while Shelley was still halfway up wondering what on earth she was thinking of buying.

As she reached the top herself she stepped off and looked around her. It was a level she hadn't visited before and she had no idea what stores or franchises traded up here. It also seemed less well kept than the rest of the mall – the first three stores she could see were all empty and one of them actually had boarded-up windows. The whole area was underpopulated and badly lit. No wonder she hadn't been up here before. Who'd bother?

So why the hell had she? No, she'd had enough of asking herself questions. She was here to do herself good. To get her mind off Chris's tragedy.

She set off at a determined rate down one of the walkways between the stores, running through possible purchases. What did she need? What did she want? She'd get her mother something as a thank-you for coming over. God, she couldn't even remember telling her mother she was going to slip out. But she must have done so, mustn't she? She looked up.

She was already in a store. Jesus, her mind was running almost completely on autopilot. It was scary. She looked behind her. The plate-glass doors at the entrance to the store were sliding shut. Presumably she'd just walked through them. But she had no memory of that at all. Though there was no resurgence of the paralysing panic that had gripped her on the escalator, Shelley thought that perhaps the best thing she could do would be to find a pay phone, call home, and tell her mother to come and get her. Autopilot may well have brought her safely this far, but now that she was aware of it, she really didn't wish to trust it to get her home. She was sure it was all right. She was sure the doctor would have a word for it. Trauma-Related Amnesiac Pattern, or something. TRAP. Trap. Hey, that was pretty good. Maybe she could get a job in the medical industry as an acronym maker. But before any decisions about career change she'd better get herself home – and before she could do that, she'd better find out precisely where she was.

She looked away from the entrance doors to glance around the store. And that was the first moment she felt a fear other than that fear of short-term memory loss; the store was totally deserted. More than deserted; empty. She was surrounded by glass display cases of various shapes and sizes, and that was it. No customers, no staff, no Muzak, no merchandise. Even beyond the closed glass doors, Shelley could see no one walking the corridors of the mall.

For one terrible second Shelley felt held in place, as if fear and distress were six-inch nails that had been suddenly hammered through her feet, rooting her to the floor. She gasped but, ripping herself free, walked hurriedly back toward the automatic glass doors and reached the touch-sensitive mat that normally triggered them.

The doors didn't open.

'No,' Shelley breathed, instantly regretting making any noise at all in that silent, empty space. She rushed to the doors themselves and tried to pry them open. They could have been welded together for all the impression she made.

She turned back around to look into the store, telling herself not to panic, that there would be something nearby to force the doors, or a plainly visible phone, or a storeful of smiling assistants eager to assist. Scratch that last one, she thought, there was some undercurrent to it she didn't like. A sealed store full of dark-suited strangers with fixed smiles and distant eyes descending on her, their first customer in centuries, wasn't all that reassuring an image.

But of course the store was still empty when she turned around, and she told herself to get a grip. Jesus, it wasn't that big a deal – if nothing else, somebody would eventually pass on the other side of the doors and she could ask them to call security. Then she noticed that one of the glass cases, which she could have sworn was as empty as all the others a few seconds ago, had some kind of display in it.

She was at a bad angle to see the item properly, and walking down and around to bring it more clearly into sight would mean leaving the relative comfort of the glass doors and their view – albeit a limited one, of the outside world. Nevertheless Shelley's need to view the case was stronger than her reluctance to walk back into the strange emptiness of the store. Seeing it would lend some sense to the day, would allow her to give a name to the place where she was trapped. If it was a clock, then she was stuck in an abandoned watchmaker's, if a set of pans, then a hardware store – either of which sounded better than a limbo franchise, a nothing store, a shop that specialized in emptiness and traded in absence.

Carefully, Shelley walked away from the doors toward the aisle and angled herself around toward the glass case. She looked in. It wasn't a clock. It wasn't a set of pans. Sitting on the third glass shelf in the display cabinet was something very odd. Strangely beautiful, but very odd. Shelley was reminded of those small plastic or glass paperweights sold as novelties in tourist towns, things that you shook to bring a plastic snowfall down on a plastic skyline. Shelley'd seen an old movie once in which that fat guy from the commercials dropped one of those things in slo-mo before croaking. Well, this thing was like one of them but much bigger and much more carefully made.

It was a rectangular glass box framed in lacquered wood. Shelley had to crouch slightly to bring it into direct line of sight. Inside the glass was a perfectly rendered red rose standing alone in a thin bed of dark soil. There was a trick to it; as Shelley moved her head slightly some kind of optical technique provided a backdrop of a midnight blue sky and a bright and swollen moon. Maybe it was a hologram, Shelley figured. Certainly there was no real background; from some angles – such as straight on – you just saw the rose and directly through the glass behind it. But from *here* – crouched down and with your head at a slightly canted angle to the box – you got what looked like a perfect representation of a night scene. Well, almost perfect; Shelley didn't pride herself on an intimate knowledge of the natural world, but she was pretty sure some flowers closed themselves up at night, unlike this crimson beauty, which stood open and unafraid in its boxed midnight. It was exquisite. And

150

probably very expensive. This must have been a great store, Shelley thought, wonder what else it sold?

The beauty of this item had managed to soothe Shelley's nervousness about the emptiness of the rest of the store and the whole of this level. She remained happily crouched down, staring at the midnight rose as something else began to happen within the confines of its box. The dark soil in which the rose stood began to change as Shelley watched, modulating into a lighter shade. At first she didn't understand what was happening and then realized, as she saw tiny traceries of white begin to form around the green stalk of the flower itself, that she was watching a highly sophisticated version of the plastic snowstorms that raged in the cheap paperweights. It wasn't snow here – she was being shown a representation of a night frost creeping around the rose.

It was stunningly well done. Shelley had no idea what new technology made it possible but assumed it had to be Japanese. The problem was, it was so well done it made Shelley sad. The intricate patterns of the frost, which had their own delicate and finely detailed beauty, were of course killing the rose. The soil became a stiff and harsh strip of frozen sterility, the stem of the rose moved from a pliant and pulsing green to a brittle glasslike translucence, and the flower itself, as the speckles blossomed all over it like cancerous white cells, seemed to shrink and shrivel in on itself, losing its bloom and its fullness.

Shelley was about to turn her head away, reluctant to see the end of the process, when a voice suddenly broke the silence behind her crouched figure.

'Perfect gift for the gal who has everything.'

Shelley's heart pounded in her chest and she felt her throat constrict in fear. She straightened up instantly and swung around to face the speaker.

As she gained her full height and completed her turn, her former fear of an unknown stranger seemed as nothing. With a terrified gasp, she slumped back involuntarily against the glass case, her jaw slack, her eyes wide.

She was staring into the smiling face of Chris Tempest.

Shelley felt the scream of terrified denial building in her

151

throat, but before she could let it out, Chris raised her hands, palms outward, in a calming gesture.

'Shell, Shell. It's all right,' she said, her voice soothing and knowing. 'It's a dream, Shell. A dream. You're dreaming this. Don't be scared.'

Chris's eyes were tender and concerned. They were a little amused, too, but Shelley was prepared to let that pass. Nobody can help being a little smug if they're in on the gag and you're not, and Chris looked neither ghostlike nor aggressive, which was really all Shelley cared about at the moment.

In fact, Chris looked great. She was dressed as she had been when Shelley had last seen her, and her body was apparently unmarked by the violence that had met it shortly after that last sight. She was smiling at her friend, and the affection in the smile outweighed the amusement.

Shelley felt the terror begin to slip quietly away like a tactful guest giving ground to a new arrival. The new arrival in this case was a nostalgic and loving warmth that suffused Shelley's body as she stared in wonder at her friend. She blinked at Chris, the smallest reflection of her friend's smile beginning to grace her lips. 'What?' she said. 'What do you mean, dreaming?'

'I mean you're dreaming, stupid. What do you think I mean?' Chris replied. She gestured around at the glass emptiness of the store. 'You don't think this is real, do you? Do you have any idea what this kind of space is worth in rental? There aren't any empty units at Ghirardelli Square. There's no seventh level either.'

Shelley nodded slowly. She knew that. She'd known that all along. She'd just tried to deny it because otherwise it didn't make any sense. And now here it was not making any sense and it didn't matter after all because she was dreaming. It was funny, kind of. She began to laugh, the sort of relieved laugh that comes after an adrenaline rush or some mild substance abuse.

Chris was still talking. 'I thought you'd feel safe here,' she was saying. 'I was told to come and talk to you, so I figured I'd put you in a comfortable environment. And I know how you *love* to shop, so Ghirardelli seemed a good idea. You must have

152

been a little too anxious. I couldn't keep it perfect. Sorry if it got a bit creepy.'

'Wait a minute. Wait a minute,' Shelley interrupted. This was all going too fast. What the fuck was going on? 'What do you mean? What are you talking about? Is this *my* dream or yours?'

Chris smiled. 'It's yours, Shell. It's yours. But I'm . . . kind of in charge at the moment.'

Shelley raised a hand to break in again. 'Hold on,' she said. 'Before we go any further, there's something I've got to do.'

Before Chris could ask, Shelley stepped forward and wrapped her arms around her dead friend. She pulled her close, kissing her cheek before burying her face in Chris's shoulder. She began to sob, not in sadness but in a rich and terrible joy at this opportunity to say goodbye that the real world had denied her and the dream world now gave.

'Oh Chris,' she said, amid her weeping, 'I'm so sorry. So sorry. I'll miss you.'

Chris returned the embrace, pressing her hands against Shelley's back and closing her eyes in pleasure. 'It's all right, Shell,' she said. 'It's really all right.' She moved her hands to Shelley's shoulders and, giving them a comforting squeeze, gently pushed the still-weeping girl back from her.

Shelley blinked through her tears, beginning to wipe them away, already a little embarrassed at her display and relieved when Chris continued in a more businesslike tone.

'Or, it *will* be all right if you help us. You know, this place is appropriate, after all. I *am* a salesgirl, Shell. I've got to sell you on something. You want to take a walk with me?'

Chris took Shelley's hand and, turning her around gently, led her toward the glass doors, which parted easily for them. They led directly to a wide escalator running upward, but Shelley didn't mind that the geography of the mall had changed. It was a dream mall, so it was fine. She felt safe with Chris. They stepped onto the escalator.

'Morningstar's got to be stopped, Shell,' Chris said as the escalator carried them upward. 'He's a really fucked-up son of a bitch, and he's been taking out his psychosis on the world for too damn long.'

'What's he look like?' Shelley asked. 'Did you see him when . . . when he . . . ?'

'When he killed me? Yeah, I saw him. Good-looking bastard. *You'd* probably get wet for him. You know, that power-broker soap-opera look. Classy suits and cannibal eyes. Like Blake Carrington with black hair and balls. I *warned* you about that type, didn't I?'

Chris laughed, and despite the incongruity of what they were talking about, Shelley felt herself smile at Chris's usual ability to synopsise a situation. Before she could ask a further question, she was distracted by the play of sunlight on Chris's face. She looked up. The escalator was depositing them on a sandy beach. The sea sang in the distance and a late-afternoon sun shone down on them.

Shelley threw a glance back down the escalator to try to make sense of this, but it was already lost in shadow. She went with the flow and followed Chris out onto the beach.

They were alone there and Shelley looked around at the beach in pleasure. Rock formations broke up the sweep of the sand at intervals and seabirds added occasional counterpoint to the low whistling constancy of the sea, whose song sounded as rich, as deep, and as green as the sea itself looked.

'This is where I died,' said Chris.

Shelley looked at her, at the strange, almost affectionate expression on her face. She'd accepted now that she was in a dream. An odd dream, that was for damn sure, but a dream was all it could be and consequently she found herself moving into that fatalistic acceptance that governs behaviour in most dreams, even though, in *this* one, she was fully aware of the fact that it *was* a dream.

Because of this acceptance, she put aside any questions her conscious self had about the dream itself – like, how *come* Chris was 'in charge' as she'd claimed, or how *come* she felt that she was in some kind of genuine contact with her dead friend, that they were having a real conversation, that her sleeping self *wasn't* writing both parts – and instead concentrated on questions arising within the dream. Such as the delicate matter of Chris being wrong about where she'd died.

'But the alley . . .' she said tentatively. 'You were found –'

'Yeah, yeah, yeah,' said Chris, almost impatiently. 'But you get a choice. Or, well, you don't exactly *get* a choice, but if you make a choice, if you're lucky enough to be calm enough to make a choice, then . . . then you get a choice. Oh shit, I don't know how it works. My body may have died in that alley, but my soul made its passage here, because I've always liked it – it's one of the little quieter stretches above Pescadero, you recognize it? – so it was comfortable for me. Well, maybe "comfortable" is putting it a bit strong, but you get the idea – maybe you'll be able to choose to go over in the ski-wear section at The Gap, ha-ha.'

Chris broke off for a second as a look of panic swept over Shelley's face, then rushed on to calm her. 'No. No. Not *now!* God, I'm sorry. No. Jesus, you've got *years* before . . . oh no, I'm not meant to give you any clues. Sorry. Anyway, look, you're not really here to talk about me. Like I said, it's Morningstar. He's got to be stopped. And you've got to help stop him.'

They were still walking along the sand. The birds were still singing. The sun was still shining. The breaking waves of the sea were still stroking at the shore and slipping away like the strong but gentle hands of a patient and powerful lover. It was one of the Dream Country's safe havens. There was no peril here, only peace and warmth and solitude. Shelley knew this. Nothing was going to hurt her here. But nevertheless, at Chris's last words, she felt a stiletto of fear, tiny and chilling, slip its way past those defences of sunlight and birdsong to slide into her unprotected heart.

She stopped walking. Chris, a pace or two ahead, stopped as well and turned back to look at her.

'*I've* got to . . . ?' Shelley asked, a tremor of uncertainty in her voice. 'What do you mean, Chris? What can *I* do?'

Chris smiled, a smile that was both sympathetic to the fear and reassuringly dismissive of it. 'You won't have to see him, Shell. You won't have to get anywhere near him. Somebody else will do that. You've just got to . . . open a door.'

Chris narrowed her eyes a little and turned her head slightly to look at Shelley from a more oblique angle. 'Could you do that, Shell?' she said. 'Could you open a door?'

Shelley stared back at her beautiful dead friend. She didn't answer straightaway. Couldn't answer straightaway. The question itself seemed pretty simple – hell, yes, anybody can open a fucking *door* – but she could sense there was a buried significance beneath the question. What kind of door? Open it how? And who – or what – was going to come through it?

Shelley wasn't used to adventure. The bravest thing she'd ever done – well, apart from that thing with the paddle and the cuffs Adam had talked her into a year or so ago – had been to make the move from Redwood City to San Francisco. Courage wasn't a currency she had to deal in in her everyday life and she wasn't sure how her reserves stood. What she was sure of, though, was that whatever it was that Chris was asking her would draw heavily on them. Courage was what was required, if only imaginative courage, if only the courage to say yes to the opening of a door from the Dream Country.

Shelley swallowed nervously. 'Yes,' she said.

2

June 19

The lobby of the Hyatt Regency at the Embarcadero was designed to impress. It made no bones about it. Not for it the understated elegance of some European hotels that hide their pride behind an old-world facade as if to say, 'Impressive, *moi?*' and then blushingly acknowledge it in shy displays of oak panelling and crystal chandeliers. No, fuck that. The Hyatt swaggered. Its pride was the unselfconscious pride of the scholarship athlete whose chest measurement equals his number of working brain cells. If the Hyatt had stomach muscles, it would almost certainly invite you to feel them.

The lobby was far from vulgar. It was well designed, intelligently lit, and comfortable. It was just very big. Even on the busiest days, its long marbled check-in desk could never seem crowded. Even when host to conventions, its floor space could never have the feel of a departure lounge for a busy flight. And those glass-fronted glittering elevators gliding continuously up and down the breathtaking height of its many floors could only ever seem attractive and elegant.

If you weren't staying there, it was designed to make you wish you were, and if you were, it was designed to make you feel pretty bloody special.

That is, unless it was your first time there and your only previous experience of hotel living had been twenty-dollar franchise motels. Then it didn't make you feel special at all, just unworthy and embarrassed.

Vinnie, seventeen years old and not born to money, wasn't feeling special. He was staring into the impassive face of a desk clerk and trying hard not to let his nervousness show. 'Could you check again?' he asked, striving for the right vocal effect —

157

one of bored annoyance rather than the humiliated panic he assumed he was actually projecting. 'Buchmann, Vincent,' he repeated helpfully, hopefully.

The clerk, a hollow-cheeked and bespectacled young man whose bald head – acknowledged by a close cropping of what little hair remained rather than vainly disguised by careful brush-and-grease work – conspired with his dark brown uniform to lend him an authority his years and his station in life did not really deserve, raised a marginally exasperated eyebrow and pressed some keys on his computer console.

'Could you confirm the spelling for me,' he said, pausing subtly before adding an obligatory 'sir.'

'B-U-C-H-M-A-N-N,' said Vinnie, spelling his surname out for the third time in as many minutes. He cast a nervous glance to his right, where a middle-aged woman was registering without any trouble at all and where the clerk dealing with her was not only a pretty dark-haired girl not much older than Vinnie himself but was dealing with her guest in a manner that was just on the pleasing side of obsequious.

The elder woman caught Vinnie's eye and smiled uncertainly. Vinnie mugged an exaggerated expression of amused anger in an attempt to establish some kind of this-side-of-the-counter solidarity. 'Tsk. Happens all the time, doesn't it?' the expression tried to say. 'God. These hotels, eh? I don't know . . . honestly!' He followed this up with a warm smile. The woman's face froze into the expression we reserve for our primal fear of the hopelessly insane and hurriedly turned her head back to the pretty young clerk.

The clerk attending to Vinnie pulled his hands theatrically away from his keyboard and accompanied the gesture with an exasperated tut. He gave a minimal shake of the head as Vinnie looked at him. 'No. I'm sorry,' he said. 'We have no reservation in that name.'

He looked at Vinnie expectantly, ready for further instruction. Vinnie swallowed. He had no idea what to do. God knows, none of this was exactly his idea anyway. He'd just agreed to . . . ah, maybe that was it. Genuinely blushing now, he asked

158

the clerk a further question. 'Um, how about Masterton?' he said.

The clerk pulled a slight face and set to the keyboard again. A couple of seconds later, he had something. 'Right,' he said, 'Masterton. Party of two. Reservation held by AmEx.'

'Right,' agreed Vinnie.

The clerk kept his eyes down at his computer, still reading off information and sharing it with anyone within earshot. 'Mmmm. Room 1533. Fifteenth floor. Miss Masterton checked in about an hour ago. And pre-paid her bill.'

Vinnie was glad to hear that last bit. But he was far from sure that he liked the way the clerk said it. And – maybe it was his imagination – but hadn't he stressed that 'Miss' in a distinctly old-fashioned manner?

The clerk lifted his head and caught the eyes of the girl behind the counter with him. Vinnie couldn't see his face, but he could see the tiny flicker of amusement in the girl's beautiful blue eyes as she quickly turned back to her own customer. He wished that he could be somewhere quiet with his bald clerk, somewhere where he would never have to stop punching him in the face.

Something of this move from embarrassment to anger must have shown in his eyes as the clerk turned back to him because there were no more jokes, just a businesslike politeness. 'You'll want your own key, of course, sir,' he said, and producing something from a machine beside his computer, he handed it to Vinnie. It looked like a credit card with a spectacular attack of termites. Vinnie held on to it with purposeful familiarity as he waited for his key.

There was a moment of silence between Vinnie and the clerk, culminating in a small puzzled expression on the clerk's face. 'Was there anything else, sir?' he asked. 'Do you have much luggage? It is only a one-night reservation . . .'

Before Vinnie could reply, the female clerk spoke to her customer. Her voice was a little louder than it need have been. 'Here's your key, madam,' she said. 'It's electronic – just slide it in the slot on the –'

'I'm quite familiar with them, thank you,' the middle-aged woman interrupted, a trifle testily.

Vinnie's eyes darted across to the girl behind the counter as she handed the woman a hole-punched card similar to his own. Turning back, the girl met Vinnie's glance for a fraction of a second, the ghost of a warm smile on her face.

Vinnie grinned and, with an all-but-imperceptible nod, registered his gratitude. He looked back at his own clerk. 'No,' he said. 'Everything's fine, thank you. Room 1533?'

'Yes, sir,' the clerk replied. 'Fifteenth floor. There's a nice view from that room.'

Vinnie nodded, turned away, and began to make his way across the lobby – suddenly less imposing, suddenly *his* – toward the cylindrical glass elevators.

From the relative seclusion of an armchair beside what, in the context of the lobby, was a potted plant, but what anybody in their right mind would call a tree, Shelley Masterton watched him walk. She'd wanted to check him out before meeting him in the room. Jesus, he was young. What, eighteen maybe? Younger?

She'd been up to the room once and left her overnight bag 'there. It was a nice room. Hell, it was a great room; she was just too nervous to be enthusiastic. She was glad she'd decided to spend the money, though. If she'd copped out and rented something tacky, she might not have been able to go through with it. Room 1533, though, was good; classy, spacious, cable TV, *huge* bed, and a view of the waterfront taking in the clock tower and large scaffold-supported letters spelling out PORT OF SAN FRANCISCO. Spelling it out *backward* from her point of view of course, but what the hell, long as it kept the sailors happy. Yeah, it was a good room, a fine room, and if you were going to rendezvous with a total stranger and fuck his brains out, you might as well do it in style, right?

She still couldn't quite believe she was here. Still couldn't quite believe she was going to do it. Still couldn't quite believe it wasn't another of Chris's dreams that she'd somehow walked into – eyes falsely open, body falsely clothed – while in actuality she lay, shut-eyed and naked, in her bed at home. But she knew it wasn't. There'd only been the two; the first one on the beach and the second when Chris had simply sat in her bedroom

160

beside Shelley's bed, speaking as gently and as persuasively as the first time. No, Shelley didn't think she'd be seeing Chris again this side of eternity. She'd only come that second time, in fact, because Shelley had asked her to.

The thing on the news had prompted it. After the first one, when everything had begun to white out and the rushing had begun in her ears, when the beach and the sky and the sea and Chris herself had begun to disappear, and Chris's last cry – 'Shell, when you wake up, you'll want to dismiss this as *just a dream*. Don't! Please don't!' – had begun to fade even as she shouted it, Shelley had woken in a normal room on a normal afternoon with a normal mother shaking her.

'Shelley. Shelley!' her mother had been calling, her face, as it swam into focus, twisted in concern. 'It's all right, darling! It's all right.'

'No. No, it's not,' Shelley had blurredly mumbled. 'I've got to open the door.'

Even as she'd said it, as reality flooded in on her, a reality of her bedroom, her bed, her mother, and a world where the dead are permanently silent and don't take their friends for walks and ask them to open doors, she'd felt ridiculous, and when her mother, misunderstanding but eager to make her feel at ease, had rushed to the bedroom door and flung it wide, Shelley didn't correct her, didn't say that that wasn't what she'd meant, didn't say that that wasn't the door in question.

It had been four o'clock when her mother woke her up – alarmed, apparently, by the whimperings and sobs coming from her bedroom – and by six that evening Shelley had without a doubt, and without guilt, done what Chris had asked her not to: dismissed it as just a dream.

Also by six that evening she'd decided she'd done enough lying down and had wandered into the other room to watch some TV with her mother. The news had just begun on the local station, and suddenly both women found themselves looking at another brick wall and another red and sticky Morningstar signature.

Shelley had gasped instinctively and her mother had leaped for the remote control.

'No,' Shelley had said, 'leave it on. I want to follow this until they fry the bastard.'

The news had trotted out the latest facts almost blandly — after the novelty of Chris's non-pattern-fitting murder, this one must almost have been a disappointment to the media. Then they named the victim.

Henry Rose, they said. Henry Rose, Shelley repeated in her head. Henry Rose. Rose. *Rose.*

Shelley had suddenly been freezing cold. *Freezing* cold. She'd heard of the phenomenon but never assumed its literal truth until that moment. But it was as if her room had been transported instantly to the Antarctic and some idiot had left the windows open. She'd glanced at her forearm and been completely unsurprised by the goose bumps she saw there.

Rose. A dead rose. She remembered the elaborate paper-weight in her dream and the elaborate death of the rose it contained. What the fuck was going on? She'd dreamed of this man's death in some dreamlike symbolist way. Chris hadn't been lying. It hadn't been just a dream. And this precognitive proof had been planted there to jerk her out of a denying wakefulness into a genuine awareness.

Insane it may well have seemed if Shelley had stopped to consider it, but she didn't. Like a sudden conversion to faith or the devastating and unexpected arrival of love, this new knowledge *invaded* her. It didn't invite debate, it didn't woo, it didn't seek to persuade: it possessed her. All she knew was that somehow the dream world had imparted knowledge to her that could have come from no other source and that therefore the dream world was not simply the storehouse of memory and desire she had always assumed it to be. It was something bigger, something more real. Chris was no projection of Shelley's own pain and loss. She *existed* in that dream world. And as a representative of that world, she'd come to Shelley for help. And Shelley had promised that help and then nearly betrayed her.

She'd remained seated until the cold shock of revelation passed and then, making excuses to her mother, had gone back to her bedroom, closed the blinds against the early-evening summer light, lay down on her bed, and willed herself to sleep.

162

She wasn't even sure if she'd been asleep at all when the dragging sound caused her to open her eyes. She'd gasped. Chris was pulling a chair over to the side of the bed.

'Thanks, Shell,' she'd said, 'thanks for coming back,' and sat down in the chair.

'Is this . . . ? Am I . . . ?' Shelley had asked, confused by the fact that she was still in her room.

'Yes. You're dreaming. You're asleep. You're actually lying on your side and facing the other wall. I didn't bother waiting till you'd put yourself in some location. We don't need that to talk. I could have come this way this afternoon, but I didn't want to freak you out, make you think you were seeing a *ghost* or something.'

Chris had laughed. Shelley had laughed, too.

'I saw. On the news. The rose. I remembered,' she'd said in a rush of words, eager to let Chris know of her understanding, of her belief. 'I want to help. I want to open the door.'

Chris had nodded. 'See, what it *is*, Shell, is that this is the only way we can make contact,' she'd said. 'That's the trouble. She's been trying to get at the Matador – that's Morningstar, that's his real name – through his dreams, but it's no good. The pig gets away. His own fear saves him. Pulls him out. She needs a way to reach him in his world, *your* world. She –'

'Wait a minute. Wait a minute. Who's *she*?'

Chris had made the kind of face a child makes when it's got a secret and wants to prolong it. 'Ah!' she'd said. '"Mystery, lo! Betwixt the sun and moon, Astarte of the Syrians: Venus Queen, ere Aphrodite was –"'

'What the fuck . . . ?'

'Rossetti. Dante Rossetti wrote that. Some Brit junkie with a wop name.'

'Jesus, Chris. I thought Jackie Collins was the heaviest reading you did.'

'Yeah, it's true. But now . . .'

'They have a *library* where you are?'

'Don't get smart. No, it's like . . . I don't *need* to read anything. It's like I . . . know it, anyway . . . I know *lotsa* shit now. Did you know Jefferson had a real bad pimple on his ass when he was sworn in? Did you know poets were the unacknowledged legislators of mankind? Did you know Heather – Little Miss Not-Till-the-Seventh-Date – used to have sex with her high-school principal? Did you know Divine was a *man*? Did you know –'

'Yeah.'

'What?'

'I knew Divine was a man.'

'You *knew* that?'

'Yeah. I knew that.'

'Oh. I didn't know that. Isn't it *wild*? Anyway . . . did you know that in 1374, the –'

'Chris. Chris! It's really great that you know all this stuff, that you're one with the universe and all that hippie shit, but could we get back to the point?'

Chris had reined in her galloping words and looked at Shelley more seriously. When she spoke again, her voice had become a little flatter, a little less like the Chris that Shelley had known at work and at play. 'Okay. The point is this: He's unreachable in his dreams, so he's got to be faced on this plane of reality. So dream must become flesh. So flesh is needed. A sacrifice is needed.'

Oh. That had been a bad word. Shelley hadn't liked the sound of that at *all*. Her dream body had flinched as Chris said it and she'd stared at her calm twilight visitor with frightened eyes.

'Don't worry,' Chris had said. 'It's not what you think. We don't need a victim . . .'

She'd paused then and looked at Shelley in a curious way, pregnant with meaning. It was at once appraising, affectionate, and . . . *envious*. Envious. As if this special paranormal creature who sat and spoke like Chris Tempest saw a potential in the confused and nervous human before her that was to her at least as strange and wonderful as anything Shelley saw in her.

'We need a mother.'

164

3

Vinnie slid his card key into the slot above the handle on the door of room 1533.

There was an electronic whirring noise from within the brass housing of the handle and a small green light began to blink above the key slot. Vinnie removed the card and turned the handle down sharply. Whaddaya know? The door opened. Vinnie decided the burst of pleasure he felt at this was decidedly unsophisticated. He leaned on the door and began to push it wider and was suddenly seized by an etiquette attack. If the girl was here, maybe he should have knocked? Apart from anything else, she was paying for the fucking room.

Feeling very klutzlike, he froze. Half in and half out of the doorway, one foot still in the corridor, he pulled the door back toward him a little and rapped on it with his other hand. 'Miss Ma . . . ?' Shit. Vienna Boys Choir or what?

He cleared his throat. Half an octave lower, he repeated, 'Miss Masterton? Shelley?'

There was no reply from the room. He glanced self-consciously at the number on the door. Sure, his key had worked, but who knows with these electronic things? Maybe he could open every fucking door in the hotel. No, the number was 1533 all right.

'It's Vinnie. Vinnie Buchmann.'

Still nothing. He moved the door forward again, but cautiously. Maybe she was in the shower or something. If he heard it running, he'd leave for a while. He didn't think surprising her naked and dripping would be the best introduction. Sitting there casually channel-hopping the TV and waving a lazy hand as she emerged from the bathroom . . . no, not a good idea.

As the door swung open, revealing a small vestibule leading to a wide archway beyond which was the room itself, another thought hit him. Maybe she was already in bed, stripped and languorous, ready to greet him with a slow barroom smile and siren eyes full of sexual challenge. Jesus Christ, he wouldn't be able to cope with that. He was nervous enough as it was. His throat constricted and his stomach felt hollow and tremulous. Biting his lower lip once, he walked on frightened feet through the archway and into the bedroom.

It was all right. The bedroom was empty and the shower wasn't running. There was no naked person in the large double bed that dominated the room. On top of the bed, though, was a small overnight bag that looked like it hadn't even been unpacked yet. In an unthinking gesture, Vinnie laid his hand on the canvas surface of the bag as if doing that was somehow a way of breaking the ice, of establishing intimacy. Hello, Shelley, he could say, you don't know me, but I once stroked your suitcase . . . so – where d'you wanna do it? Yeah, right.

He looked down at his hand, still resting on the bag. He couldn't deny that he felt an impulse to open the bag up and sift through the contents, to check out her brand of mouthwash, to sniff at her choice of perfume, to feel the textures of lace and cotton between his fingers. He didn't do it, though. The imperative was not so much moral as pragmatic; if her bag was here, then she couldn't be far away, and to have her walk into the room to find him with her camisole pressed to his face would not, in all probability, be the best note on which to start their collaboration.

He shifted his own small bag off his shoulder and put it down on the bed next to Shelley's. Wait, though. What kind of signals did that send out? Did it seem presumptuous? Territorial? Would she glance at his bag nestling beside hers, curl her lip, and walk away? Jesus Christ, get a grip! She'd call the whole thing off because he'd put his stupid *bag* down next to hers!? Come on! Vinnie pulled himself together and then, once he knew he was completely calm and was doing it simply because he *preferred* it that way, he lifted his bag from the bed and placed it instead on the surface of the . . . *thing* – what do you call a chest of drawers that doesn't have drawers? – on the opposite wall.

166

Doing this brought him opportunely in line with the big rectangular wall mirror. He stood still and took stock of himself. What would she think? The part of him that he thought was mature told him that that didn't matter, that they were here for a bigger reason, but the part of him he mistook for callow and would one day understand was not, knew that of course it mattered, knew that without attraction, without connection, big schemes – be they metaphysical or merely sociological – were just so much hot air. The invisible lines between people, the currents of desire or affection, those are the strings that pull the world into whatever shape they decree. Everything else – religion, politics, ambition – is at best metaphor and at worst vicious displacement.

The naive and truthful heart of Vinnie Buchmann knew this and always had. It would be years, though, before the confusions of adolescence would allow his mind to accept its simple profundity, to relearn what it had known in childhood. Even so, despite his conscious assumption that it was irrelevant and foolish, he began to pull and tuck at his clothes, to comb his hair, to wonder if he had time to go to the bathroom and freshen up, to look at himself and hope he proved acceptable. Appearance, of course, wasn't the point. In his nervousness and his youth, however, it was the only analogue Vinnie could find for his desire to have Shelley like him, for his hope that they would connect with each other. He stared at himself.

He was short for his age, but his body was lean and well proportioned. His face would never give Mel Gibson cause for concern, but there was nothing actually *wrong* with it – all the bits were in the right place and none of them did anything unusual, though his nose would occasionally get flaky and red when sun-touched or windblown. He was as fond of junk food as the next seventeen-year-old, but he indulged that fondness carefully and his skin was grateful and therefore noneruptive. His eyes were his best feature – surprisingly dark for a pale-skinned redhead, they were also bright and eager, luminous with a native intelligence and a warm soul.

In short, he was an average-looking healthy teenager. He would never turn heads on a California beach, but equally he'd go very hungry were his chosen profession to be that of carnival geek.

There was a soft footfall back by the door followed by the quiet but sharp rat-tat-tat of fingernails on wood. As he swung away from the mirror toward the door, Vinnie just had time to see his reflected face assume the kind of stricken pallor that it was used to wearing when the nurse would open the door to the dentist's office and smilingly inform him that Dr Robson was ready for him now. Jesus, it was ridiculous! He imagined telling Erik and Mark about it; yeah, guys, there was me, a hotel bed, and a beautiful female stranger – and all three of us knew that what was going to happen was spelled S-E-X . . . oh, and the other thing, the bit you'll really like is – I'd rather have been having abdominal surgery! Is that a killer? Am I a stud or what?!

His head full of the imagined derision of his friends, Vinnie saw Shelley for the first time.

Oh God, she *was* beautiful. Oh God, she was *old*.

Not *old* old, of course, just a vital and terrifying five years more old than him. Not I-can't-do-it-it'd-be-like-fucking-my-grandmother old, but oh-jesus-god-in-heaven-she'll-know-every-thing-I-don't-and-laugh-at-me old.

Shelley was half leaning into the room, one forearm still resting on the wood of the door where she'd tapped her fingernails. The upper half of her body leaned forward and her head was angled slightly to let her face peer through the archway to look at Vinnie. Her mouth (God, her mouth. He was going to *kiss* it.) was open in a warm smile of greeting and her green eyes sparkled as she looked into the room. The angle of her body made her breasts press slightly against the black silk of her blouse (God, her breasts. He was going to . . . No. Stop it!) as she tilted her head a little in an unspoken question. Vinnie stood silent and frozen. She spoke.

'Vinnie?'

'Yeah. Yeah. Er . . . Shelley?'

She nodded, smile still intact. 'Right,' she said.

'Oh,' he said.

There was an uncomfortable pause as Vinnie wondered if

168

he'd run out of conversation already. Then he realized Shelley was still hovering in the door. 'Jesus! Come in. Come in.' He smiled apologetically. 'I mean – it's your room. You're paying for it.'

Shelley's smile disappeared, replaced by an anxious expression. 'Does that bother you?' she asked, and the concern in her voice was a comforting thing to Vinnie because it let him know she was as on edge as he was despite her beauty and her years. He hastened to answer her.

'God, no. I'm grateful. I . . .' He paused, embarrassed again. Did that sound wrong? Oh, fuck it, maybe he should just be honest. She seemed nice. She'd understand. 'I'm so . . . I just don't want to say the wrong thing, you know?'

The smile returned and Shelley nodded as she finally made her way into the room. 'I know what you mean,' she said. 'I'm nervous as hell.'

'Really? That's *great*,' Vinnie said in a rush of relief, and then stopped himself again. He pulled a wry face at her. 'Well, shit. What I mean is . . . it's not *great* but . . .'

'It's all right,' Shelley said. She'd walked into the room and now they stood, about four feet from each other, both of them unsure as to whether they should move closer, sit down, talk awhile, whatever.

Shelley looked at the boy. She hadn't lied. She *was* as nervous as hell. But she felt a little better now. It was easier for her. She was the elder, and Vinnie's nervousness, hollering its presence in his face, his stance, his voice, was clearly stronger than her own and consequently made her feel more in control of the situation. Not at ease exactly, but at least within sniffing distance of it.

This relative calm allowed her the luxury of pity. Vinnie looked terrified. Standing there, silly grin on his face, probably wishing he was playing softball or drinking illicit beer with the boys. She stopped herself right there. It was *nice* that he was nervous, too; God knows, her imaginings had given her far worse scenarios – some sleazoid beast, charged with lust and the kick of a free fuck, grinning knowingly at her in an inappropriately proprietary way. No, this was much better than it could have been. She felt a sudden burst of affection for the boy. He'd been picked just like she had, and she trusted Chris, trusted the dream world, to have picked wisely.

Whether it was the calm, the pity, or the affection, or some mix of all three, she wasn't sure, but something propelled her into action. She closed the distance between them, almost allowing herself the luxury of amusement as she saw Vinnie's eyes widen at her approach, and reached an arm around his shoulder.

'Listen,' she said, and then realized she wasn't sure how to say it exactly. 'Why don't we . . . I think . . . what I mean is, let's break the ice before we both freeze. Kiss. Let's kiss. Why don't you kiss me? Then we might be able to sit down and talk without feeling we'd shatter if we moved.'

She smiled up at him, the one arm around his neck, the hand of the other resting gently on his hip – nothing too sexy, nothing too standoffish – a tiny gap between their bodies that he could choose to close if and when his fear let him take her up on her invitation.

Vinnie stared down at the upturned face of the girl. The girl with her arm around his neck. The girl with the most gorgeous green eyes he'd ever seen. The girl with her body a tantalizing, exciting inch away from his own. The girl whose mix of fragrances filled his senses and made him both dizzy and aroused.

He was still terrified – in fact, his body had actually started shaking now and he was damn sure she could feel it, tense his muscles to control it as he might – but there was also a growing warm glow, a cocktail of excitement and comfort. He was glad Shelley was smaller than he. It wasn't an issue with him normally, but the edge her years gave her – at least in his mind – was mitigated a little by the fact that he could look down at her smiling face. That he could slip an arm easily about her narrow waist. Could pull her that vital quarter inch closer. Close his eyes. Bend his head. Place his lips on her waiting, smiling, perfect mouth.

Shelley let him continue the kiss and accommodated herself to it. His mouth was slightly open, so hers was, too. His tongue wasn't particularly brave, so hers stayed relatively modest. But

170

it was a nice kiss. Friendly rather than passionate, but with a palpable sensuality and an undeniable undercurrent – an erotic charge that was as much the result of the strange and formal circumstance that brought their mouths together as it was of any personal electricity.

They held the kiss for six seconds, the last enriched by a mutual pressing together of their bodies and a single thrilling pass of tongue against tongue.

They stepped apart and back. Vinnie smiled and swallowed, still tasting her, still breathing in her scent.

'Good idea?' asked Shelley, though she knew from his responses it had been.

Vinnie nodded in confirmation. He drew in a deep relaxing breath and nodded again. 'Yeah,' he said. 'I feel . . . I mean, apart from the fact it was really nice anyway . . . I feel more together now.' He laughed self-deprecatingly. 'Less likely to run screaming from the room, you know?'

'I'll take that as a compliment . . . I think,' Shelley said as she eased herself into one of the armchairs close to the bed.

Vinnie laughed and sat down on the edge of the bed. He tried not to look at her dark-stockinged legs as she crossed them, the short black skirt riding teasingly up her thigh. 'Sorry,' he said. 'I didn't mean . . . No. You're gorgeous. You really are. And in fact, if I saw you in a bar or something, I *would* be too scared to talk to you. But that isn't what I meant. It was the formality. The expectation. I wanted to scream at him for talking me into it.'

'Who was it?' Shelley asked.

'My father.'

'Your father?' she repeated, and then, telling herself to tread gently, 'Your . . . *dead* father?'

Vinnie nodded. 'Henry Rose,' he said.

'But . . .'

'Yeah. Divorce. My mother married again when I was a kid.'

'Yeah? Me too. But I kept the name. I'd be a Katz now, but I'm still a Masterton. Don't really know why. Dad's a jerk.'

'I didn't really know mine. He had visiting rights, but . . .

you know. Fact, he's used 'em more since he died. Nah, just kidding. But . . . was it *your* dad who . . . ?'

'No. No, he's alive. It was a friend. A good friend.'

'Uh-huh.' Vinnie accompanied this noncommittal sound with a nod. He wanted to ask if the good friend was a guy. A lover. But not only did he feel it was none of his business, he recognized that the stab of jealousy that had gone through him at the thought of it being a man was absurd and unjustified – which didn't mean that he wanted to be stabbed again should the answer be yes.

There was a moment's silence between them, which Shelley broke with a question it had never occurred to her to ask Chris. 'Did you ever wonder why they didn't just give us his name?'

'Who? Morningstar?'

'Yeah.'

Vinnie pursed his lips and shook his head slowly. 'I don't know. I didn't think . . . I guess it has to be this way. I don't think they'd want us to go after him ourselves, anyway. The guy's too good. He's the best there is at what he does – but what he does isn't nice, you know?'

'What?'

'Wolverine. The X-Men.' He gave her a curious glance. 'Don't you read comic books?'

Shelley almost laughed at the question but managed to stop herself; the age difference between them seemed to have stopped bothering him and she didn't want to spoil the relaxed friendliness growing in the room by renewing his nervousness. So she simply shook her head.

Vinnie assumed an exaggeratedly incredulous look. 'You don't?' he said. 'How in the hell did you cope? When you were visited?'

'I don't know what you mean.'

'I mean – I'm used to this shit. I read it all the time. Other planes of existence. Visits from the dead. All that stuff.'

Vinnie was talking at his most animated now, his voice rising and falling in emphasis, his hands lending visual support to his rapid and excited speech. Shelley liked it. He was completely at ease now, and she gave an inward giggle at the thought that

172

the kiss, though it had done its job, may have been less effective at relaxing him than an enthusiastic mention of the latest issue of Casper the Friendly Ghost. Vinnie was still speaking.

'So I shoulda been ready. But it *freaked me out*! God knows what I'd've been like if I didn't own a complete set of Phantom Stranger! How did you . . . I mean . . . you a "Star Trek" fan or what?'

He grinned at her, his rapid-fire speech concluded. His pale skin gained colour when he was excited, Shelley noticed, but it wasn't the blotchy red patching that some redheads suffer from at times of passion or exertion. Jesus, she thought, if I was a redhead and could keep myself permanently on the edge of excitement, I'd save a fortune on foundation cream. But that wasn't answering his question. Star Trek? Get real.

'No,' she replied. '"Laverne and Shirley" reruns?' She shook her smiling head even as she said it. 'No use?'

Vinnie laughed. 'Not really,' he said.

Shelley shrugged her shoulders. 'Then I guess I'm just user-friendly as regards the haunting scene.' She dug into the small handbag she had with her and pulled out a pack of cigarettes. 'I'm trying to give these up,' she said, waving the pack at Vinnie. 'No. Bad psychology. I *have* given these up. But I bought a pack in the lobby for . . . you know, later . . . and I – would you like one now?'

Vinnie looked thoughtful. And tempted. 'I . . . don't know. I've never had a cigarette.'

Or a girl, Shelley thought in a sudden flash of insight that his nervousness wasn't just the situation, wasn't just her, it was the Act itself. Wisely, she didn't ask him if that were true.

Instead, as he stood up and leaned over to reach for the pack, she let it slip from her fingers and closed her hand about his. She pulled him closer, arching her body upward to meet him, her free hand finding and stroking his upper thigh as he balanced himself and braced his other hand on the back of her armchair.

Before they could read each other's expression, before Shelley could see in his eyes the confirmation of his inexperience or he see in hers the relative coolness of her decision to make it happen now, she pressed her face into the side of his neck and ran her wet tongue along one of his veins.

'Take me to bed, Vinnie,' she whispered into his ear, punctuating her speech with small kisses. 'Make it nice for me. Make me feel good.'

His only audible answer was a sigh, but his actions shouted an emphatic yes. He took his arm from the back of the chair and pressed it along the line of her shoulders. His other hand he shook free of her grip and tucked it low beneath the curve of her ass. He lifted her clear of the chair, keeping her face pressed to his neck.

Shelley, secure in his grasp, lifted her legs from the floor and, spreading them wide, wrapped them tight around his hips, locking her ankles together behind him. She felt a warm flush of embarrassment that due to her movement her skirt was now practically around her waist, but the alchemy of arousal was there to work its magic and transform shame into excitement.

Vinnie accommodated himself to her weight, pressing her tightly to him. His hand slipped underneath her skirt to support flesh and silk. It was partly for balance, Shelley knew, and partly to feel her. But that was all right. That was all right. Whatever the reason for their being here, she was open to his exploration and she mustn't expect him to write desire out of the itinerary. She moved a little on his hand and sighed into his ear to show him it was okay as he turned smoothly back toward the bed.

Miraculously free of awkwardness, they sank onto the bedcover without essentially changing position, except that Vinnie moved his hand from the spread of her cheeks to stroke at her side, his thumb just stopping short of the swell of her breast on each stroke.

Shelley manoeuvred her legs, each foot in turn working a toe into the heel of a shoe and prizing it free. She kicked them loose. Vinnie knew it was this practical-minded removal of shoes that made her legs move so, but he didn't care — the by-products were a deliciously arousing movement beneath and around him and the sensual sound of her dark stockings rubbing against the denim of his jeans.

Vinnie lifted his head from the crook of her neck and brought

174

his mouth to hers. With the perfect timing of natural instinct, his hand cupped her breast and massaged it as their lips parted for each other and their tongues probed wetly and sensually in each other's mouth.

Shelley slid her hand down his back and pressed against his butt, forcing him more urgently against her. She pulled her tongue back, tracing it across his lips as it left him, and moved her head to one side. 'Take something off,' she murmured, her voice rich and low.

Vinnie leaned up from her and made as if to unlace his sneakers.

'No,' she said, urgency in her voice, 'just the important ones.'

She took her arms around his body to the waistband of his Levi's to demonstrate what she meant and unsnapped the button. She drew the zipper down eagerly but carefully, mindful of the straining erection behind it. A hand at each hip, she forced the jeans down to midthigh level, carrying the boxer shorts with them. His cock sprang into view, hard and pulsing, accompanied by a moan of pleasure from its owner.

Vinnie'd gotten the idea. He rolled to one side, allowing his hands access to her brief silk pants and, breathing heavily with the fury of his desire, slipped them off her as she raised her hips to help him. He drew them over the stockings and down, staring wonderingly at her legs as she raised them slightly to let him complete the process.

Shelley was unbuttoning her blouse as Vinnie did this. She popped the central clasp on her brassiere and moved the cups to either side, freeing her breasts, and as Vinnie moved back toward her she grabbed at the base of his sweatshirt and pulled it over his head. He raised his arms to assist and she let one hand complete the removal while the other cupped his balls, her fingernails tickling gently at the back of the scrotum between his thighs.

As Vinnie was freed from the sweatshirt he leaned down again to unclasp one of her stockings from the garter belt.

'It's all right,' Shelley said, adding with a laugh in her voice, 'You can leave them on. You're allowed to enjoy this, you know.'

'Oh. Sure,' Vinnie replied in a voice that would have been confused had passion allowed it the luxury.

He doesn't get that, Shelley thought. Guess it's an older guy's thing. She was charmed. And ready as hell.

She opened her legs again and pulled at Vinnie's body to make him roll back between them. She stared with delight at his eyes as they focused, with the fixed gaze of a mystic or a junkie, on the spread of her thighs and her moist waiting pussy. It *is* his first time, she thought, and cradled his cock with one hand to help him inside her as her other arm went around his neck to pull their faces together again.

Vinnie moaned into her mouth as her tongue ran itself across his teeth. He was enfolded and caressed by her as his hips began to move him inside her.

He'd had lingering virginal doubts about how it would feel, even whether it would hurt, and lingering virginal fantasies about how good it would be, but nothing he had dreamed or feared had prepared him. At one and the same time it felt like nothing he'd ever experienced and like the most familiar, most right, most homelike sensation he could imagine.

He was no stranger to orgasm of course, so he knew the destination to which he was heading, but now he was on a different train that ran on different tracks because being inside Shelley was very different from being inside his own hand. It was both gloriously selfish and liberatingly self-dissolving. While he was acutely and blissfully aware of every exciting point of contact between their bodies, he was also, and simultaneously, freed into a bodiless and dreamlike sea of sparkling pleasure in which his soul swam and tingled as if burning with a joyful fire that was nourished rather than extinguished by the ecstatic waters around it.

He was in the land where fire and water met, mated, and fed on one another.

He was where the elements reclaimed their hidden unity.

He was ... Oh God ... He was having his nipples sucked. Oh Jesus, that was good.

He looked down. The sea of spiritual ecstasy was still sweeping through him and it was undeniably fabulous but it was no

176

more fabulous than the sight of Shelley's beautiful blonde head burrowing into his chest or the feel of her flicking tongue and her teasing nibbling teeth.

Shelley raised her head to look at him. Her eyes glittered beneath lids heavy with pleasure.

'Don't stop,' Vinnie pleaded.

'My turn,' Shelley said, tilting her head to one side. 'Here. My neck. Kiss me.'

Vinnie bent to his task eagerly and began sucking and licking the taut muscles and veins of her exposed neck down the side below her ear.

Shelley moaned and surrendered herself to the crescendo she felt building inside her. She relaxed her body totally and let the boy do all the work, her limbs slack around him, her mouth open, her eyes closed. It was on its way. Lights danced behind her closed lids. The rushing of her blood sounded throughout her body like a song from a memory of heaven. She was nowhere and everywhere and tiny and entire and fused and dissolved and all her scattered atoms vibrated with joy and screamed with life.

Vinnie saw her mouth tremble. Words escaped her as if she was almost unaware she was speaking.

'Oh ... I'm coming, Vinnie ... I'm ... can you feel? Can ... ? I ... ohhhh ...'

That was it for Vinnie. The sight and sound of this exquisite creature in the abandonment of ecstasy was the key that unlocked his own floodgates. He poured forth the juice of his passion into her, each spasm of pumping release accompanied by a soul-deep drowning wave of pleasure that forced cries of bliss from his mouth even as it milked his body.

Vinnie rolled to his side, carrying Shelley with him, so that they lay side by side on the bed, legs still intertwined, bodies still pressed tight, as the last wave receded, leaving them beached on the shifting and languorous sands of satisfaction.

'That was ... you're ... I ...' Vinnie tried to say, and Shelley silenced him with a small pouting kiss.

'Sshhh ...' she whispered. 'Just lay still.'

She'd been here too many times. She didn't want him giving

voice to nonsense phrases that five minutes of recovery would have him regretting. They'd shared the beautiful madness and that was enough. To pretend sanity was not going to reclaim them was not just foolish but painful. Vinnie was young. He didn't know that yet. But boys learn fast. Several sad stories in her past could testify to that. It was better, she'd found, simply to lie in the sweet warmth of each other and hold off on words until their distinct and separate personalities had returned and evicted the single selfless creature that had temporarily possessed their bodies.

Vinnie was very good. He lay content and silent beside her, breathing deeply of her skin and running an occasional hand over the smoothness of her back. When she could tell they were human again, Shelley turned slightly away from him so that her face looked up at the ceiling of their room. She kept her arms around him, though, in case he should mistake relaxation for rejection.

Hardly disturbing the silence of the room, she let out a long sigh, slow and delicate, which transformed itself into speech before the end of the breath. 'Did you ever play that game?' she asked. 'The one where you get a letter and you all have to come up with words beginning with it – like trees, countries, presidents? You know the one I mean?'

'Uh-huh,' Vinnie responded, 'I think so. Like, R comes up, so it's Redwood, Russia, Roosevelt?'

'Yeah, right. I was at a party once, and we all got bored with the categories, so we made up our own. Fun stuff, drunken stuff, you know. It was like, Diseases You'd Most Like to Avoid, Ugly Person on Prime-Time TV, shit like that. One of them was Things You Like After Sex. So if C came up, you could say Cigarette, B Backrub, S Shower, and so on. Anyway, one round O came up and I put –'

'Oral?' Vinnie guessed.

Shelley giggled. 'Well, that *was* one of the first things to come to mind. But you lose points if other people get the same thing and I knew that was going to be a popular choice.'

'So what did you put?'

'Oblivion.'

Vinnie looked puzzled for a second and then nodded slowly. 'Yeah, I know what you mean. I'm wiped out.'

Shelley glanced at him quickly and wondered whether to shake her head, whether to tell him she meant more than that, that she was talking about a real wish to disappear, to escape the thousand tiny disappointments that welcome you home from fuckland. But he was seventeen. She couldn't. It'd put her right up there with that bitch in kindergarten who'd given her the hot news about Santa Claus. No, he wanted to hear other stuff.

'I'm wiped out, too,' she said, investing her voice with a sated purring quality that, if not exactly fake, was certainly exaggerated a little for his sake. 'I'm glad you didn't see me in a bar and get scared off, Vinnie. I'm glad this happened.'

The boy beamed. He tried to hide it but he couldn't. 'Me too,' he said. 'I'm glad this happened . . .'

He paused than, as if the other significance of their encounter had only just returned to his mind. 'What *else* is going to happen?' he asked, in a different voice. 'What's going to happen *now?*'

Shelley shrugged. 'I'm not sure,' she replied. She reached one arm out to the side of the bed and pulled the bedspread up, folding it back on itself to cover them. Freeing herself of the rest of her clothing and snuggling in close to Vinnie, she gave him a soft kiss on the mouth and added, 'But maybe if we sleep on it, they'll come to tell us.'

4

But they didn't.

What happened instead was that at about four in the morning Shelley suddenly woke up from a dreamless sleep. She woke with the kind of clean break from sleep to consciousness that most of us stopped experiencing when we were ten years old, Shelley included; her normal waking process these days was to be dragged foggily upward by the loathsome screech of her unsympathetic alarm clock into a time – thirty minutes long on a *good* day – of dull-eyed and clumsy bad humour. This was different. One second she was deeply and completely asleep. The next she was not. She woke knowing precisely where and who she was with a clarity that it normally took her a shower, a juice, and a black coffee or two to achieve. There was neither drowsiness nor confusion to accompany her from one state to the other. There were no vestigial dream images playing through her mind. There were no protesting limbs begging her eyes to close themselves again.

There was only the agonizing pain.

Shelley's stomach felt like it had been repeatedly kicked – and kicked hard – from the moment she'd closed her eyes to the moment she'd opened them again.

It was an overwhelming, all-encompassing agony that centred, sharp and bright-edged, in her belly but echoed throughout her whole being in dull brutal waves. Its intensity made her feel sick, though the pain itself seemed not to relate to nausea so much as to that dreadful ringing shock that follows direct physical assault.

Its suddenness, its strength, its mystery, terrified Shelley. A few seconds passed while she did absolutely nothing but lie there, disabled by the pain and paralysed by the fear. Vinnie, as a sideways glance told her, was lying on his side facing away from her and snoring gently. She was about to call his name when a fresh spasm of pain shuddered over her, rolling through her like a wave wielding razors, and convinced she was going to throw up, she threw the blanket aside and clambered to her feet, intending to reach the bathroom.

She'd covered about half of the distance when something stopped her. With the instinct of the sick – who call for things not knowing why they will be of help to them, only that they will – she headed instead for the large window that looked out onto water and sky.

Framed in the window, a supporting arm pressed against each side of its wooden frame, Shelley stared out helpless and confused at the night. There were lights along the dock and a few distant spots of luminous colour rose and fell on the water to mark the slow passage of bay traffic, but essentially the lower half of her view was blackness. It was the sky that was alive. Brilliant with stars, it hung before the hurting girl like a tormenting paradigm of lost peace and cold immeasurable splendour. Through her agony, through her nausea, Shelley was suddenly besieged by another sensation as an inexplicable and elusive nostalgia swept through her. For the briefest of instants, she transcended her pain, transcended even her sense of self, as she stood and yearned: staring at stars, and homesick.

The pain wouldn't let her forget it for long, though. Its stabbing insistence brought her rapidly back to herself, and for the first time in the twenty or so seconds she'd been awake, she looked down at her stomach, afraid of what she might see. It was less bad than she'd feared, but it wasn't good. Her stomach was swollen. The swelling was not massive, but it was clearly visible, and her skin was stretched tight and shiny across its distending bulk. What was worse, though, was that the swelling wasn't constant – her stomach was moving. In time with the spasms of pain, it was rising and falling in a throbbing pulse like an abscess about to burst.

An involuntary moan escaped from Shelley's mouth, chased there by the atavistic terror that the sight of her transformed body induced in her. In the small part of her mind that wasn't held ransom and gagged by that terror and by pain, its vicious sidekick, Shelley had an idea of what was happening to her. She'd been told a mother was needed. But how could this be happening now, so quickly, so unnaturally, so painfully? Whatever emissaries from another plane had acted as their dating service, she and Vinnie were normal humans who'd enjoyed a normal fuck, so what in God's name was going on? Shit, she was scared. Another whimper crawled out into the silent room.

'Shelley?'

Vinnie's voice was clouded by sleep, but the concern in it was apparent. Shelley heard the fumbling, rustling sounds of his still-sleepy body moving against the blanket as he sat up in bed, but she didn't even try to look around. She couldn't. Her body was too busy suffering the pain and her mind was too busy trying to answer the questions it had asked itself to let her do so much as throw a comfort-seeking glance at him.

'Shelley? Are you all right?'

The voice was clearer now and its concern more sharply focused. Shelley was about to attempt an answer when something else happened.

Great, she thought, now I'm fucking delirious. It had to be that. It had to be that the agony was so great that her mind was wandering. It had to be hallucination because what she thought she was seeing couldn't be happening. It appeared to her as if a narrow shaft of light was shining down on her from the night sky outside. It was the strange silver light normally associated with a bright full moon, but there was no moon visible, and even if there had been, it would have to have been blanketed by clouds to give this effect of a single escaping beam. But there were no clouds, either. Just the stars.

Shelley stared outward and upward. The shaft of light seemed to become diffused in the middle distance so that her eyes couldn't trace it back through the night to a direct source, but if she plotted lines back from the point at which the brilliance dissipated into the surrounding darkness, they would seem to indicate that the root of the light that bathed her was a fairly bright star relatively low in the sky. This was of course impossible and she gave it no further thought – not because she was particularly averse to considering the impossible but because

182

something else was happening that to her seemed of much greater importance; as the light enfolded her the pain in her belly was disappearing.

She heard the sounds of Vinnie crossing the room behind her and managed to gasp out an answer. 'Don't. Don't,' she said, breathing each word out between the waves of pain, which, though diminishing in intensity with each successive stab, were still strong enough to silence her as they passed. 'It's getting better. I think. I think it's going. Stay there.'

'But what the fuck's going on?' Vinnie asked from somewhere close behind her, his voice now as much confused as concerned. 'Can't I do anything?'

'No. Just stay there. It's all right.'

The pain, still coming in waves but now as small as a tooth-ache, was no longer blinding Shelley to other things. She didn't know precisely why she was telling Vinnie to stand back, but she knew it was important that this light had free play over her body. It was part of the same process she and the boy had started when they made love. She was able to answer her own earlier question now, even if the answer would seem silly in the cold light of normal life. It *hadn't* just been a normal fuck; she'd been stupid to think it had been. It was a ritual act performed for magical reasons. And now the ceremony was continuing.

Shelley stood there, the pain now almost a memory, and was filled with a strange sensation. It was pride, she thought, except that there was a paradoxical humility there, too. She felt at one and the same time that she was the centre of things (*of all things, of everything*) and that she was merely the tiniest part of an awesome unknowable system, and curiously, it was the former that made her feel humble and the latter that made her feel proud.

'Shelley . . . Your stomach . . . What's happening?'

Vinnie was still paying lip service to normal human reactions, but she could tell he felt it, too, or he would be grabbing at her, stroking her brow, calling an ambulance, whatever.

The pain was gone completely now, though Shelley's stomach was still expanding and contracting. She was about to risk a backward glance at Vinnie when the silver light disappeared. For a second the world seemed magicless again and Shelley felt the loss like an amputation. She didn't, however, have time to worry about it because suddenly her stomach was flat again and an overwhelming feeling filled her innards like a massive peristalsis. There was no room for thought, only surrender. She spread her legs wide and gasped for breath as she felt an irresistible movement begin within her. Dimly she heard Vinnie's answering gasp as something gave and a wet, warm rushing poured out of her.

'Oh God,' Vinnie muttered from behind her. She heard the barely hidden disgust in the voice and it frightened her to think of what he was seeing. She didn't know yet because her eyes had shut instinctively as the flood continued. She was powerless before it. She simply had to let it happen. It reminded her of something, though she wished to God it didn't, reminded her of clinging to toilet bowls with her head hanging loose and her mouth helplessly open as an out-of-control and alcohol-enraged stomach flung its contents away from her.

Then, suddenly, shockingly, it was over. Whatever had had to pass from her body had passed. She was Shelley again. She was sealed again. She was human, normal, and frightened again, and she found herself staggering back from the window to be caught in Vinnie's arms.

She swung herself around, and burying her face in his chest and wrapping her arms tight around him, she let all the tension and shock go in a series of massive gulping sobs as he held her firmly, one hand stroking at her back in soothing, comforting motions, the other wrapped in her hair, pressing her face against him.

'It's all right, Shelley. It's all right,' she heard him say through her weeping. But she wasn't sure that it was. There was some-thing hidden beneath his words. Shock? Disapproval? Revul-sion? She allowed herself a few more seconds of the bliss of ignorance, of the physical comfort to be found in his warm, firm body, and then tried to turn herself around.

The subtext of his words – the doubt, the disgust – seemed confirmed by the way he tried to hold her in place until she was forced to actually push her way out of his embrace in order to turn to see for the first time what it was that they, and the forces that moved them, had conjured.

Like a freak tadpole, pale and overgrown, it thrashed and writhed on the floor, wriggling slickly in the deep red shallows of a steaming blood pool. It was startlingly white, except where the blood stained it crimson, and about the size of a skinned rat. Two tiny black spheres at one end of the thing's unformed body were presumably eyes, eyes no bigger than – and gleaming as wetly as – individual eggs in a scoop of caviar. It had four dwarfish limbs swelling out of its body, and the body itself continued beyond the lower limbs as if its matter was still in flux and was leaking into its lower half to give the impression of a tail.

Shelley gasped. The same revulsion that had fuelled Vinnie's gasp earlier was part of it, but in her case there was also a terrible sense of loss, of something wonderful having gone wrong.

A crippling and impotent pity seized her as she watched the thing writhe. A flash memory burned through her mind: a wasp in her apartment last summer. She'd always hated and feared them and had grabbed the can of bug spray in an instinctive panic and used nearly half of it when the wasp had settled on her window. It had taken two minutes to die, vile little insect legs twitching in agony, stinging itself in fury and pain as its body contorted, accompanied all the time by the hideous alien sound of its tortured buzzing. And throughout those two minutes, Shelley had found herself moving from the xenophobic rage that had doomed the creature to a terrible pity that had almost made her feel sick. And the very alienness that had made her kill it became the heartbreaking barrier between her and anything she could do to ease its pain, and she found herself longing to be free of her phobia not, as she often had, for her *own* sake but for the sake of the things she feared.

She felt a little like that now. The thing wriggling in the pool of her blood was horrible and alien to her. She wanted to be far from it. It revolted and frightened her. But at the same time it seemed so helpless, so uncomfortable, that she yearned to make things well for it. Her sympathy transcended the barriers of otherness, but the otherness effectively barred her from acting on her sympathy – what could she do? How could she help? She didn't think she could even get *near* it without fear or disgust making her puke.

Vinnie had slipped his arms back around her from behind while she was looking at it. She kept her eyes on the thing on the floor but shrank back against his body.

'What can we do?' she asked helplessly.

She sensed Vinnie's head shaking slowly from side to side as he attempted to formulate an answer. Before he could give voice to anything, however, Shelley cut him off. 'Look. The light,' she said.

The impossible beam of starlight was back in the room, bathing the twitching creature in its glow.

'Can you see it?' Shelley whispered, still half-convinced it was a product of her delirium.

'Yes. I see it,' Vinnie replied, his voice as hushed as hers.

They stood together silently, Vinnie's grip on Shelley's shoulders relaxing as the silver beam cast a magical ease over the scene before them, softening the harsh and horrible reality of blood and writhing in its supernatural wash of light, a light that in its cold-chrome brilliance shouldn't have seemed warm and soothing but somehow did.

It wasn't just the human distress of the two observers that the brightness calmed; almost as soon as the light touched it, the creature's manic wriggling slowed down and its movements became apparently conscious, became almost sensual, as it rolled and turned in the healing glow like some alien vacationer basking languorously in the warm and soothing light of a distant foreign sun.

'Thank God,' Shelley said, letting out a sigh of relieved tension. She didn't understand what the hell was happening but whatever *was* happening was clearly the right thing.

'Fuck me, it's *growing*,' said Vinnie, his tone as relieved as Shelley's but with an added air of incredulous wonder.

He was right, Shelley saw as she looked more closely. Or partly right. The creature wasn't just growing, it was *changing*.

The limbs swelled to more appropriate proportions. The atavistic tail shrank back in toward the mass of the body. The hideous black pinpoints in the unformed head sank into the flesh as a white transparent jelly formed around them. Five tiny digits blossomed out of the end of each limb and began to flex in the silvered air, and then, almost stopping the hearts of the awestruck couple watching the process, a tiny hole opened somewhere below the eyes, and as lips budded and swelled around it the embryonic mouth let out a full-blooded cry of life and awareness.

'It's a baby,' Vinnie said, though even as he said it it was no longer true. The process began to speed up, accelerating what had resembled a newborn child through the toddler stage in a matter of seconds. And three seconds after *that*, what to all intents and purposes looked like a seven-year-old girl raised herself elegantly from her prone position and sat, straight-backed and cross-legged on the hotel-room carpet, staring calmly and benignly into the shocked eyes of Vinnie and Shelley.

A slow smile crossed the child's face. Or rather the movement from impassiveness to smile was slow. The smile itself, like every other part of the girl's body, was quickly growing and evolving. The mouth that finally smiled was a different mouth from the one that had begun to smile, and when it parted its full and sensually heavy lips to speak, it was something else again. It was the mouth of a mature, full-breasted, slim-figured young woman. A beautiful young woman, sitting calmly in the same position her prepubescent self had moved into hardly five seconds earlier.

'Thank you,' she said.

Her language was English, her accent American, and her body and face a dream of nationless beauty.

She seemed to have very little in common with Shelley or Vinnie in terms of appearance, and although they could, they supposed, be called her *parents*, their reaction to her now was far from the loving and protective superiority a brand-new mother or father might be expected to feel. Apart from anything else, she seemed older than both of them – though the process that had taken her there appeared to have stopped now, leaving

187

her looking about twenty-five years old – and the magical nature of her transformation made them both feel very small and very young in the face of her. There was also something about the woman herself, something that survived the vanishing of the starlight around her, something that shone almost as brightly from her luminous grey eyes, that seemed to demand a quiet and humble respect.

Shelley had no idea what to say. 'You're welcome' didn't really seem to have the appropriate air. She'd just seen something incredible, something that made her feel . . . she didn't know, she didn't have the words . . . made her feel . . . *different.* Fundamentally and forever different. From the moment she'd first met Chris in her dreams, she'd felt as if she was heading to some kind of . . . show. And here it was. Here was proof that life was richer than she'd ever thought, that the universe was stranger and more wonderful than she'd ever allowed herself the pointless luxury of yearning for. Life was something more than hot hands and cold hearts, vacant hours and paychecks, it was about secret patterns and hidden sentience, about miracles and revenge.

Receiving no reply to her thanks, and her eyes flashing a forgiving understanding of their dumbstruck silence, the woman stood up.

Shelley heard Vinnie suck in a deep breath, and for a second she was almost jealous. Because the breath was not indicative of wonder alone – there was a strong undercurrent of naked and honest desire at the sight of this beautiful unclothed creature.

'Perhaps you should leave now,' the woman said. 'Your part in this is over.'

There was no argument. Vinnie took his arms from around Shelley and they both began to move slowly toward the bed. They didn't meet each other's eyes as they dressed hurriedly in the clothes they had discarded earlier. Vinnie picked up his bag and was already heading toward the door as Shelley paused and unzipped her own.

She took out the change of clothes she had brought with her and laid them on the bed, and then, rooting further, pulled out a few bills from her purse and dropped them on top. She raised her eyes to meet those of the woman, who had come a little closer to her as she did this. Her voice was small and embarrassed.

'I don't know if . . . you probably don't . . . I thought . . .'

One hand held her bag, the other waved in the air in nervous accompaniment to her nervous speech. The woman raised her own arm and lightly brushed Shelley's hand with her fingers. 'Thank you, Shelley,' she said. 'I appreciate it.'

The two women held each other's gaze for a moment, reading secret and unspoken feelings, and then Shelley smiled, nodded once, and turned away to join Vinnie, who held the door open for her, followed her out, and closed it behind them.

The early morning air outside the Regency was cold and fresh, and a strong wind came off the bay to whip Shelley's hair around her face as she and Vinnie stood together on the sidewalk. They had been silent in the elevator, silent in the lobby, and now were silent still as the night gave way in the distance across the water to the rich and heavy blue of the incipient dawn. Finally Shelley spoke.

'You got a car? I'm parked here. You want a ride?'

Vinnie shook his head. 'No,' he said. 'Thanks, but I think I'm going to walk for a while.'

'Uh-huh,' Shelley replied. They looked at each other for a moment longer, and then prompted at the same moment by the same instinct, they lowered their bags and pulled each other close. They kissed and the kiss was warm, but it was an ending not a beginning. It was the farewell embrace that soldiers on a dockside will give each other when they are back from a shared experience in a foreign land, a caress that said, 'what we have seen and done will bond us forever, but you will go your way and I will go mine.'

They broke the kiss and stood apart.

'Good-bye, Shelley,' Vinnie said.

'Good-bye, Vinnie,' she replied, and turned left toward the valet parking area, toward a quiet drive home, toward a career change, a long and loving relationship, a house in Sausalito, a natural daughter, a life lit from within by the memory of the

189

miraculous, and a peaceful and healthy old age. When they brought in the cake on her seventy-fifth birthday and she felt Death lean down beside her to help her blow out the candles, she fell into the dark promise of his arms with the romantic abandonment and flirtatious readiness of a virgin embracing adventure.

Vinnie turned right toward Fisherman's Wharf, already busy in the half-light of morning, and on to a college career where he discovered other young men, long dead, who, like him, had been blessed by passing madness. His book, *The Unguarded Moment: Transcendence in Romantic Literature*, made his name in academic circles and he ended his years as a professor somewhere in the Midwest, a legendary educator, an inspiration to six generations of writers, actors, and lunatics. The only words on his tombstone were those of the last stanza of Edgar Allan Poe's 'To One in Paradise.'

In room 1533, the naked woman sat on the bed. She did nothing but breathe and look and listen. She was in an ecstasy of sensation. Running through her body, singing in her veins, throbbing in her heart — *her* heart — was life. Corporeal life. Physical life. There was bone and sinew and muscle. There was skin and lash and teeth. There was movement in time and space. There was flesh and its ready potential for pleasure or pain. There was change and decay within her at every passing second.

She blinked.

She stretched her fingers.

She sighed.

She laughed.

She spoke his name and hers.

'Morningstar,' she said.

And then she was silent and still again, and the only sound in the hotel room was the strong and steady newborn beating of her ancient heart.

In other parts of the city, in other nighttime rooms, other hearts were beating.

If it were somehow possible to still for an instant the world's other musics, to silence mouths, machines, and Mother Nature, and to listen only to the hearts of its millions beating in the night, then their counterpointing rhythms alone – crossing, conflicting, converging – would be sufficient to make a song that wordlessly told of the whole of human experience.

There would be the strong beats of young life. There would be the weak sounds of aged and weary hearts dancing already to the staggered rhythms of death. There would be the tempos of stress, of romantic love, of fury and exertion. There would be the bombastic pounding of confidence, the steady ticking of security. And here and there, making their own unique beat-skipping dislocating contribution to the sonic mixture, would be the hearts that throbbed to the freezing rhythms of mortal terror.

It was this last song that Jonathan Frost's heart sang that night as he lay awake in his own part of the city, his eyes open to the darkness of his room.

He had been asleep earlier, but now, in the hour before dawn, in the hour they call the hour of the wolf, he lay awake, keeping himself conscious despite the tiredness of his body. He stared unseeingly through the darkness of the curtained bedroom to a darkness beyond that. A deeper darkness; less physical but no less natural, a darkness of the heart and soul.

Tonight he had walked in the rooms and chambers in which he was used to walking in his nightmares and had found himself alone. No beast-headed revellers, no harlequin women, no buried monsters were there to confuse, to indict, or to torment him.

The dream halls were deserted. Their echoing oak-panelled geographies were filled only with shadows and decay. Through the cobwebbed silences of implacable rooms, he moved alone, occasionally passing discarded items, signs of the departed masque; a clouded glass of mildewing wine; a stiletto shoe of silvered leather (buckled and strangely swollen as if recently forced to accommodate a foot of curious shape, of alien anatomy); a long black whisker crusted at one end with dried and darkened blood; a desiccated rose.

These, and a new fear – a fear different from the growing sense of dislocation and anxiety that normally scarred his dream life – were his only companions as he trod his familiar but newly charged path through the vacated halls.

That older fear (alienation, accusation, persecution) was one to which, over the months of spring and early summer and the increasing frequency of his nocturnal visits, he had accustomed himself. This was new. Present in the dream itself but infinitely stronger now as he lay awake and alone, this was a fear rooted in a terrible overpowering sense that something dangerous had slipped its leash. That something vicious and hungry – and previously caged – had found a secret path between its bars and now was staring at its ignorant keeper from a shadowed place, flicking its tongue, flexing its claws. It was a sense that something had escaped him. A fear that he had been outwitted.

Or outflanked.

June 21

After her arrival in San Francisco in the early hours of the previous day, she had slipped quietly away from the Hyatt Regency dressed in the clothes that the woman had left for her. She had walked and observed. Finding herself quite taken with the appearance of the St Francis Hotel on Powell Street, she had installed herself there.

She had registered as Ms T. Astare, and after correcting the desk clerk's spelling and explaining that no, she was not a distant relative of Fred, she had been shown to her room on the seventh floor. When the uniformed and elderly porter who had escorted her upstairs (and who could hardly keep his hands, let alone his eyes, off the curve of her hip) had asked if she had no luggage, she had replied distractedly that she was sure something would turn up and he had gone away quite content, not even realizing until late that night that he had received no tip.

She had eaten and drunk a little. She had watched some TV. She had remained in her conservative clothes (a tight halter top and black denim shorts) and walked herself up and down Broadway, finding her amusement in the competitive cries of the barkers employed by the many sex clubs that thrived in that area.

'Roll up! Roll up!' one would shout. 'Three women, a petrified snake, and a water buffalo!'

'Ah, the buffalo's got da mange and two a'da women are dead,' a rival would insist. 'Come *over* here! Come *over* here! We got Sadie and the telegraph pole! We got Ellie-Mae and the entire Russian army!'

'All-girl! All-girl!'

'All-boy! All-boy!'

Later she had returned to the hotel and spent a quiet night. The day, too, had passed uneventfully, and now she was ready to begin her evening's work.

She took a long warm shower and padded back, naked, into the bedroom. What to wear? Carefully laid out on the surface of the coffee table were seven matching dark wooden boxes, each nine inches long, seven inches wide, and three inches deep, each free of decoration save for a delicately carved stellar motif in the centre of each lid. She stared at them for a time, undecided, and then went finally for the one nearest to hand. She lifted back the hinged lid and smiled at the contents. She placed the fingers of her right hand into the box and took hold of the silky material therein. Carefully, she drew out the costume and carried it across to the hotel bed and began to dress herself.

First the white stockings and, drawn over them, the bright yellow pantaloons, loose and flowing but tied tight just below the knees. Then the simple black slippers and the voluminous bright yellow top, drawn tight above the wrists to accord with the trousers, and decorated below the left breast with three red diamonds in a triangular formation. Next came a blue turban into which she tucked all her hair, and finally a slim black mask, useless for preserving anonymity but aesthetically enhancing.

She took herself to the room's full-length mirror and examined the finished effect. She smiled broadly and bowed low to her own reflection in the elaborate eighteenth-century manner.

Bobby Corvino left his fifth-floor room and made his way to the elevator. The bodyguards would be waiting in the lobby and the limo would be waiting outside, engine running and ready. Somewhere across town, forty thousand fans were waiting for him and the Fiasco Brothers to take the stage and rock their cares away. He'd eaten, drunk, shot up, and was ready to go.

He watched the light pass behind the numbers over the elevator door, making their way from 7 to 6 to 5 and then, with a soft mechanical sigh, the elevator door began to open. He stepped in impatiently before it was fully wide and glanced around. There was one other person in there with him. His heart sank.

Some crazy fan had got past the jerks on the desk. At least, that was the first explanation that sprang to his admittedly self-centred mind when he saw the weirdo chick in her panto-mime drag who was already occupying the cubicle. But she didn't squeal when he walked in, she didn't giggle or press upon him a book or a limb to be signed, she didn't start removing her clothes and telling him how long she'd loved him. He didn't know whether to be pleased or disappointed.

'I'm Bobby Corvino,' he announced. 'Got a gig tonight.'

The chick just smiled.

Bobby developed another theory. 'Hey! You going to a cos-tume party?'

The smile broadened and flowered into speech. 'Something like that,' she said. Bobby couldn't place the accent, though the voice was sweet to him and dreamily familiar. He was suddenly sorry she wasn't a fan. Maybe he could make her into one. Maybe he could take her to the gig. Jesus, she looked good. Screw taking her to the gig. Screw the *gig*. Maybe she could take him wherever *she* was going. Fuck it. Maybe they could both take the elevator back upstairs. Maybe ... his fucking *head* was spinning. How much had he had to drink ... ? Maybe they could just stay in the elevator.

'Hey ...' he began to say.

'Lobby,' she replied as the doors slid open and she walked out of the elevator.

Dressed as she was, heads naturally turned in the lobby as she made her way across it to the hotel's main entrance, but walking as she was with the natural confidence of those correctly dressed for specific occasions, the stares were primar-ily of admiration and appreciation, not surprise or amusement.

Bobby Corvino stayed behind in the elevator for a few seconds, blinking his eyes and getting his balance back. The two ex-heavyweights employed by the record company to look after its investment approached the cubicle and stared quizzic-ally at the rock star, one of them even making as if to follow his erstwhile fellow passenger. Bobby shook his hand in the air to discourage him.

'It's okay. It's okay,' he said, and it was true. His head was clear now. It was the other thing that was bothering him – and he certainly wasn't going to mention that to them. He had just discovered that he was the owner of a proudly pulsing erection. He didn't understand it. He thought the smack had taken care of all that years ago. He wondered if he had time to get rid of it somewhere warm and moist before the gig. He looked at the clock in the lobby. It was eight in the evening.

It was eight in the evening and still warm and bright. Donovan Moon felt like shit and had been feeling like shit for the past nine days.

He was alone again in the apartment on Liberty. Matt had a married sister in Sacramento, and four days into this nine-day period, four days into living with a depression and a silence that used to call itself Donovan Moon, he had announced his intention of making a fraternal visit. The silence remained unbroken, hardening around Moon like a shell around a creature reluctant to be born. Moon knew that it should be shattered. That he should smash it from the inside and crawl back blinking into life, but he was afraid. Afraid to talk, afraid that the slightest opening up would shatter not just the silence but him with it. That everything that he was holding in would be released in a traumatic explosion, and he wasn't ready for that. So Matt wasn't dissuaded. And Matt went away. And Moon had had five days to feel worse.

Nothing from Frost. Nothing in the papers. Well, Rose's body had been discovered, and for a day or two Morningstar was hot news again. And Moon had stared into the televised face of Commissioner Schulman as it begged anybody who had information, anybody who was sheltering this disturbed individual, to contact the police. And that didn't make him feel a whole lot better. But Frost's promised climax, the showdown, the main event that had bought Moon's silence and stalled his integrity, was only where it had always been. In a hypothetical future somewhere inside the head of a lunatic. This disturbed individual.

Fuck it. He was going to call the cops. He stood up and went over to the small table by the fireplace. His hand was actually on the receiver when the instrument rang. Probably Frost not believing in coincidence again, he thought, and lifted it to his ear. A female voice he had never heard before came out of it.

'Look at the window,' it said.

He looked at his window. His top-floor window.

And at the woman's face staring through it at him.

There was no fire escape outside his window. No balcony. Nothing except air. And a woman's face. His blood turned to water and he felt an overwhelming need to sit down. But he didn't have time. The woman held his gaze and, without fanfare or exaggeration, lowered her eyelids. Instantly, inexorably, Moon's own eyelids followed suit and everything went black.

He opened his eyes again. Something very strange had happened. Or at least for about a second he *felt* something strange had happened. But then he couldn't think why. Everything appeared normal. There was nothing strange about sitting at the bar in Sam's Place on Twenty-fourth Street. He did it all the time. It was perhaps a little unusual that he should have his overcoat on, but so what? He shook his head as if to clear it of something and then looked around. The place was deserted except for him and, at the far end of the bar from him and assiduously cleaning glasses, Sam himself. The place was dimly lit, which is how he liked it. But he didn't like it much now. And he was glad he had his overcoat on. It was cold.

Sam walked down behind the bar to where he was sitting and placed a long glass in front of him. 'There ya go, Donny,' he said. 'I've been asked to give you this. It'll fortify you.'

'Thanks, Sam,' Moon replied automatically, and then, more consciously, more carefully, '. . . er . . . cold in here.'

'Whaddayexpect? It's dark.'

Moon swivelled on the bar stool. Sam was right. Behind the large plate-glass window that faced out onto the street was only blackness. He swung back to face the bartender. His earlier sense of something not being quite right had returned. It shouldn't be dark yet. It was only . . . 'What time is it?' he asked.

Sam went into a whole oh-Jesus-Christ-we're-late routine, grimacing, sucking his teeth, slapping his palm to his forehead. 'God, you're right, Don,' he said. 'Here we are chewing the fat and not thinking of the time at all. Shit. Better throw it down, old buddy. The car's outside.'

'Car?'

'Yeah. Car. Car. C-A-R. Get with it, Donny. C'mon. Drink. Drink.'

Sam made hurrying motions with his hands, and Moon, still confused, downed the large bourbon in one. He began trying to work out what it was that was different about Sam, and as he rose from his stool and made to turn for the door, he realized what it was. Sam no longer looked like a man waiting to be astonished. Moon paused, quizzical but unsure of what it was exactly that he wanted to ask.

'Sam . . . ?' he said.

Sam raised an eyebrow but Moon just shook his head and turned away. He was halfway to the door when Sam shouted to him. 'Hey, Don!' he called. 'You wanna see 'em before you go?'

Moon really didn't think so, but his reporter's blood turned him back anyway.

'They're through,' Sam said in a tone that was excited and happy but had the satisfaction of a man beyond astonishment. 'Just like she promised. Look!'

He peeled his lips apart and leaned his head slightly back to assist Donovan's examination. But it wasn't necessary. They were quite apparent. Donovan nodded, smiled, and headed for the door.

'Oh. And don't talk to the chauffeur,' Sam shouted to the opening door. 'He's dead.'

But this, too, was superfluous. Donovan could see he was dead. He was sat cross-legged on the sidewalk of the dark, deserted, and unusually foggy street, his back resting against a lamppost, his head resting impossibly on an unhunched shoulder. His face was peaceful but terribly pale, and rendered a strangely disturbing muted orange by the unnatural light of the street lamp, running down his throat from two tiny punctures and disappearing under his shirt-collar, were two tiny streams of blood.

The street lamp shone also on the blue-and-grey beauty of

Frost's Bentley, and as once before, Moon saw the backdoor swing open for him. But the chauffeur was dead. This time it *was* magic. No. No, in fact, there was someone in the driver's seat, but whoever it was was shadowed, not quite clear. Donovan walked forward and placed himself, as once before, on the fine red leather of the car's interior and attempted to make the driver's acquaintance, as once before, via the rearview mirror.

'Oh shit,' he said. The driver cast no reflection.

A light ripple of laughter came to him from the front seat. 'I'm sorry,' said an attractive female voice. 'I couldn't resist it. Just a little joke. There. Can you see me now?'

And indeed he could. He found his gaze held by two reflected eyes that seemed oddly and tantalizingly familiar to him. Their owner's voice spoke again.

'Don't call the police. Call Frost.'

The mirrored eyelids closed and, instantly, inexorably, took Moon's with them. And everything went black.

Donovan opened his eyes. Why was he looking at his window? So it looked like a perfect summer's evening. So he could check it out *after* he'd made the call. He wasn't familiar enough with Frost's number to punch it without looking. He dropped his eyes and made the connection.

'Frost,' said the voice.

'Nah. Too warm. Might get a bit of fog later, but –'

'Your banter is as obvious as ever, Mr Moon, but I'm pleased to find you so jovial.'

'Frankly, so am I. And a little surprised. Because when I decided to call you, I was feeling really ... no ... wait a minute –' Donovan broke off for a second, confused. Something was wrong. *Was* it Frost he'd been intending to call? Hadn't it been someone else? 'I was going to call the ...' Donovan stared at the receiver and then back up to the window, as if that could shed some light on the matter. Frost's voice, alert and on guard, cut back in to his thoughts.

'Moon? Moon!'

Moon shook his head, feeling whatever it was he'd been about to grasp fleeing away like a vaguely recalled dream put to flight by black coffee and breakfast TV. 'Yeah. Yeah, I'm here . . . Fuck, am I drunk or what?'

'I don't know. Are you?'

'Two beers at lunchtime. Not a drop since.' That was the truth, but he could . . . could he? . . . almost *taste* Jack Daniel's on his lips. He shook his head again, both in an attempt to clear it and with anger at himself.

'I think you had better come over, Mr Moon,' Frost said.

'Why?'

'I don't know. What made you call me?'

'I don't know.'

'I think you had better come over.'

'Why?'

'Mmmm. Perhaps my choice of recorder has been . . . approved. I'll send the car.'

A sudden stab of irrational and unfocused fear went through Donovan. 'No!' he shouted. 'Don't send the car!' Why the fuck not? 'It's okay. It's okay. I'll get a cab. I'll see you soon.'

He put the phone down quickly. He noticed he was wearing his overcoat and couldn't remember putting it on, but what the hell, it gave him less time to change his mind. He checked his pockets for cab fare and cigarettes and left the apartment. He was glad he'd had that drink. It had fortified him.

He flagged a cab. He lit a cigarette. He enjoyed a peaceful ride across town. He watched the summer twilight settle over San Francisco. He wondered what the hell he had to feel so good about. But he didn't have to wonder long. They pulled up outside Frost's building, and the present tense became the past as Moon's temporary intoxication was replaced by the familiar nervous depression of the past nine days.

He paid off the cabdriver, and as the money changed hands he was suddenly seized by a strong and unheralded wish that he had been brought here not by this anonymous and bored-looking stranger whose parting smile was a purely formal response to a tip but by somebody he *knew*, somebody to whom he could say good-bye. That feeling, that hypothetical *good-bye*, had implications he didn't like at all, and he practically ran across the street to the building in order to avoid being tempted to call the cabbie back and ask him to take him to Twenty-fourth Street instead. Yeah, things would just be starting to happen at Sam's Place around now, he thought. Though, for some reason, that thought, too, disturbed him, so he let it go and concentrated instead on watching the uniformed security guard on the other side of the glass doors operate the release switch that opened them. He walked into the main foyer of Frost's building, which, of course, he hadn't seen before, but he smiled a little as he recognized from Frost's own office the conventionally impressive elegance of the Successful Company of the Successful Man.

The guard who had opened the doors for him, a middle-aged man who looked as if his job had been found for him by a Hollywood casting agency that specialized in the Fatherly Elder Cop, motioned Donovan over to a closed-circuit video camera perched above the small desk at which he could check spurious

visitors against an appointment book when he wasn't busy
flashing his Fatherly Elder Cop smile at the typists and secre-
taries.

The snout of the video camera sniffed at Donovan, and presumably as a result of its inspection, the guard's cell phone,
slung low on the hip in a brown leather holster, began to buzz.
Moon couldn't remember seeing a video monitor – or, indeed,
anything so pushily high-tech – in Frost's room, but it seemed
he must have had one hidden away somewhere, for when the
guard drew his phone, it was Frost's voice that issued from it.

'Yes. That's him,' it said. 'Send him up.'

'Okay, Mr Frost,' the guard drawled.

'And Deke . . .'

'Yeah?'

'Then I want you to secure the building and leave.'

'You sure, Mr Frost?'

'Quite sure, thank you.'

The upstairs phone clicked audibly in the guard's handset.
Deke shrugged and holstered it with a flourish. Donovan felt
sure that had he been alone, Deke would have spun it around
two or three times first, but he resisted the urge to grin. He had
no wish to offend the man, and besides, he rather approved of
the Dennis Weaver two-tone moustache. So miming an 'after
you' with his hands, he followed Deke to the elevator and,
miming a 'thank you very much for all your trouble and I
hope you get home safely' with his grin and his nod, saw him
disappear as the elevator doors closed between them.

He pressed the unmarked button in the cubicle and wished
fervently that there were some kind of manual-override button
so that he might slow the elevator down to something reasonable – the speed of light, say. But there wasn't and so he simply
endured the launch. At least it's over quickly, he said to himself.
But there was no one to prod, no one to whom he could point
out that the whole reason it was *unpleasant* was just how
quickly it *was* over. And it wasn't really a very good joke anyway. And he was doing it again: filling his head with rubbish
to avoid worrying about why he was here and what was going
to happen.

The elevator stopped. His stomach caught up. The doors opened. He left the elevator and strode down the corridor, throwing open the double doors to Frost's room with an insouciance he wouldn't have dreamed he was capable of on his last visit.

'Hey, Jack!' he shouted. 'You got the garlic? I . . . Shit!'

In an instinctive reaction Moon threw himself bodily onto the hard wooden floor and then looked up sheepishly as Frost lowered the double-barrelled shotgun into the business end of which Donovan had found himself staring as he'd entered the room.

'No,' said Frost, in exactly the same tone of voice he would have used had Donovan been standing casually in front of him rather than stretched out inelegantly on the floor with his hands over his head. 'No garlic. I told you last time, didn't I? All that crap is so much . . . crap. Garlic. Crosses. A cross doesn't spit shot the way this fine Purdey does. And garlic, though pungent, isn't as sharp as a stake. I know where I put my faith, Mr Moon, and that is in things that deal death with proven efficiency – and that don't rely on the religious background of the creature I am exterminating. Anyway, do please get up. I was simply making sure you came through those doors alone. Drink?'

Donovan lifted himself up from the floor and made to dust himself off, but there was no need. Frost's floor was scrupulously clean. He followed Frost across the room to the same desk, the same two chairs, and the same two drinks as before, but rather than sit opposite Frost as the executive lowered himself into the seat behind the desk, Moon stood in front of the picture window and looked down.

'Doesn't it all seem a little . . . inappropriate to you?' he asked tentatively. 'I mean, look; it's just getting dark, but the evening's still warm. There're lights on the water, boats on the bay. People are out on the streets. There's a little drinking going on, a little dancing. Bands'll be playing somewhere, there're movies –'

'Yes,' Frost cut in. 'People are out on the streets. There's a little murder going on, a little mayhem. Junkies will be scoring somewhere, there're snuff movies. Somebody is certainly being assaulted somewhere in the city as we speak. Before the night's out, what do you think? Couple of rapes? One murder? Two? Come on, Moon. You're a reporter. What do you think? How many obscene phone calls? How many beatings? How many dead?'

Before replying, Moon turned away from the window and walked to the side of Frost's desk.

'How many dead?' Frost repeated.

Moon rested his hands on the surface of the desk, leaned toward Frost slightly, and looked down at him. 'You mean disregarding any little adventures we may have ourselves?' he asked.

Frost made a face. 'Oh, very good, Moon,' he said. 'I'm sure you were a wow in your school debating society. But in answer to your first question – no, I don't find it inappropriate. Don't let the summer fool you. Evil isn't seasonal. And it doesn't take vacations. It doesn't rise with the moon or set with the sun. It doesn't go out with the tide or come in on the wind. It is always here. It is always now. It *is*. Always.'

There was a moment's silence. Moon nodded a little nervously and glanced back down the length of the room to the doors. He took his hands off the desk, stood up straight, and sighed.

'I would appreciate it, Frost,' he said, 'if you would stop talking in *cues*.' He swung an arm in the doors' direction. 'That was such a great lead-in, I was waiting for the fucking *door* to burst open then!'

Frost looked at the doors and then at Moon's dramatically pointed arm. He raised a cynical eyebrow. 'Or then?' he said.

Moon pulled his arm in rapidly and, in concert with his other one, used it to make a muted placating gesture toward Frost. 'All right,' he said. 'All right. Let's just forget it. Okay? Change the subject. You got any hobbies?'

All the lights went out.

The darkness was complete. It was as if someone, somewhere, had had his hand on a single switch that controlled all the lights in the world and had just flicked it off. It was as if light was suddenly impossible. It was as if there was no light left. The darkness was complete, but it was short-lived. The hypothetical switch flicker flicked it back on as quickly as he'd flicked it off. Go to a light switch. Press it. Off. On. That's how long the darkness lasted. No time at all. But when the lights came back on, each man could see in the other a reflection of the terror that had gripped him. A terror surely out of all proportion both to the event and to its duration, or so Moon told himself, and continuing the soothing process, he assigned a reason to the blackness as quickly as possible: power-station switching, he decided. Happens all the time. A fractional absence of power as the load is shifted from one station to another. You hardly notice. It's just circumstance made it scary that time. It was nothing.

'It was nothing,' he said.

And then all the lights went out.

Donovan moaned. Frost gasped.

And then all the lights came on.

Both men were breathing quickly and audibly. Frost looked up at Donovan and managed a sneer.

'Nothing,' he echoed, his voice rich with irony and undercut with tension. But Moon needed to believe it even more than he had the first time and nodded emphatically.

'Yeah. Nothing,' he insisted, and elaborated: '*Nothing*. It's the power stations. Swapping loads. It's nothing.'

'No,' said Frost, 'you're wrong. Something's happened. Something's here.'

'Don't be ridiculous. Nothing happened. Nothing's here.' But still, catching a little of his host's nervousness and adding it to his own, he looked around the room. He wasn't making sure, he told himself. He was just reassuring Frost. 'Frost,' he said, 'the room is completely empty.'

He was disregarding Frost and himself, of course, and disregarding Frost and himself, he was telling the truth. The room was completely empty.

And then all the lights went out.

And then all the lights came on.

And when all the lights came on . . .

The room was full.

The room was full.

That long bare stretch of room that Donovan had found so imposing when first he had come to Frost's tower seemed considerably less imposing when its self-conscious sparseness was ignored and violated by the sudden presence of three hundred people.

Particularly when those three hundred people were dead.

And they *were* dead. Donovan was quite sure of that. To begin with, many of them were in more than one piece. Some, in fact, were so thoroughly dismembered that moving must have been very difficult for them. Fortunately none of them *was* moving. Yet.

It was just as his nostrils, twitching in disgust and breathing in decay, gave him confirmation, had any been necessary, of the nature of these nighttime visitors that Donovan even thought to look at Frost. He had, up to that point, been taking the matter entirely personally – an understandable but profoundly unattractive stance – and he was glad to remind himself that the responsibility of host lay not with him, but with Frost.

'Friends of yours?' he asked hopefully.

'I've met them all. In most cases, once and once only,' Frost replied. He remained sitting behind his desk, but Moon saw his eyes flicking back and forth across the graveyard crowd, scanning the tombstone faces, peering beneath the various stages of decay to recognize the remnants of features he had once seen *in extremis*.

Moon gasped. 'These are . . . *all* yours? You . . . *All* of them?' he said, surprised to find room among the terror and disgust for astonishment and disapproval.

'*All* of them,' Frost confirmed, and Moon was unsure which

quality in the voice, under the circumstances, frightened him more: the hatred or the pride.

He should have known from Frost's story. He should have realized what a foul and abundant harvest Frost had been able to reap over a career of thirty years. But even had he done the necessary piece of hell's addition, he would still have been unprepared for this sudden and putrescent visualization of its total. His horror and disgust at Frost and his achievement multiplied, but a creeping contempt for himself was their unwelcome companion; he realized that much as he might intellectually wish it otherwise, emotionally he preferred the company of one civilized killer to that of hundreds of his victims – especially when the slaughterer's skin was pink and that of the slaughtered white, grey, or green, depending on how long ago they had first made Frost's acquaintance.

Donovan Moon, like all of us, was not above exaggerating those qualities in himself that he admired or thought others would find admirable, but he was wise, or pessimistic, enough never actually to invent characteristics to which he had no claim at all. He would, for example, when drunk or desirous of seducing, happily boast of his wit, his literary abilities, his profile, or his capacity for liquor, but you would never catch him claiming to be brave.

So it was not courage that kept him conscious and continent when the dead came, and he would never pretend that it was. No, what it was – and God, how he welcomed it – was a growing sense of his own irrelevance to at least this stage of the night's drama. The gathering of the resurrected seemed to have eyes only for Jonathan Frost. Perhaps, Donovan thought, they couldn't even see him. They certainly weren't *looking* at him. This made it easier for him to look at them. Not calmly, he would never claim that, but at least without a completely paralysing panic.

Frost had been catholic in his exterminations. They were a very mixed bunch. There were men, women. There were children. There were Caucasians, Asians, blacks. Some were very old. Some were very young. There were fat corpses, thin corpses, tall corpses, short corpses. There were well-dressed

208

corpses, corpses in rags, and naked corpses. There may well have been corpses that, in life, had been disfigured or crippled, but given the vigorousness of Frost's approach to mutilation, this was difficult to ascertain without a closer examination than Moon was prepared to undertake at that time.

It was clear that they had all remained the ages they had been when Frost found them, but change had not left them alone. It had simply substituted a different form of decay. Growth, wrinkles, and hair loss had been replaced by pallor, gangrene, and the stench of putrefaction.

More than half of the bodies were headless, and while some carried their heads with them, others, armless, too, had to rely on the kindness of their companions for this service. Each of the antique chairs that sat in that part of the room had a head perched on it, and one of them a severed hand as well. A profusion of limbs lay scattered here and there upon the floor, and among them, and most distressing of all, there were a few torsos, headless, armless, legless, that shuffled and wriggled like fat, bloated worms, leaving a trail of foul-smelling slime behind them as their rotting bodies rubbed against the floor.

And every eye in or out of every head on or off every body was fixed on the man behind the desk. Moon tried to read the expressions therein and thought he detected loathing, anger, and not a little residual fear, but he realized he was finding them there only because he was looking for them. The faces of the dead are blank, their motives a mystery not revealed by any tattletale expression. Like Buster Keaton or a first-rate poker player, their faces are stone on which we may carve whatever our imagination tells us. A perceived malevolence, an imagined grin may be nothing more than the rictus of death left unchanged through the years in the grave.

But whatever dark secrets lay locked behind their ossified eyes, whatever shadowed desires hid in their petrified hearts, their *immediate* motive, Donovan realized, was about to become clear, because now they began to move. Slowly and with difficulty – their minds having forgotten how to insist, their limbs how to obey – this nightmare gathering of impossible creatures began to stagger their way toward Frost and him.

Now Donovan felt a little less complacent about his standing as a disinterested party. The amount of fear an object can induce is directly proportional to its proximity and direction. Sufferers from arachnophobia can, with an effort of will, remain in the same room as a spider, provided it is headed rapidly in the opposite direction. Should, however, the spider take it into its furry little head to turn around, the story is quite different. And so it was that Moon discovered in himself a phobia of which he was previously unaware: He was very frightened of dead people that moved. Particularly when they moved in his direction.

But fear, normally a great incentive to movement, was no use to him; he was standing to the right of Frost's desk, and behind him there was no exit, save through the picture window and then straight down for twenty-five floors. The only way into and out of the room was the double door at the far end, and between him and it came a rapidly diminishing empty space and three hundred zombies.

Their advance was grotesque and ill-disciplined. Some shuffled, some slid, some staggered. But the gap between the living and the dead was growing smaller all the time. Donovan's legs at last gave way and he crumpled to the floor, saving himself from being laid completely flat only by catching hold of the edge of Frost's desk as he fell. He steadied himself into a sitting position, his legs stretched out in front of him, but he knew that terror had robbed him of the power to stand. He began shuffling backward on his palms and buttocks, keeping his eyes fixed on the dead, heading for the solidity of the wall somewhere behind him, even though he knew it was pointless. He began to repeat the word *no* continuously and tonelessly and he had no idea whether this constituted a plea for them not to do whatever they were going to do or a denial that any of this was happening. Probably both.

'For fuck's sake, Frost! *Do* something!' he cried.

The Matador hadn't moved. The Purdey sat untouched atop the desk where he had laid it earlier and he sat still behind the desk, both palms resting on the green leather surface. Unlike Moon, however, he was able to pull his eyes away from the advancing undead and he turned his face to the frightened reporter.

'What exactly would you like me to do, Moon?' he asked in a tone that, given the circumstances, was impressively contemptuous. 'Kill them again?'

Terrified as he was, Donovan wasn't falling for that one. For them all to be inanimate, and preferably invisible, again was something he devoutly wished, but he had no intention of causing them undue offence by *saying* so.

He was saved the effort of constructing a tactful answer by a disturbance in the crowd. Those nearest to Frost had stopped their advance about two feet from the desk, and now there was some kind of collective shuffling going on in the middle of that front row. Something was being made way for.

A tall and reasonably intact male figure emerged from the gap his fellows had created for him. None of his limbs was missing and his head was still on his shoulders despite huge entry and exit wounds on either side of his neck. His decay, however, was very advanced and his skin had long since left the liquefying stage for that of desiccation. He resembled some foul papier-mâché creature; should you have the gall and the stomach for it, it looked as if you could tear off the dried remnants of his skin in scabrous strips. The eyes had disappeared long ago, but the black pits where once they had shone seemed still to stare, to focus, to follow all the rules of sight. Their attention was unwaveringly on Frost's face, almost as if their owner were challenging him to a staring contest that the paper man could not lose, having no eyes to blink or lower.

Moon was now, of course, some way behind Frost, having made his way as far as the wall, and was unable to see with what degree of strength he met this unfair challenge. But he could see the head not waver and he could see the arms not tremble, and though he realized this was, if anything, proof of Frost's insanity, he envied the man the strength his madness gave him.

This face-to-cadaverous-face confrontation lasted nearly thirty seconds, and it was only as the next stage was about to begin that Donovan saw that it had been more than merely contest. It had been dialogue. Not a word had passed Frost's lips or a sound (Moon thanked Christ) escaped the mummied maw of the creature, but some kind of communication had been going on. Or studying. What was Frost making of his handiwork? What was his handiwork making of him? And which found the other more alien? In whom was the contempt more profound?

Suddenly, in this frozen tableau of life, death, and speculation, there was movement. The creature's hand shot up from its side and thrust itself toward Frost, who finally reacted in a way to which Moon was able to relate; he threw himself backward in surprise and shock. But the hand, once in position in front of Frost's startled face, made no threatening gesture and held no weapon. It was not empty, though. Hanging from it, held by hair still black and abundant and tangled in the paper man's cracked and defleshed fingers, was a severed head.

It was as old as he that held it and similarly shrunken of skin. But unlike him, it made no pretence to life. The sunken eyelids were closed and did not flicker, the silent mouth was sealed and did not sneer.

It had once been Laura, of course. Moon realized that right away, and so, presumably, did her cousin, her killer, who, rigid against the back of his chair from the shock of the head's sudden appearance, gasped and slumped down in the face of the slower, surer horror: the realization of who it had been.

Nobody moved. The assembled dead kept their eyes on the Matador, watching his reaction, savouring his shock, and waiting for something more. For a second Moon thought Frost was about to break his silence, but he was never to know what words he may have spoken, what sobs of regret or snarls of defiance he may have given them. Suddenly, with a speed and a strength terrifying in their contrast to the painful slow movements the creature had made previously, the paper man flung himself forward, grabbing Frost's shirtfront and pulling him bodily across his desk until his face was two inches away from Laura's own. Her eyelids flew open and the same black empty pits she shared with her dead lover stared at the man her cousin had become. The dehydrated mouth ripped itself apart and the

212

few remaining yellowed teeth followed suit. A voice, like a dentist's drill in its ability to find a nerve and hurt it, coughed itself out of the black void behind those teeth.

'Johnny,' it grated.

And then she kissed him.

The paper man's hand had flown from Frost's collar to the back of his skull, and now, like some eager pimp from hell, he was pressing Frost and Laura together, holding them firm and close.

Moon could see Frost's head and neck muscles tremble, could hear the choking noises of denial in the back of his throat. Worse, he could see the dead head's cheeks puckering and twitching as the dried lips opened and closed, opened and closed, contorting themselves in an obscenely unmoist parody of passion. The journalist found himself praying that the tongue had entirely decayed away. The thought of such a blackened husk of dead flesh probing the wet and warm interior of a living mouth was almost enough to send him finally to the other side of consciousness in a nausea-driven faint. But before he could convince himself against his will that that *was* what was happening, the paper man, having held them there for a full five seconds, suddenly pulled them apart, let go of Frost, and still holding the head, stepped back two paces from the desk to watch Frost scream.

And scream he did. At last, flung back into his chair, eyes screwed shut against the horror, hands twitching unconsciously in the air, Frost screamed loud and long. The Matador's mask had been ripped from him and the man beneath it was lost, too. This was a scream of naked human anguish. Open, vulnerable, terrified, the sum of all the screams Frost had spent a lifetime denying, it rang in the room like the final despairing scream of a torture victim who has gone beyond pain to gaze into the terrible uncaring abyss of a world without salvation or respite.

This was what his audience had been waiting for. And they were deeply attentive. Moon was reminded of the manner in which businessmen watch strippers: the face as impassive as the veneer of worldliness can make it, but the eyes drinking every detail, the memory taking notes to be recalled in private moments of pleasure. Here, too, the audience wasted no energy on expressions of delight, but their absorption was complete and their relish implicit. The manifestation of Frost's suffering was not in itself more than a minute long, but they had eternity to play it back. A small thing to take, perhaps, but the comforts of the grave are few.

Eventually, after first descending into whimpers, the scream stopped, the hands fell into the lap, and the eyes opened. And Frost came back.

He stared again at the hosts of the departed, and suddenly, with a speed that matched that of his humiliator, he was on his feet and the shotgun was in his hands. With neither hesitation nor careful aim, he jerked both triggers toward him. Moon had no time to protest, having time only to become convinced that they were both about to die, and prepared to scream. But the sound of the gun was quicker. There was a deafening roar, and simultaneously, all the lights went out.

All the lights came on.

Donovan bit off his scream and caught his breath. The room was empty of those without pulse. The far wall of the room and the double doors were pitted with scores of tiny holes where the shot had scattered. The echo of the shotgun's scream slowly died away, and the gun itself, spent and silent, lay again on the desk. Frost stood still. Donovan stood up. And the doors flew open.

10

Afterward, Donovan was to wonder often why he hadn't laughed. What had happened to bathos? Where was it when you needed it? It was a *clown*, for God's sake. Midnight's clown, perhaps, but a clown still. Standing in the doorway was a beautiful girl in a carnival costume. And *this* was the follow-up to that brain-numbing collection of ambulant decay? But he didn't laugh. And he didn't sigh with relief. And he didn't move. He didn't do anything. He just watched her walk.

She moved like a Japanese actor. Outside time. It may have taken an hour for her to cross the room, it may have taken seconds – it was impossible to tell, for the attention she commanded was complete, and though clocks may have stopped or sprinted, neither of the men in the room would have been able to notice.

She moved with utter seriousness, with a face at least as impassive as those of the dead who had come before her. She offered no threat, made no promise, other than any her observers might choose to infer from her silence. She simply moved forward and eventually, after the time it took, she stopped moving forward and stood before Frost's desk in approximately the same place the paper man had stood when he made *his* contribution to the night.

Hers began with a smile. A radiant, warm, and to Moon's immense pleasure, unthreatening smile. Then she bowed low, elaborately and gracefully, and standing again, looked expectantly at Frost.

'I've killed women before,' he said as if in warning.

Donovan moaned. This was not, he thought, the charming opening gambit that the situation required. Whoever or whatever this young woman was, her company was to be preferred, surely, to that of Frost's previous visitors? Perhaps he should bring into play the famous Moon charm and smooth things over a little. Then he looked into the fathomless cold that Frost's remark had brought to her eyes and decided that perhaps the most useful thing he could do would be to imitate a particularly quiet piece of furniture.

'You have all the grace of a stuck pig, Frost,' she said. 'I could have all your friends back here in an instant, all quite keen to have a piece of you as a souvenir. And I could make very sure that there was enough of you to go around.'

Frost's voice was like chilled vitriol, a mix of cold determination and an eager dark lust. 'And I could have a stake through your black heart and your pretty little mouth bubbling blood even as they did it. Killing the queen is the best way I know of destroying the nest.'

An incongruous sweet laughter blessed the room as the woman tipped her head back to release it. Donovan felt like he had heard it before somewhere. It put him in mind, of all things, of Frost's Bentley and he assumed with a vague regret that his sanity must have slipped quietly away without a proper good-bye.

'That's so pathetic,' the woman said.

Without taking her eyes off Frost, she raised her left hand and clicked her fingers. Suddenly Moon, who had been labouring under the misapprehension that he was imitating a hat stand, found that what he in fact was imitating was a tape recorder. His mouth opened involuntarily and Frost's voice came out of it.

'It is neither a myth nor a disease, Mr Moon. It is an ideology. An ideology of indulgence and disorder.' Another click of the fingers. 'Disorder' – *click* – 'disorder' – *click* – 'disorder.'

She lowered her hand, the voice stopped, and Donovan decided he would rise above complaint.

'Disorder,' she said. 'You said it yourself. Isn't that why you kill them? And yet here you are, claiming hierarchies for chaos. Inconsistent. And is that how you see me? Queen of the Vampires of Summer? Sorry. I've played that joke once tonight, but I'm afraid *you* don't deserve comedy. For you –'

'I'll –'

216

'*You won't do anything, you little shit!*' And suddenly her voice was like thunder and both men froze like forest creatures waiting for the lightning. 'You'll just stand there and *watch*.' Her tone changed to a sly and ironic contempt. 'It's what you like best, isn't it?'

The thunder had passed but the paralysis remained. Donovan found that he no longer had to tell his limbs not to tremble, his muscles not to twitch; that decision had been made elsewhere. Only his eyes were in his control, and making them perform a painfully extreme swing to his left told him that the same was true for Frost. His one thought of gratitude amid the outrage and fear that this state induced was that his sphincter was equally hostage to whatever alien power held him. He turned his eyes back to the motley-clad source of this power and suddenly his own heartbeat threatened to deafen him and he felt his face become icy cold as all its blood fled.

The woman stood exactly as she had stood before, arms hanging undemonstratively at her side, her left leg a little forward of her right and its knee slightly bent. The only difference was that now both her feet were forty inches above the floor. She was standing in midair.

As the men watched, helpless to do anything else, she raised both her legs effortlessly and crossed them over each other, so that, still impossibly above the floor, she sat cross-legged – except that her knees remained a few inches lower than her hips as if she perched on two or three cushions invisible to her audience. Despite its blood-freezing strangeness, it was not a particularly threatening posture and Moon took the opportunity to look at her more closely – something he would not have done had she not, like the dead who came before her, had her own eyes fixed firmly on Jonathan Frost.

A centre of alien power she may have been, but Donovan could see in her physical form only the grace and the delicacy – even the fragility – of a dancer. Her yellow costume hung sensuously over her body, the trousers moulding themselves to the long, smooth curves of her thighs and calves and draping loosely beneath, as if the outfit still believed in gravity even if its owner did not.

Donovan looked at her face, pale and decorated only by the small smile and the smaller black mask, cut close enough to the eyes to give almost an impression of neatly but overenthusiastically applied eyeliner. The eyes themselves were . . . pale blue? . . . pale green? . . . grey? He'd never met anyone with grey eyes before. But then he'd never met anyone who could float, either. The eyes were grey. Or perhaps they were silver. The lips were full but without the corrupting sullenness that sometimes mars such fullness. She was . . . what was she . . . ? Oh yes. Strange it should take him so long to realize. She was beautiful.

And now she was revealing more of her beauty. There was an opening, it appeared, below the waistline of her clothing and she was spreading it to show them her flesh, pink, glistening, and framed with down. Donovan was still in a stew of fear, but it was suddenly seasoned by the spice of excitement.

Her fingers were long and slender. She began to stroke herself, slowly at first and then with a mounting speed and a mounting pressure. Fingertips began to disappear inside her, at first irregularly and then settling into a regular loving rhythm, syncopated by the romance of the thumb and the clitoris. Moon realized that the pulse he could feel in his neck was aligning itself to the tempo of her pleasure, that his pounding heart told the measure of her ecstasy's beat.

But it was more. The room itself appeared to be dimming and brightening, dimming and brightening, as if it, too, was helplessly focused on her fingers' dance. And now each brightness was brighter than the one that had preceded it, and each seemed to swell earlier out of the shrinking darkness between. The room and its contents were no longer visible. There was only the woman and her pleasure, floating in a bed of pulsing light. The bright whiteness no longer alternated with darkness but with different colours, so that the watchers' eyes grew confused. From white to red to white to yellow to white to blue to white again. And though the changes were rapid and chained to the rhythm, the effect was perceived not as a flickering but as a rich, protean flow.

And as the speed of her fingers increased, so did the speed of the changes. And as the speed of the changes increased, so did the richness and the luminescence of each revealed colour until Moon felt he would be unable to cope with whatever it was she was heading toward.

And now the light was free of her fingers and was making its own dance. Faster and faster until it *was* a flicker. Faster still until it was like a multicoloured strobe. Faster still until terrifyingly, beautifully, speed and stillness were one, and Donovan, in the eternity between two heartbeats, saw all her colours at once and heard his blood singing in his ears.

And then the world came back.

There was the woman, still in midair. There was Frost and Donovan himself. There was the still-warm night breeze, and there were the stars. They were on the roof of Frost's building.

Donovan stared about him wildly, his head and arms swinging freely as he tried to take in where he was. His body was obviously his again, but he was too confused to celebrate the return of free will. It was true. He and Frost stood on, and the woman hovered above, the plain concrete of the building's flat roof. Night had fallen, but the moon was bright and the sky was cloudless and brilliant with stars. The woman uncrossed her legs and straightened them, and then, upright, glided gracefully down the two or three feet to the roof as if balanced on the invisible fingertips of God.

As her feet met the concrete she turned and faced Moon directly for the first time. Her face was again impassive, but Donovan felt she was in search of a response. For a terrifying few seconds his mind raced madly as he tried to think of one that was the most appropriate and the safest, but as he saw her face illuminated by her answering smile, he realized he was already giving it; his own mouth was swollen in an open and unambiguous grin, which felt as if it had been resident on his face for minutes. He let reason go and was unafraid. Then he heard the scream. He spun around to his left.

Frost, too, looked beyond reason, but the unwilled expression *he* wore, unlike Donovan's, was the grimace of the predator and his cry the roar of the beast. He had never looked less civilized. Even when he had been death's messenger, his face had slipped, at the most, to a very human sneer of a very human contempt. Whatever animal rage may have boiled unconsciously within, it had always been human disgust that drove his matador hand so conscientiously. Now, his nostrils flaring, his mouth full of challenge and fury, he began a run across the twelve or thirteen yards that separated him from his tormentor, his right hand drawing, with practised malice, a wickedly sharp and solid wooden stake from the inside pocket of his jacket.

'No!' Donovan screamed, and began to run himself, desperate to stop him, knowing that he couldn't, knowing that from a standing start he had no chance at all of reaching Frost before the stake reached the woman's breast.

The woman herself seemed almost surprised by this sudden and mad attack, and Donovan, with a sinking heart, saw her throw her arms up in what he took to be a futile gesture of panic or surrender.

What happened next could have taken only a second – for Frost was still moving toward her and pain was still in his hand and death was still in his eyes – but to Donovan it seemed almost leisurely, as if time was operating on two levels. He saw the woman's hands above her head. He saw behind and above her the clear night sky and the backdrop of stars. He saw her palms turning to face each other. He saw three stars visible between and behind them. And then the hands came together, each passing in front of one of the stars, alternately obscuring and revealing them as they passed, until they met, mutually obscuring the third star. The hands, still pressed together, dropped to the woman's breast and Donovan saw three things. He saw Frost practically at the woman, less than two yards separating them; he saw the woman with her palms pressed together like a devotee at prayer; he saw the star missing from the sky.

Frost stopped. He blinked. Once. Twice. His hand came down slowly and the stake clattered to the roof. He took one step back. There was a woman on his roof with a star in her hand.

Moon stopped. He blinked. Once. Twice. There was a woman on the roof with a star in her hand.

Holding her hands cupped together, the woman stretched her arms toward Frost. Gently, slowly, she began to lower her hands. Frost's eyes followed helplessly. When her hands were at about waist level, she stopped. Then carefully, like one who holds a treasure, she opened her palms to share the wonder with Frost.

For one cold, detached moment Donovan found himself reminded of that strange effect a regular patron of the cinema like himself might see once every ten years or so: A single frame becomes trapped in the projector, seared by the heat of the lamp, its bubbling, blistering agony magnified many times and held on the huge screen for all to see. A frame whose normal time before our eyes is but one twenty-fourth of a second makes real and entirely its own the illusion it is normally merely a constituent part of; it becomes a moving picture. First it swells and seems to expand. Then it turns brown, and bubbles – two, twelve, forty – appear over its surface, and finally, from the centre outward, it blackens, cracks, and disappears. Like a cancer cell, its ambition is admirable but the result of its revolution is the end of the big picture.

The pursuit of this conceit took Moon perhaps two seconds, longer than the inspiration for it lasted. Frost's face had indeed swollen, changed colour, bubbled, cracked, and disappeared, but it had taken less than a second to do so. Muscle, flesh, and skin, along with hair, blood, mucus, and eyeballs were blistered away. Only dry, off-white bone remained. Everything else had been wiped clean. Eradicated. There was a mild stench of cauterized flesh, but this came entirely from the new and smoking lip of Frost's skin, which was about halfway up his neck. Above this there was absolutely nothing, not even a lingering odour, to show that the death's-head that grimaced there had only moments before been disguised by flesh and features. Below the inch and a half of naked neck came, grotesque in their new context, a collar, a tie, and the well-dressed and completely intact body of a forty-eight-year-old man.

For a second Frost was still. Then he took two staggering steps backward, steps like the heavy-footed lurching of a punch-drunk fighter whose body has yet to realize that he's already been knocked out. Donovan had once visited an abattoir and his sickened heart was reminded now of the terrible stagger of the cattle after the electric killing blow. But it wasn't as simple as that. Frost's body didn't collapse immediately after those steps. His skull, like a grey and shrunken jack-o'-lantern, dark gaping holes for nose and eyes, long and lipless teeth, swivelled on the still-fleshed neck and gaped at Donovan. Moon tried to tell himself it was accidental, but the rationalization, like a hide-bound ideology, ignored the evidence that didn't fit; the mouth that, tongueless, tried to speak, the hands that, helpless, reached toward him.

The reporter shook his head from side to side and made nonsensical but meaningful moaning noises at the thing of pity and terror before him. But this was useless; it had no eyes to see him shake, no ears to hear him moan. It had turned not to Moon but to its memory of where Moon had been when last it saw him. Centuries ago, when it had sight. Aeons before, when it had been a creature of sense. In hell, time is relative.

Moon found it hard to imagine a worse horror than the hands – would they still be warm? – of that abomination making contact with his shaking and pallid self, but what happened next *was* worse. The imploring hands stopped short before ever finding Moon's flesh. They moved back toward their own body and fastened on the suited chest. It was then that Donovan guessed what was going to happen and found it within himself to wish that he had seized those hands and held them to his heart forever rather than let them find the dreadful secret they were about to find. Because Frost, of course, had yet to realize the full extent of his transformation. He knew he had been rendered senseless – his eyes had lost their power, his ears had heard their last, the world no longer smelled or tasted of anything – but he did not yet know in how profound, how obscene a manner this had been accomplished. The inquisitive hands moved inexorably upward. And found out.

Donovan stood very still. He was breathing, fast, through his mouth. His eyes seemed to beg to look away, but he couldn't let them. It would somehow compound the cruelty to deny the wounded monster a human witness to his last agony.

The hands reached, touched, clenched, and dropped away. The arms followed, hanging limply at Frost's side. The body did nothing. The skull, though, despite its silence, was eloquent, It flung itself back violently, as if to see the sky from where its doom had come. And then, the dénouement of some dark pantomime, the jaw opened in a silent scream of human dis-belief and the Soul's despair.

Moon could stand no more. He began to cry. Tears blurred his vision and streamed down his cheeks. Huge, inelegant sobs staggered from his lungs and out of his mouth. His nose ran, his mouth slobbered. He turned to the woman. 'Please . . .' he begged. 'Oh, please . . . please . . .'

Her eyes, like Moon's, had, until this moment, remained fixed on the creature she had made of Frost. Now they flickered briefly toward the distressed journalist. Through the haze of his sorrow-clouded vision, Moon thought he may have seen an all-but-imperceptible nod.

Instantly the monster collapsed, all life, natural or otherwise, finally fled. It was probably ten seconds since the burning.

Donovan felt the nauseated relief we feel when a mouse, squealing and speared in a trap, finally shudders itself into silence and eternity. Long beyond our help, we wish its death on it as the only release it can have. Looking down at the skinned head and the suited body, Donovan realized that for Frost the trap had been sprung long ago and was of his own devising. His tears had ceased to fall, but he felt a new wetness on his face. He looked up. A summer rain was falling. The wind was changing.

He looked at the woman. His throat constricted in a sudden, choking panic. She was opening her hands again to show to him what she had shown to Frost. No time for good-byes, he thought, and pictured Matt. Then he saw it.

Resting in the palm of her right hand was something that was at once reassuringly familiar and beautifully alien. Like something from dreams, it seemed to Donovan to be both strange and yet profoundly known – as when fear or passion reminds you you have a pulse. It was the size of a small pearl and, as far as he could tell, of the same spherical shape, but the light that pulsed within it was of such a brightness that he could not be sure. It defined itself by its denial of definition. But it was warm and it soothed him.

The woman closed her hands over it again, and Donovan thought as he lifted his eyes with the movement of her hands

224

that he caught the ghost of a smile on her face as she brought the star toward her yellow blouse. He watched calmly and without judgment as she placed it on her breast, broochlike, as an ornament and a delight. He observed without judgment as she was raised again above the roof and began to move back and upward, at an angle of forty-five degrees, bisecting the right-angle he made with the world.

Her unmoving body moved effortlessly through space, and Donovan felt neither surprise nor fear at her movement but merely a sense of undefined loss.

For a second it looked as if the world was not to mark her passing; then Moon felt the concrete shift beneath his feet. He remembered his first earthquake and the rippling walls of the Marin County motel he had been in, and glanced around himself wildly for a doorway to stand in. But he was naked to the world's trembling and all he could do was to spread his legs a little and hold his arms out like a nervous skater seeking invisible balance rails.

From below, a city-wide symphony of car alarms and howling dogs, massive and cacophonous, rose to assault his ears. Then, as if the rest was but a prelude, the major theme broke in and its chosen instruments were roaring earth and screaming buildings. The growling of the ground – huge, deep, and demanding – had the terrifying half familiarity of a buried nightmare threat, suddenly unleashed into endless power and vast insatiable hunger. Concrete and steel howled and groaned as great unseen forces twisted and heaved them. The city was suddenly dark, its infrastructure succumbing to the writhing world. The only lights were on the river and they were rising, falling, and rolling in awesome patterns as small ships struggled with angry tides, violent enough to have terrified ocean liners.

Donovan pulled his gaze back to Frost's roof. The world had become water and Moon stared in paralysed terror at the ripples and waves in the concrete beneath him. Hideously, Frost's fallen body was being buffeted by this impossible current, its stripped skull rolling back and forth between its shoulders, its lifeless fingers tapping out unwilled rhythms on the roof it had owned.

The rain that had a moment before been a summer drizzle began to sting the backs of Donovan's outstretched hands, driving its way down from heaven to earth as if fleeing the wrath of clouds. He glanced toward his right hand but could hardly see it – the sky was suddenly dark and ominous. He raised his face to the sky, squinting against the painful fusillade of the rainstorm, and gasped in atavistic terror.

Blackness hung above San Francisco, crouching like an unimaginably huge beast waiting to pounce. From nowhere, and suddenly, the sky was dense and suffocating with heavy, black, roiling thunderclouds, pregnant with fury and power. From horizon to horizon they stretched, utterly obscuring stars, moon, and empty sky. Black clouds perched over San Francisco, over Oakland, over Marin County, over the whole of the Bay Area, over – as far as Donovan knew – the whole of the West Coast, the whole of the world. For the brief moment in which he first saw them, they were as malevolently silent as a hovering hawk before the swooping kill. But they could not hold their silence for long. Donovan had thought nothing could be louder or more awesome than the sound of the earthquake still raging beneath his feet. But then the thunder spoke.

Moon didn't know how his ears could acknowledge such violence without his eardrums exploding. He had never heard anything so loud in his life. Twenty years before, his father had taken him across the continent to watch men launch a rocket to the moon. Now he felt as if a thousand Saturn Fives were lifting off from each of his shoulders and that the roar of their release would never be stilled. He assumed that on the streets people would be screaming. He assumed that no one would assume that this was a regular storm. And he assumed that if the entire population of northern California were standing behind him and howling as one, he would never be able to hear it above the thunder cracks. He was surprised he could even think over the terrifying clamour, and at his next thought, he almost wished he couldn't. Where's the lightning? he thought. Shouldn't that have come first?

Almost as if in apology for its tardiness, lightning lit the world. Like its presaging thunder, it was bigger and more furious than anything Donovan had ever seen. Huge forks of lightning stabbed at the quaking earth while devastatingly bright sheets of it illuminated the scenes around and below Moon's rooftop viewpoint in rapid explosions of light.

Everywhere, at every flash, new cameos of chaos were revealed to the terrified journalist. Overturned cars – flipped onto their backs by the quake, wheels still spinning like confused insects whose legs scrabble helplessly for purchase in empty air. Glassless windows disfiguring high-rise buildings and staring blindly out at streets and sidewalks covered with powdered and shattered glass like a sudden fall of ice and snow of impossible sharpness and cruelty; fallen lampposts, fallen billboards, fallen wires – some spitting blue and gold showers of electric death as they flung themselves in angry and spastic dance steps on the road with the fury of dying wasps against windows. And everywhere, people – huddled together in doorways, frozen in solitary fear in the middle of streets, running crazily in panic terror for impossible safe haven – all of them with arms flung over their faces, above their heads, imploring hands outstretched not in any gesture of protection but in the gesture of prayer – or, more properly, prayer's older, darker brother, a gesture held in blood-memory from ancient cave-dwelling grandfathers who first raised their arms to the sky in beseeching submission to the implacable anger of gods.

To see this anarchic terror grip a city and its people so thoroughly and so quickly would have been bad enough, but it was made worse for Moon by the nature of its revelation; not only did the flashes of lightning catch these moments and present them as seemingly frozen tableaux, but the unrelenting frequency of the dazzling stabs of light gave them an almost stroboscopic intensity, making them into a manically fast slide show of catastrophe photos.

Further, the light itself, though explosively bright, was far from the photo-flood white that Donovan had seen before. This light was a bilious yellow, smearing everything he was seeing with a ghastly ochre, a sickly ominous tone he thought he knew from nightmares.

The deafening claps of thunder had neither slowed nor

227

softened and the deep and distressing rumbling of the quake still provided a hideous bass to the cacophonous symphony above. Donovan realized he'd been keeping his balance instinctively against the shaking roof while the storm raged. As soon as this realization hit him, however, as soon as this balance became conscious, it was gone. The crazy current of the concrete tide had him and he was thrown to one side, his arms windmilling helplessly against the dark and heavy air, his mind crying out silently in panicked protest at the swaying of the high rise and his suddenly perceived proximity to the edge of its roof. Down on one knee, the other leg stretched awkwardly and painfully, he grabbed instinctively at the roof, clawing uselessly for purchase as the lightning lit his helplessness and the thunder laughed at his terror.

He was still a good ten feet from the edge of the roof, but that was still too near. He flung himself flat against the roof surface, pressing his body to the pulsing movements of the concrete like a man in a cold bed pressing himself to the warm back of his lover. But the stone was cold and unresponsive, and the pelting, bulleting rain continued to smash into his back and legs. He closed his eyes and lay his cheek to the stone, suffering the rain's assault, beyond protest, beyond action, as nature raged above and below him.

He had no desire to lift his head, he had no desire to open his eyes. But something made him do both those things. Something made him look back up to the sky and find something he'd forgotten.

The woman was still there. Hanging impossibly in the sky, her legs once again crossed calmly beneath her as they had been when she had staged Frost's last performance, she was moving – without effort, beyond logic – upward and backward, the star she had attached to herself lending a sweet silver glow to her calm and poised body as it moved inexorably to the heavens. Both the path she was carving and the woman herself seemed indifferent to the storm that was raging around her. Like a still centre in a turning world, she was the calm eye of this paranormal hurricane.

Donovan refocused on her, at once remembering and retrieving the calm she had given to him when she had opened her hands before her ascension, and suddenly, magically, the storm began to abate. The sheeting rain became thinner, the building beneath Moon's pressing body shuddered finally into solidity, and the thunderclaps began to be more widely spaced.

The lightning stopped, and with it the disorienting strobing of light and darkness. For a heartbeat, Moon could see nothing at all and then a different light began to return. Donovan had never thought he would describe the cool silver-blue of moon and stars as warm, but after the nauseating yellow of the storm, warm was how it felt to him as it gradually brought back to life the roof immediately beneath him and the city farther below.

The sounds of the city were now also audible, and they, too, were strangely comforting. The howl of ambulance sirens and the shouts of those in distress or those seeking assistance for the distressed were not normally sources of reassurance, but considering the sounds that had filled Moon's consciousness but a moment before, they were happy reminders of normality, of life going on, of civilization reasserting its collective white lie of order and control, its soothing pretence that chaos could be contained.

In the sky above and before him, more and more of the stars were coming back into Moon's view. The huge mass of black cloud was gathering in on itself, rolling, folding, bubbling into a smaller tighter mass like footage of an explosion seen in reverse slow motion.

The woman, though still very much this side of the clouds, was nevertheless, from Donovan's point of view, at the central point of this gathering, and as he watched it shrink into nothingness behind her, he was suddenly filled with an absolute certainty that somehow it was he who had been responsible for the storm – that it was his fear, his inability to hold on to the peace she had bequeathed him, that had let it happen. And only now, now that he was calm again, was the fury able to abate. He hadn't been content to let a miracle be a passive thing, to be quiet or intimate. It hadn't seemed appropriate.

Whether it was his twentieth-century-ness, his Westernness,

his selfishness, or just his penchant for bad movies and worse books, he expected the marvellous to be a thing of pomp and circumstance, of sound and fury. It made sense – if sense it could be called – of the fact that the same quiet revelation (an opening of the palms, a tamed star) that had given to him only wonder and comfort had given to Frost – and *his* expectations – a searing, agonizing, and grotesque farewell. The woman was all potential, her mystery all possibility – it was what the human observer contributed, the baggage of neurosis and desire he brought with him, that shaped the transcendence, that qualified the intercession.

Donovan rose to his feet, now once again in the strangely calm state he had been before the storm. The clouds had coalesced into a tight black pinpoint, dense and dark against the midnight blue of the starlit sky, and now that, too, shrank from sight. There was no thunder, no lightning. The rain was light, warm, and refreshing. The earth was solid beneath his feet. The only thing he needed to do was to watch the woman leave. He had no other pressing business, no other desires. He would watch, she would leave. This would happen. And then something else would happen. And after that, something else. And that sequence – of event succeeding event – was, he vaguely recalled, called life.

The woman moved. Up into the sky. Out into the night. Smaller and smaller she grew to his sight, farther and farther she went, true to the only important rules of navigation; over the hills and far away; second star to the right and straight on till morning; home, always home.

The star at her breast continued to shine for him long after the outline of her body was lost to darkness, until finally, finding itself in a position close enough to that which it had occupied before her call, it slowed itself to the speed of its brothers and the rules of perspective returned.

Moon had no idea where the woman had gone, nor any desire to know. In dreams, he has seen her shed her skin and mate with passing comets, but that was later and only when reason and the world had reclaimed him. Now he simply looked at the sky, put out his tongue to collect some raindrops, and ignoring the dead thing at his feet, found his way down through the building and out to the summer and San Francisco, without thought, without direction, without fear.

EPHEMERA

From the *San Francisco Examiner*, June 25

In a macabre postscript to the weekend's double punch of earthquake and thunderstorm, the body of a man was discovered atop a midtown office building yesterday afternoon. The body was fully clothed, but was horribly and remarkably disfigured. Police spokesmen dismissed rumors that the man was the latest victim of Morningstar and confirmed that foul play was not suspected. A coroner added that the cause of death – which removed all the flesh from the victim's skull, leaving the rest of his body intact – was probably a bolt of lightning. 'Irreverent as it may sound,' added Dr Kucich, 'this should be classed as an act of God.'

Distraught staff have identified the suit in which the corpse was found as one belonging to the owner of the building, Jonathan Frost. Frost was profiled in these pages a little more than a week ago and is an urban-planning consultant of some note.

Adding a little mystery to this bizarre incident, it transpires that no dental or fingerprint records exist for Mr Frost, and the body, though probably that of the designer missing since Monday, cannot be positively identified.

From *Hot Hits*, June 27

Fifties doo-wopper turned eighties hard-rocker Bobby Corvino has personally demanded that his record company recall and trash all remaining copies of his remix revival 'Dream Angel.' Attempting to quell rumors of a resurgence of the mental problems that plagued Corvino during the seventies, a record-company spokesman claimed the aging idol was unhappy with the production (by flavor-of-the-week club mixer Hophouse Jack). A brief phone call with the rock star himself, however, drew this pithy comment: 'It's just too fucking weird, man.'

From the Bay Area Inquirer, July 14

WHERE IS MORNINGSTAR?
Killing Spree Stops. Police Baffled.

Police sources admitted today that the mystery killer dubbed Morningstar, after carving his way through San Francisco earlier last month, leaving nearly twenty dead and a whole city sleepless, seems to have taken a vacation. Confessing they are no nearer to finding his identity, an officer told the Inquirer *that 'sick as it sounds, unless he breaks cover and kills again, we may never find him.' Commissioner Schulman, dismissing this, said the case is still open and the investigation proceeding.*

Dr Dan W. Fisher, the Inquirer's *resident expert on criminal psychology, had this comment: 'These people are actually tragic cases. They are invariably fueled by a profound self-hatred. Their activities are undoubtedly cries for help. It is my considered opinion as an expert that the man responsible has certainly killed himself. Probably from the bridge, which is very popular. Mark my words – next floater they find out in the bay, that'll be Morningstar.'*

From Ink Trade, May 7

Lawyers acting for the estate of Jonathan Frost have placed an injunction on a book by Donovan Moon, Blood and Desire: The Morningstar Murders and Beyond, *on grounds of defamation of character.*

The book, in which former journalist Moon claims that the missing-and-presumed-dead executive was responsible not only for a string of San Fran killings two years ago but for many more stretching back thirty years, has already generated much interest including movie offers.

234

Greenmantle Publishers is contesting the admissibility of the injunction – and quietly rubbing their hands in glee at the extra publicity.

From *Dishing It with Kimberley Rae,* August 8
(transcribed from telecast)

KR: Donovan, Hi! Well! What do I say? From – in your words, darling – washed-up hack to media event in one easy year! Big response to your book. You must have been expecting that?
DM: I guess.
KR: But tell me, how does it feel to be accused of – what did the Times *say? –*
DM: 'Fourth-rate paranoid fantasies masquerading as reportage,' 'irresponsible mumbo jumbo,' 'foul feckless speculation, perhaps drug-induced' – that's probably my favorite. There're more. Got them all off by heart. (smiles)
KR: The Frost estate dropped its –
DM: I showed them the check. (smiles)
KR: This is the money you say Frost paid you to –
DM: I gave it to charity.
KR: How about the publisher's advance?
DM: (smiles) That's mine.
KR: (smiles) Right. Now, just to remind our viewers, you claim in the book Blood and Desire *(holds it up to camera) that Jonathan Frost, a San Francisco businessman, was systematically killing vampires and –*
DM: I don't claim he was killing vampires. He claimed he was killing vampires.
KR: But you say you saw –
DM: I saw one man with fangs, that's all.
KR: But you certainly suggest Frost was the killer the media called Morningstar?
DM: I report the fact that he told me he was Morningstar. I don't speculate anywhere in the book. I don't analyze. I did a minimum of research to check his story about being English. That was verified. That was all.

235

KR: *And then there's this angel of vengeance.*

DM: Look. I don't call her an angel. I don't call her a goddess. I don't call her a drug-induced fantasy. Those are all other people's descriptions from reviews. I don't call anybody anything. All I do is bear witness. I report. I don't speculate.

KR: *But you must have a view?*

DM: Sure.

KR: *Care to share it?*

DM: (sighs) I think that . . . just this once . . . *heaven said 'enough' and stepped on something small, dark, and unpleasant.*

KR: *(frowns) Uh-huh. And the vampires?*

DM: What vampires? You want more guesses? Frost was killing 'the other.' Like all his kind do. Sometimes the other has black skin. Sometimes the other sucks (beeeep!). Sometimes the other looks like a dead mother. Sometimes the other is sexually active. Frost made his own myth – or found one to suit him. He may have interconnected accidentally with people who also inhabited that myth but he didn't need them. His own belief was strong enough.

KR: *You don't believe in vampires?*

DM: I believe in everything.

KR: *So what are they?*

DM: What do you want them to be?

KR: *How do you mean?*

DM: I mean (shrugs, smiles) . . . *Why don't you ask me about the movie?*

KR: *(smiles) More money!*

DM: And fame, Kimberley, let's not forget fame.

KR: *So who do you want to play you?*

DM: Unfortunately, Montgomery Clift is dead.

KR: *(laughs) Stay with us, please. (turns to camera, show theme starts) A man who says his wife has come back to him as a credit card. The South American doctor who is pioneering designer babies. And, via remote from London, the private nurse who claims to be looking after Elvis Presley. After these messages.*

(commercial break)

236

From *Blood and Desire*, second edition
(Two extracts from Donovan Moon's preface)

And amid all the furore, two main questions semed to emerge. And those two questions are: Are there vampires out there? And what are they like?

To the first, I'd probably give the kind of equivocal yes I give when asked if I believe in God. In other words, I'd much rather debate the terminology before answering, but if I'm only allowed a yes or a no, then it'd have to be yes. As to the second question, the honest answer is that I haven't the faintest idea. I don't know *what they're like. But I can tell you what I think they* mean, *culturally.*

I think they're a blank canvas for us, a blank canvas that we all need. I think they are redrawn by each of us and that we each paint them in our own colours. To some, they're a dream of elegant control, of sophistication and wisdom. To others, they're the hungry and unstoppable wolf at the midnight door. I'd probably see them as romantic sexual outlaws. In a strange way, I think that was Frost's take, too. That or bad children. But I think that what this means is that they don't live off us. We live off *them.*

*   *   *

I find it interesting that the woman – or the being – I saw put an end to Frost seemed to prompt much less speculation than the people Frost himself was killing. I don't know what that says about us. One letter, though, deserves mention. The young woman who wrote it has no desire for publicity and I am respecting her wish not to reveal her own strange involvement in this story. But one thing I can repeat concerns a dream visitation from a friend of hers who was one of the San Francisco victims. In this dream, her visitor referred to Astarte. My correspondent looked it up. So did I. Astarte was a goddess of the ancient Syrians, a goddess of love. In different cultures, this entity had different names. Like Venus. Or Aphrodite. Or Morningstar.

I have no comment to make on this. If I learned anything that summer in San Francisco, I learned that the world is mystery and that interpretation is personal. What I'd like is to live a life in which the mystery is enough. Unfortunately I'm human. But I try.